A Sky Full of Dragons

THE WAND KEEPERS
BOOK 1

A Sky Full of Dragons

TIFFANY McDANIEL

SIMON & SCHUSTER BOOKS FOR YOUNG READERS
New York London Toronto Sydney New Delhi

SIMON & SCHUSTER BOOKS FOR YOUNG READERS
An imprint of Simon & Schuster Children's Publishing Division
1230 Avenue of the Americas, New York, New York 10020
This book is a work of fiction. Any references to historical events, real people, or real places are used fictitiously. Other names, characters, places, and events are products of the author's imagination, and any resemblance to actual events or places or persons, living or dead, is entirely coincidental.
Text © 2024 by Tiffany McDaniel
Jacket and interior illustration © 2024 by Ayesha L. Rubio
Jacket design by Sarah Creech
Interior illustration of stars and sparkles by writerfantast/iStock
Interior illustration of scroll by Sakura28/iStock
Interior photograph of scroll by Andrey Kuzmin/iStock
All rights reserved, including the right of reproduction in whole or in part in any form.
SIMON & SCHUSTER BOOKS FOR YOUNG READERS
and related marks are trademarks of Simon & Schuster, LLC.
Simon & Schuster: Celebrating 100 Years of Publishing in 2024
For information about special discounts for bulk purchases, please contact Simon & Schuster Special Sales at 1-866-506-1949 or business@simonandschuster.com.
The Simon & Schuster Speakers Bureau can bring authors to your live event. For more information or to book an event, contact the Simon & Schuster Speakers Bureau at 1-866-248-3049 or visit our website at www.simonspeakers.com.
Also available in a Simon & Schuster Books for Young Readers paperback edition
Interior design by Tom Daly
The text for this book was set in Adobe Caslon Pro.
The illustrations for this book were rendered digitally.
Manufactured in the United States of America
0824 BVG
First Simon & Schuster Books for Young Readers hardcover edition September 2024
2 4 6 8 10 9 7 5 3 1
Library of Congress Cataloging-in-Publication Data
Names: McDaniel, Tiffany, author. | Rubio, Ayesha L., illustrator.
Title: A sky full of dragons / Tiffany McDaniel ; [illustrated by] Ayesha L. Rubio.
Description: First edition. | New York : Simon & Schuster Books for Young Readers, 2024. | Series: The wand keepers ; book 1 | Audience: Ages 8 up. | Audience: Grades 4–6. | Summary: When Spella's aunt Cauldroneyes mysteriously disappears into a growling hat the night before she is set to attend Dragon's Knob, a prestigious school for wand magic, Spella and her new friend Tolden set out to rescue her aunt and uncover hidden secrets within the school amidst threats to its academic freedom.
Identifiers: LCCN 2024005816 (print) | LCCN 2024005817 (ebook)
ISBN 9781665955317 (hardcover) | ISBN 9781665955300 (paperback) | ISBN 9781665955324 (ebook)
Subjects: CYAC: Fantasy. | Witches—Fiction. | Magic—Fiction. | Schools—Fiction. | Aunts—Fiction. | LCGFT: Fantasy fiction. | Novels.
Classification: LCC PZ7.1.M434326 Sk 2024 (print) | LCC PZ7.1.M434326 (ebook) | DDC [Fic]—dc23
LC record available at https://lccn.loc.gov/2024005816
LC ebook record available at https://lccn.loc.gov/2024005817

*This story celebrates the delightful critters
and creatures all around us, which is why I'm dedicating this
book to the wonderful creatures in my life.*

*My pet rescue dragons, Grand, Fielding, Stella,
Sammy, Teddy, and Fancy.*

*My wild unicorns, Maggie May, Dolly, Ralph,
Sparkie, and Tabitha.*

*And I can't forget the very magical hats, Sunshine,
Boo, Miss Pawpaw, Sal, and Dinkey.*

A Sky Full of Dragons

NOTE: These spells have been collected by the Before Long Witch. The Before Long Witch was born in a dragon's footprint but raised by a most wild herd of unicorns. She was named "Before Long" because she knew that before long there would be a whirling, there would be a storm, there would be a wind that blows the old ways away. She gathered these incantations, enchantments, sorcery sonnets, and cauldron prayers throughout her long life so that the ancient magic would never be lost, much less forgotten to the tides of time.

Please practice these spells responsibly.

Spell No. 9,087

Eyes for sale, pick your color,
Purple like a troll's mother.

Note from the Before Long Witch
This spell may be used for banishing Cyclops rats from your sock drawer. Can also be used to fight a troll, as Cyclops rats are natural enemies of the aforementioned. Recite spell while holding your wandle high, turning it in small circles. Spell works best when wandle has been dipped into the spit of a deranged fairy.

CHAPTER 1
The Magical Hatmaker

AUNT CAULDRONEYES MADE POINTED HATS COVERED in bright green warts for witches, large floppy hats covered in crystal eyes and moonlight for werewolves, and hats that had an edge of mist and a ribbon of rain for the ancient trees in the forest.

She made hats that smelled like an old troll's foot for trolls themselves, and plenty of hats for ogres, fairies, giants, and dragons, even the grumpy ones. She also made hats for unicorns, but when she did, she always had to cut a hole in them.

"To fit your wild and wonderful horn," she'd say to the unicorns with a giggle. Then she'd measure the spirals that come in as many sizes and colors as there are stars in the sky and dreams to be had.

It was the best day when I got to help Aunt Cauldroneyes with unicorns.

"What do you always have to have in the house for unicorns, Spella?" Aunt Cauldroneyes asked me.

"You have to have a jar of boogers,"[1] I said. "For when a unicorn gets hungry."

"You are the perfect unicorn hatmaker, Spella!" Aunt Cauldroneyes said with a neigh like a unicorn. "Especially for a hatmaker who is so young."

I had turned eight at the beginning of September and had lived with Aunt Cauldroneyes ever since she found me as a baby in the bottom of a purple cauldron during a thunderstorm. She named me Spella De-broom Cauldroneyes. She chose De-broom as my middle name after her favorite flying broom brand, and she named me Spella because she said I was the best spell she'd ever found in a cauldron.

We lived in Hungry Snout Forest, in a house made of laughing stones that Aunt Cauldroneyes had gathered herself from the banks of the river when she built the house long ago. The house had a roof that you couldn't see was purple with yellow polka dots, because of the crispy

1 * MOST THINK UNICORNS ARE GRACEFUL CREATURES WHO EAT THINGS LIKE SUGAR BALLS AND PINK DUST, BUT UNICORNS LOVE TO EAT BOOGERS. IT DOESN'T MATTER IF THEY'RE GOBLIN BOOGERS OR ELF BOOGERS OR CAT BOOGERS. THEY'LL EAT THEM ALL.

vines and crunchy twigs that covered them, like giant nests. Except, of course, when the wind blew and lifted the nests up.

Each of the nine chimneys was shaped like a long-necked goose, and they all faced different directions. In the winter, violet-colored smoke puffed out of their beaks as if they'd been eating exploding gumdrops. The windows in the house were arched with circles of glass colored in the bright shades of wild grapes, raspberries, and fairy fromps. But inside the house was the best of all because Aunt Cauldroneyes had enchanted the doors to smell and taste like chocolate.

"So the hats can have a nibble-wibble," she said.

There were plenty of hats who lived in the house with us. They had their own beds and floppy slippers and mugs for chocolate curl. Some of the hats burped. Others farted like a spitfang. The witch hats constantly cackled. The ogre hats constantly grumbled.

The little hats made of fuzzy fabric with round twitchy ears and pink tails lived in pockets and teacups like mice, while the hat we called Mr. Sea Captain had long purple tentacles he would stick out the attic windows.

"Like an octopus," Aunt Cauldroneyes would say as she waved her arms in the air.

The feathered owl hats flew over the wild wonders, chasing the mice hats until they giggled. The hats with bat wings had to be kept out of the daylight and preferred to sleep in tiny coffins. They also had a habit of biting with their little fangs.

"These will be my vampires," Aunt Cauldroneyes had said as she made the bat hats, lining them with red silk.

There was even a hat that was made of so much dirt that when you lifted her up, it was like lifting a rock and discovering beetles and earthworms on the underside.

"We'll name her Wormella," Aunt Cauldroneyes said.

While each hat was delightfully unique, they all loved dancing to Aunt Cauldroneyes' funky-clunky monster records.[2*] The hats were more creature than fabric, after all, and I was in charge of feeding them. They ate spools of sugar thread, caramel buttons, and chocolate thimbles. I had to make sure the candy stayed out of the sunlight. The hats hated eating melted thimbles.

After dinner I would walk the hats in Hungry Snout Forest. Then we would go into Aunt Cauldroneyes' library, where books flew to and from the shelves. I would sit in her big poufy chair that smelled like cinnamon, catch one of the books flying by, and read to the hats until we all fell asleep. I always pretended not to be woken by the scratchy whiskers on Aunt Cauldroneyes' chin as she gently kissed my forehead.

"*Little Spella,*" Aunt Cauldroneyes sang a lullaby, "*she's a dragon-fire poet, a wild truth's muse, September's sapphire, a little too blue. Wise as a river, deep as a well. For this cauldron's*

2 * FUNKY-CLUNKY MONSTER RECORDS MUST BE KEPT IN A LOCKED CABINET ON NIGHTS WITH A FULL MOON, OR THE RECORDS WILL CHANGE INTO WEREWOLVES.

child, a secret to tell. Dream a thousand skies tonight. Take a thousand leaps. This is your story. This is for keeps."

She would cover me with a warm quilt and say, "I love you like a sky full of dragons."

Aunt Cauldroneyes was as old as one thousand, five hundred years. She was older than that, if you believed it. Her voice was like the warmth of soup in winter, and she had pale green skin from an accident with a pickle potion when she was younger. Though, it can be said that all witches have a little bit of green in them. Sometimes the green is all over. Sometimes it's only a spot here and there. And sometimes it's just a tooth.

One of the best things about Aunt Cauldroneyes was that her wrinkles turned her whole face into one large spiderweb. A Silver Spider would crawl out from her hair and swing from one cheek to the other on glistening thread.

"Isn't she marvelous?" Aunt Cauldroneyes always laughed as the spider tickled the tip of her nose. "We've been friends since I was a little bubble."

Aunt Cauldroneyes had large eyes that reflected everything, and her two salt-and-pepper-colored braids were so long, they fell to her wide, bare feet. She would put her braids into a bowl. Using a pestle, she would crush and grind them like cocoa beans until they became a dark brown powder that she would mix with hot milk into a drink we called chocolate curl. Her hair would grow back down to her wide feet in the time it took the milk to boil.

On the night Aunt Cauldroneyes found me as a baby in the purple cauldron, lightning flashed against the sky and thunder roared like angry trolls. But not even a storm would stop Aunt Cauldroneyes from peeking into cauldrons, her shaggy purple cloak dragging on the ground behind her while her mauve shawl was pulled across her shoulders.

"You never know what you'll find in a cauldron," she always said. "I've found dragon eyes, troll nose rings, an old wizard's robe with small giggling moons in the pockets, and even a laughing jar of jokes."

We pulled a joke out of the jar every night. One of my favorites was, How do you know if your vampire dog has a case of the October sniffles?

"He keeps a coffin," Aunt Cauldroneyes was always the one to say, making sure to cough so that "coffin" sounded like "coughin'."

Aunt Cauldroneyes was known as the best magical hatmaker in the world. There was a large wooden sign nailed to the porch of our house that read MATHILDA THE MAGICAL MILLINER.

"'Milliner' is a fancy name for a hatmaker," Aunt Cauldroneyes told me when I asked her about it. "And Mathilda is my first name. I'm named after my mother, who was also a Mathilda."

Written beneath her name on the sign was OPEN MORNING TO MIDNIGHT. COME INSIDE FOR CAULDRON CAPS AND WITCHY SNACKS! PLEASE KNOCK FIRST AND WIPE YOUR PAWS, TENTACLES, AND ALL MANNER OF FEET ON THE DOORMAT.

We had every kind of creature and magical folk stopping by the house to pick up their custom-made hats. Aunt Cauldroneyes never used a wand to make hats or for her magic. I called her a spider witch because thread, in whatever color she conjured, came from her hands, like spider silk. Her fingernails were rather short, but when she clacked her tongue three times, they would grow long enough to stitch the thread. Three more clacks of her tongue, and her fingernails would once more become so short that they barely scratched the back of the hat we called Fleabag.

I would lie on my belly in the attic and watch Aunt Cauldroneyes while she sewed, and her two long braids stuck straight up. Her braids always stuck up when her fingers worked really fast. Sometimes while she was sewing, she would ask me to grab her a jar of fairywild oil to rub the fabric with, or get her a handful of kissing bells to sew onto the ribbons. I loved running over to the ancient wooden shelves lined with jars and potion bottles full of very old flashing lights and mysterious trinkets.

Everything Aunt Cauldroneyes used to make hats with, from thunderbird feathers to tickling buttons, were things she had found and collected. She was a forager. It was one of the reasons she was always looking into cauldrons.

"I knew when I looked into that purple cauldron and found you, Spella," she said to me, "that you were more special than any old potion bubble. I also knew that you would one day be a Wand Keeper, because of your shadow."

Aunt Cauldroneyes had a regular shadow of herself, but I had a shadow that was shaped as an egg about as tall as the cookie jar in the kitchen.

One time, I held a candle to the shadow. It was like shining a light onto the thin shell of a bird egg. I could see small bolts of lightning flickering on the inside of it.

"Every witch or wizard destined for the wand has a shadow of an egg," Aunt Cauldroneyes told me. "When a Wand Keeper turns ten years old, the egg will hatch a creature."

"What type of creature?" I asked as I imagined great and wonderful things.

"What hatches may be a water owl or a giant squid or a two-headed gorilla from the mountains," Aunt Cauldroneyes said. "It can be anything in the world, because you feed the creature your magic while they are inside the egg. Once hatched, the creature will be the shadow of your wand." She held her hand up in the light of the candle, casting a shadow of her hand on the wall. "They will also be your shadow. Because the eggs come from the great thunderbird, the creature will flash with lightning. Imagine it now, Spella. You journey through the world with the shadow of a unicorn galloping beside you, or a thunderbird flying high above you, or a lightning lizard slithering beside you. And whenever you need them, your creature will gallop, swim, slither, or fly into your hand and transform into a solid wand. The wand you will use to cast the very magic you had fed the creature with while they were still inside the egg."

"I wonder what my creature will be," I asked.

"A creature that will be as wonderful as you are, Spella," she said. "I bet your wand will even have your beautiful blue freckles."

She would rub her hands, which smelled like the thousands of cauldrons she had stirred, across my cheeks and over my bright blue freckles. I wasn't very fond of my freckles, starting out. The other kids in the village drew pictures of me with hag hair and wonky teeth and a big pointed chin that had goat hair on it. I didn't have any of those things, but they seemed to think that just because I had blue freckles, I was ugly all over from head to toe. That's why my only friends were the hats—and Egypt, of course.

Egypt was Aunt Cauldroneyes' talking cat. She was wrapped up like a mummy, with only her glowing yellow eyes showing. She was always tripping on the loose pieces of frayed linen that dragged on the ground beneath her. She had come from the land of the pyramids and had a habit of writing hieroglyphics on the walls in the house with black crayon. She had the even worse habit of mummifying things, from pots and pans to umbrellas and even pillows.

"I knew all the famous pharaohs," she'd say in her deep, dusty voice, waving her paw through the air. "I'll tell you about them if you give me three chocolate mice."

Chocolate mice were her favorite candy. It was how I got her to help me walk the hats. Getting the hats to go on their walk was often like herding wild animals. We had to pull the octopus hat, Mr. Sea Captain, in from the windows, his tentacles knocking things off shelves. Egypt always managed to catch all the unicorn figurines just in time. Then there was the giant hat who preferred to stay inside and knit or do jigsaw puzzles, his small gold-rimmed eyeglasses always perched dangerously on the very end of his bulbous nose. His name was Grandma's Boot.

"Grandma only ever wore the one boot," Aunt

Cauldroneyes said. "No one ever knew what happened to the other one, or even whether it had ever existed."

Aunt Cauldroneyes said the boot was what was left of her old grandmother, so she'd pulled out the stitching and unfolded the skin of it and softened the sole. With the length of a single shoelace, and the size of a single boot, Aunt Cauldroneyes had made a hat that was as giant as the life she said her grandmother had lived.

Even though he was named after a boot, the giant hat didn't much enjoy walking. I thought it was because, having once been a shoe, he had done so much of it.

"Ah, come on," he'd say. "No walk today. I just walked yesterday. Besides, I got to finish my puzzle. I only have three pieces left."

Me and Egypt would push him out of his comfy quilted cushion. He would quickly grab hold of the doorway with his long fingers and try to pull himself back toward his chair.

"You can finish your puzzle when we get back from our walk," I always had to tell him.

"Are you pushing hard enough?" Egypt would ask, her voice barely able to be heard from beneath the heavy ribbon fallen down from the hat and covering her face. "I feel like I'm doing all the heavy lifting here. And I've been mummified for over a thousand years."

Pushing the giant hat was like pushing a boulder. The fairy hats were the easiest to move. I could hold ten in one hand, they were so small. They looked like little pointed witch hats, only the points drooped under the weight of the very tiny toadstools growing on them.

The fairy hats' bits and baubles were of tiny, secretive things like the spittle of ravens or the sparkle of stars. One fairy hat could be the color of a green toad, another a flash of fuchsia. They often changed color, depending on mood, and they all had funny names like Grow-a, Fenreer, or Ow-stree. Though you might have thought they were dainty and fragile, with their tulle and sparkle, they knew how to use pine needles as swords and acorn caps as shields.

"Warriors of the winds," Aunt Cauldroneyes would say.

Each night at bedtime I ran around the house with a jar to catch the fairy hats as if I were catching fireflies. Once they were inside the jar, I would press my face up against the glass and smile in at the twinkling lights as they smiled back at me.

"I love you like a sky full of dragons," I'd whisper to them, because you never wanted to speak loudly to a fairy hat. They have such tiny ears, after all.

I always caught more of them than Egypt. It was rather hard for her to grab hold of a fairy hat, given how they would fly under her linen, causing it to glow and flicker until she was like a mummy made of lightning.

"Lightning mummy! Lightning mummy!" Aunt Cauldroneyes would giggle and clap her hands until her mauve shawl slipped off her shoulders, revealing even more fairy hats hiding beneath her collar.

CHAPTER 2
THE HIDDEN UNICORNS

I NEVER WANTED TO LIVE ANYWHERE ELSE BUT Hungry Snout Forest. Aunt Cauldroneyes said that at one time, before so many trees had been cut down, there used to be very old ones known as Anima Mundi. There, in the shallow bowls of their trunks, the trees held the raindrops from thunderstorms and turned them into stars, making galaxies in the middle of the forest.

"Can you imagine, Spella?" Aunt Cauldroneyes said. "Galaxies in something as simple as a puddle of water. That is the power of a forest."

I tried to imagine how large Hungry Snout had once been. It was still vast enough to get lost in, but Aunt

Cauldroneyes said that was still too small when you have creatures like dragons who take up many acres by themselves, and herds of unicorns who need wide-open spaces to gallop.

"When I was a little bubble," Aunt Cauldroneyes said, "there used to be Star Spiders.[3*] They were Silver Spiders that were so sparkly, you could see them miles away. They dropped down on webs they created in the sky, and they would lay their silk across my hair like diamonds."

Aunt Cauldroneyes spun silver thread from her hands. It sparkled against her skin. She giggled and let the strands crisscross down my hair.

"Am I all shiny now, Aunt Cauldroneyes?" I asked, skipping around her.

"Yes, little dear. You are all shiny now." She laughed, then her large eyes grew weary.

"What happened to the Star Spiders?" I asked, grabbing her hand and gently squeezing it. I knew that always made her feel better.

"Oh." She sighed and laid her other hand over her heart. "Folks thought the spiders were so shiny because they were made of jewels. So they plucked them from their webs in the sky. But no matter how many spiders they took, they never found any diamonds. By the time anyone realized

---

3 * Sᴏᴀʀ Sᴘɪᴅᴇʀᴀʀᴇ ᴀʀᴇ swordsmiths and can weave a sword out of web, though it will take them several months. That is the slow and steadymagic of a spider sword.

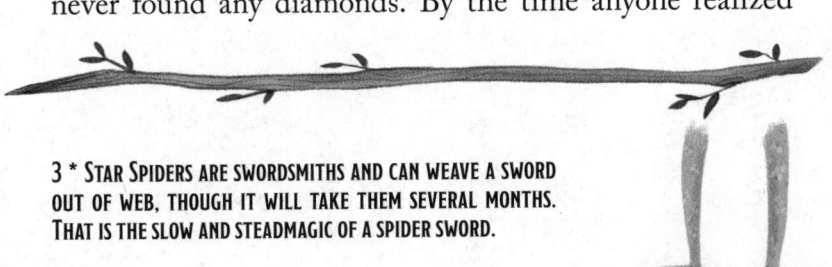

they would never become rich by trapping something shiny in their hands, it was too late. The Star Spiders had been hunted to extinction."

I saw tiny silver legs poke out from one of her braids.

"All except one." Aunt Cauldroneyes smiled as the Silver Spider came out of her hair and crawled to her cheek. "She is the last of her kind, Spella. She came down on a string of web all alone. I've let her live in my hair ever since. It's safer than the sky. Though, I know she doesn't like it as much." Aunt Cauldroneyes tenderly touched the spider. "Once you've sewn webs across galaxies and lived amongst the stars, living in an old woman's hair isn't as shiny of a life."

Tiny buttons, in shades of blue, fell down Aunt Cauldroneyes' cheeks. The buttons were her tears.[4]

"Don't be sad, Aunt Cauldroneyes," I said as the Star Spider collected the buttons.

She started to hang them in Aunt Cauldroneyes' braids as if the buttons were blue beetles in a web.

"I bet that one day the skies will be full of Star Spiders again," I said, gently squeezing her hand once more, "because you won't stop fighting until they are."

Aunt Cauldroneyes had long been a supporter of plant magic and had taken me to marches with her, protesting

[4] * SOME WITCHES CRY TEARS OF BUTTONS, WHILE OTHERS MAY CRY TEARS OF CAT WHISKERS OR FERN SEEDS.

the use of animals in spells. For centuries witches and wizards had used things like dragon's tongue, toad eyes, and unicorn horn in their cauldrons. But Aunt Cauldroneyes said it was cruel to steal a dragon from the sky. She said it wasn't right to capture a phoenix for his ashes or a unicorn for her horn.

She shared the history books with me about the origin of magic and how the first witches and wizards had used plants, not animals, to cast their spells.

"Roots and trees, leaves and seeds, are all a witch or wizard will ever need," she always said. "Magic is a living force. If we feed it blood and bones, we turn it into a curse. Remember this, Spella."

I loved foraging with her in the forest. We always took the frog hat with us. He would hop around and use his long tongue to pick up herbs, nuts, and rocks.

A couple of days after my eighth birthday, we headed out to the forest. I always made sure to wear my vest anytime I went into the forest. Aunt Cauldroneyes had made it for me out of leftover scraps of fabric. It had spots of shaggy fur and patches of purple corduroy. She had sewn pockets on both the front and the back of the vest, hanging each with small star charms. The pockets were always stuffed with things I had collected. And I always collected the most things from the forest.

As Aunt Cauldroneyes and the frog hat hopped their way through Hungry Snout, I ran up ahead to a tall purple oak and laid my hands upon the tree. My blue freckles instantly glowed as the bark moved in slow swirls as if it were a potion in a cauldron being stirred. I started to write with my fingers across the bark in a language known as Elflock.[5*] Not even Aunt Cauldroneyes, as old as she was, knew how to read or write it. But for as long as I could remember, I had been able to. The words were written in long, twisting lines like roots. It was why Elflock was known as the ancient language of the trees.

As I wrote the last letter, the words sparkled with light and the oak's branches started to shake with the earth beneath our feet. I stood back beside Aunt Cauldroneyes and the frog hat as we watched the mighty oak break free from the ground. Dirt and rock fell away as the tree rose higher and higher until a woodland unicorn, snorting and huffing, climbed up out of the earth. The oak tree was now revealed as the horn upon her head.

The woodland unicorn's body was made out of whirling roots and sticks. Her mane and tail were leaves in the same shades of green as her eyes. She smelled warm and nice, like the earth after a rain. Clumps of mud fell from her as she took a step. I looked at her wonderful hooves. They were made out of boulders. Fluffy moss grew out of the cracks in them.

"I have not seen a tree speaker in a long time," the woodland unicorn said with a neigh that echoed across

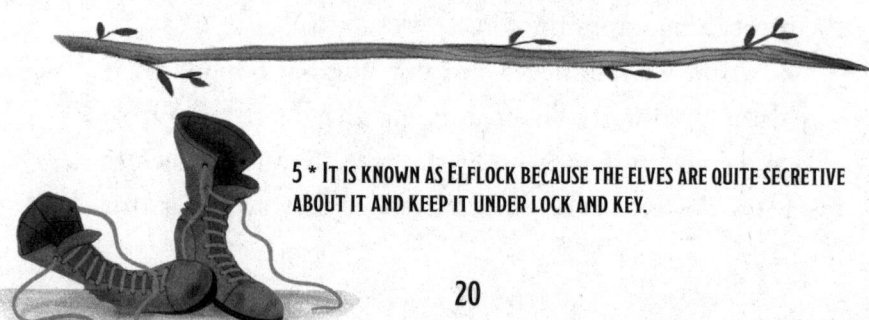

5 * It is known as Elflock because the elves are quite secretive about it and keep it under lock and key.

the forest. She was so tall, the frog hat tumbled backward as he stared up at her. Aunt Cauldroneyes laughed and picked up the hat.

"Those in my herd who have already met you call you Spella," the unicorn said. "Is that your name, tree speaker?"

"Spella De-broom Cauldroneyes is my full name," I said. "And this is my aunt. Her name is Mathilda Cauldroneyes."

Aunt Cauldroneyes bowed to the woodland unicorn, who did the same to her, causing the tree on top of the unicorn's head to shed some leaves. I caught one in my hand and put it in a pocket on my vest. I knew the leaf was like having a lock of the unicorn's hair. For the next hour, as the frog hat hopped around, we listened to the ancient giant speak about her life in the forest, about galloping beneath the ground with her herd.

"Every time you see a tree," the unicorn said, "it is the horn of me or one of my sisters. And every time you see a forest, it is a herd of us galloping beneath the ground." She smiled, and her teeth were made of small, flat rocks. "It is said that our galloping is what turns the world."

"It is indeed what turns the world," Aunt Cauldroneyes said as she laid her hand on the unicorn's boulder hoof. The moss in the cracks responded by blooming little white flowers.

"I shall be happy to tell my herd that I have spoken to you both." The unicorn neighed and tossed her mane of leaves back. "Goodbye for now, Spella De-broom and Mathilda Cauldroneyes."

She stepped back into the hole she had made when she

climbed up out of the earth. Dirt gently fell in on her as she disappeared into the ground, and the oak tree lowered back down to settle into place on top of grass that instantly grew to cover the spot.

Aunt Cauldroneyes let the frog hat hop out of her arms and dusted off the tree's bark the way she would the hats after they'd gotten too muddy in play. Then she said to me, "You were born knowing how to read and write the ancient Elflock language. It's a rare gift to have. What you can do is very special, Spella."

"It's nothing special," I said, lowering my head. "I have funny hands, is all. It's probably why my parents left me in the purple cauldron when I was a baby. They didn't want me."

"I don't know why they left you in the cauldron," Aunt Cauldroneyes said. "But I do know it's not because they didn't want you. You have to remember, Spella, it was not a silly old shoebox they left you in but a cauldron. You act like a cauldron is one's place to keep dirty socks. Little dear, only the most treasured things are put into cauldrons. Spells and prayers and all of one's hopes and dreams. And secrets. Oh yes, plenty of secrets."

She smiled and wrapped one of her long braids around my shoulders like a warm scarf.

"Did you know that if a cauldron is ever in water, it will float?" she said. "And if it is ever tossed up into the sky, it will fly. A cauldron will keep you warm when it has to, and cool when you need it to. Whoever put you into that cauldron did so with love, little dear. And not because they didn't want you."

"You really think so, Aunt Cauldroneyes?"

She squeezed me tight in a hug and said, "Yes, I really do."

"There's a feather!" the frog hat said as he hopped by. He made a *ribbit* before sticking his long tongue out and wrapping it around the fallen feather. He carried it to Aunt Cauldroneyes.

"Oh, look here, Spella." She took the feather and held it up. "It's from a River Eagle." She flew the feather through the air. Drops of water rained down from it. "It's said that the River Eagle is born from the surface of a river and that its feathers are created out of the ripples at the water's edge."

She turned to me and asked, "What is that word you always say, little dear? When something is especially cool?"

The word "cool" always sounded funny in her old voice and made me giggle.

"Was it 'awesome 'possum'?" she asked. "Or something like that?"

"Not 'awesome 'possum,' Aunt Cauldroneyes! Toadfire."

"Oh, yes. Sorry, little dear." She turned back to the feather. "This feather is toadfire."

I watched the water drop softly from the feather.

"I've read about the River Eagles," I said, remembering the stack of books I always kept by my bed to read at night. "There are fewer than a hundred left in all the world."

"That's right, little dear." Aunt Cauldroneyes' tone deepened. She stared down at the feather as if she held something heavier in her hand. "Fewer than a hundred

River Eagles, when once there had been so many, the surface of the rivers constantly rippled. Tell me, Spella, why have so many of the eagles disappeared?"

"They were stolen out of the skies," I said, remembering the sadness of the passage in the book.

"Yes." She spoke quietly as water from the feather dripped between her fingers. "It was believed if you captured a River Eagle, and squeezed their feathers into your spells, then you would capture the power of water. And everything that reflected in it would belong to you. You'd be able to walk across rivers, lakes, the sea. Turn a single drop of it into silver."

She held the feather up toward the sky and asked, "What do we say now, Spella? What do we say when we find a gift in the forest?"

"Thank you, kind eagle, for dropping your feather for us to find," I said.

She tucked the feather down into one of her pockets and said, "A forager is a woman of many pockets. Remember this now, Spella. Always have one more pocket than you think you'll need."

"I think I have enough already, Aunt Cauldroneyes." I patted the ones in my vest, bursting with things I had collected over time, like polka-dotted rocks and barking twigs and the fluffy fuzz furls from the forest, which I thought looked like pieces of storm clouds.

I showed her the pockets in my shorts that were stuffed with buttons and spools and enough chocolate mice for Egypt to eat on long walks in the forest. I tapped my boots until little critters popped their heads out above the flannel lining and through the holes in the toes. Some two-headed lizards even peeked out between the bootlaces. Lastly I showed her the headband I had made out of a scrap of fabric. In the top of it I'd sewn a little pocket, just big enough for one of the mice hats to pop in and out of.

"See," I said, smiling. "I have enough places to hide all the slobbering toadstools[6] and dead men's toes."

"Dead men's toes!" Aunt Cauldroneyes laughed. "What an old witchy thing to say." Then she smiled and said, "A forager is a *girl* of many pockets."

She grabbed my hand, and together we hopped through the forest with the hat like three frogs finding their way home.

[6] * THE SLOBBER FROM A SLOBBERING TOADSTOOL IS SWEET AND EXCELLENT TO ADD TO TEA.

Spell No. 13,001

The clouds drift on a ghost whale.
Midnight comes when the waves are pale.

Note from the Before Long Witch

If you're a pirate and need to create wind to sail your ship across the high seas, this spell is for you. The wind will come sure enough, but be prepared to hear its whole life story, for the winds love to chat more than a three-eyed gnome. This spell can also be used on washday when you have to launder your pet dragon's favorite blanket. This spell will dry the blanket instantly, and your pet dragon will be sure to stop misbehaving and melting the neighbor's begonias.

CHAPTER 3
DO GHOSTS WEAR HATS?

THE ATTIC WAS THE TALLEST TOWER ON OUR HOUSE.

It was crooked, with a lean to the east, and was full of fabric and lace that floated above our heads and all the way up into the rafters of the ceiling. There were long slender buttons with legs like a centipede's, and they would climb onto the floating fabric, only to jump down on top of Aunt Cauldroneyes' head. She would frighten so badly, she'd nearly trip over her braids. Then she'd laugh and hold her arms open as she said, "I love you all like a sky full of dragons."

The attic would speak back to her in flutters and sparkling whispers.

I adored going up to the attic. It had chairs, tufted and

puffed, with little skirts that hung over wooden legs, so the giggling mice hats could run beneath them to hide from the owl hats flying above. There were enough plump chairs for all the hats to sit in whenever they tired of running with me and Egypt beneath the floating fabric, past shelves of glittering jars full of bits and baubles, like pumpkin puffs and fire feathers that Aunt Cauldroneyes would sew onto the hats.

Sometimes the octopus hat, Mr. Sea Captain, would pick me up in one of his tentacles and fly me through the air, before setting me back down where the braver of the hats were already in line for their own turn. In our magical house the attic was the most magical room of all, and there was always a glow and warmth coming from the hat covered in flames who sat in the big stone fireplace.

"That hat once belonged to a dragon," Aunt Cauldroneyes told me. "That's why he's part fire."

The hat loved it when I roasted mallowfluffs in his flames, and he was ever so careful not to burn them. Aunt Cauldroneyes would blow on the mallowfluffs to cool them down before handing them out to the hats who crowded over, waiting for their treat. The bat hats would speed by to pierce one with a pointed fang, before flapping up to the rafters, where they hung upside down and smacked loudly.

It was in the attic that Aunt Cauldroneyes made all the hats. During the eight years I lived with her, she taught me how to make them, too. But I didn't have thread in my hands or sewing needles for fingernails. I had to learn the old-fashioned way. I made the mistake of starting with edible thread, which smelled so much like sugar cookies that the bat hats kept flying around me and eating it before I even got to make one stitch.

Worst of all, the big buttons I liked best kept hiding from me in the drawers.

"Why don't they like me?" I asked Aunt Cauldroneyes.

"Oh, little dear." She chuckled. "They like you."

"Then why are they hiding from me?"

She turned over the tin in her hand. "Because, Spella, you've opened the can of shy buttons. They hide from everyone, even your old aunt Cauldroneyes."

One of the buttons peeked out at us, before shrieking and running to the back of the drawer.

"Let me show you which of these will be best for you to start with," Aunt Cauldroneyes said as she pointed out items on the shelves. "That jar has moonfoam in it. Very easy to sew with. There's a canister of pumpkin seeds. Though, I always have the habit of eating those before I can even sew them on. That bottle holds the pieces of an old sea map. Excellent to add to a pirate's hat. There's a box of clock hands. Next to it are some twirlblasts. We'll save those for when you're a little better with the needle."

Aunt Cauldroneyes pulled up an old wooden chair for me beside hers. Together we sat at the sewing table. It was scratched with scissor marks from centuries of use and had nooks and crannies where lost thimbles made their homes. As the thimbles peeked out and watched, Aunt Cauldroneyes taught me the double and under stitch, the over and out, the flippity pull, and all the ancient knots, which she said she preferred to the modern ones.

As I learned more and more about magical hat-making, Aunt Cauldroneyes gifted me with a wooden sewing box that had a handle carved with my name. The grain in the honey-colored wood of the box looked like big owl eyes, and each of the little drawers had tiny golden keys hung with shimmering blue tassels. She stocked the box with hopping pincushions,[7*] burping buttons, singing scissors, and all the thread I would ever need. Inside the box were tiny doorways for the thimbles to walk through from one drawer to another, and if you opened the top lid, a little spinning hat popped up like in a music box.

The box was always by my side as I worked at the sewing table. I knew in the beginning that Aunt Cauldroneyes sewed slowly so I could keep up with her. But soon her hands stitched as fast as lightning, her two braids sticking straight up. Even though I wasn't as fast as her yet, she said, "You're a natural hatmaker, Spella. It's as though you were born to the needle and thread."

Sometimes when we were sewing together, I would wonder if I was born to it. *Would my grandmother have taught me to sew, the way Aunt Cauldroneyes did? Would my father have laughed at the shy buttons? Would my mother have*

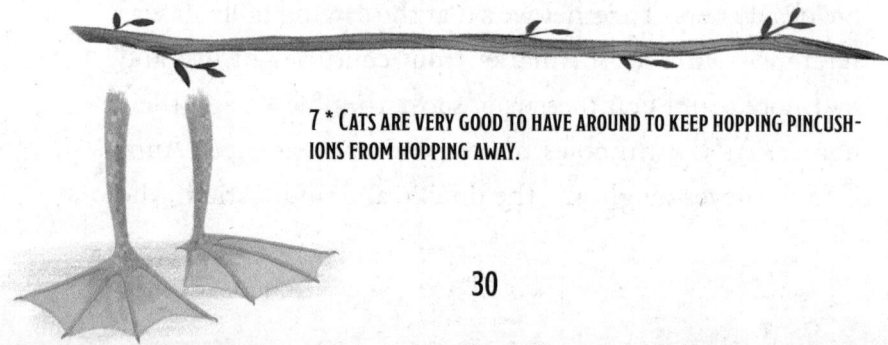

7 * Cats are very good to have around to keep hopping pincushions from hopping away.

danced in the floating fabric? Would I have brothers and sisters to roast mallowfluffs with in the fireplace?

I always felt closer to Aunt Cauldroneyes as we worked on the hats, but when I looked at the thread coming out of her hands, I knew I wasn't like her. I had the hands of my mother. The fingers of my father. And yet, I didn't even know their names. All I did know was that they had left me in a purple cauldron.

When I thought too much about it, my sewing would get so slow, it would stop, and Aunt Cauldroneyes' braids would drop down to lie across her shoulders as she asked, "What's wrong, little dear?"

"Nothing," I'd say, quickly picking the needle and thread back up. "I just forgot my counting. That's all."

Then the bat hats would fly over and tickle my hands with their fangs until I laughed and called them, "Silly little vampires."

The hats who lived with us, like the bat hats, were never given away. Only the hats that were custom-ordered by magical creatures and other folks were the hats that left to go home with their new families. But we always sent each off with plenty of goodies to remember us by.

I'd get the round hatboxes down from the shelf. The boxes were just as beautiful as the hats themselves. Me and Aunt Cauldroneyes would wrap the boxes in fabrics like velvet and silk printed with old-fashioned flowers such as fairy fangles and wistereyes. And I'd always tie each box with the tongue of a Frobby Beast.[8*] When Aunt Cauldroneyes first told me about the tongues, I imagined someone reaching into the creatures' mouths and yanking their tongues out.

"Certainly not!" Aunt Cauldroneyes said with a hearty chuckle. "A Frobby Beast grows a new tongue every day, so their old one drops off to the ground. The tongues come in a variety of colors and are as soft as satin and tie into a bow quite easily, even though they tend to flop about from time to time."

Aunt Cauldroneyes would leave me to pack the hats in the boxes while she went downstairs to make cookies to send the hats off with. She knew all their favorites recipes, after all.

As soon as she was gone, I'd take a hat back out of the box and go to the mirror in the corner of the attic. The mirror stood taller than me in a dark wood frame carved with rosebuds and toadstools. As I stared at my reflection, I would put the hat on to see if it felt like who my family might have been.

When I put on a hat Aunt Cauldroneyes had made for a unicorn, I pulled my long hair through the hole for the horn, but my hair only fell limp instead of standing up straight and tall. It didn't look right. My mother and father weren't unicorns. I put on the hat for the werewolf, but it howled too much. My mother and father weren't wild wolves. When I

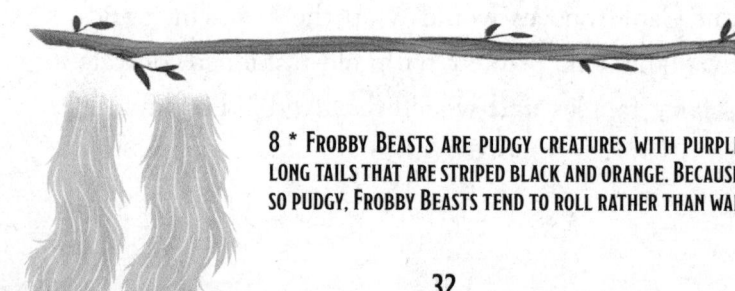

8 * FROBBY BEASTS ARE PUDGY CREATURES WITH PURPLE FUR AND LONG TAILS THAT ARE STRIPED BLACK AND ORANGE. BECAUSE THEY ARE SO PUDGY, FROBBY BEASTS TEND TO ROLL RATHER THAN WALK.

tried on the goblin hat, the green slime made my skin sticky. My mother and father weren't goblins.

I had tried on just about every hat. Then came the day Aunt Cauldroneyes said ghosts had put in an order requesting matching hats for a family photo.

"Ghosts!" I said. "Do ghosts wear hats?"

Aunt Cauldroneyes laughed as she pulled a dusty box down from a top shelf in the attic. The box was marked with delightful words like SECRET and MYSTIFYING. Written above a hole cut into the lid was FEED WITH DUST.

Aunt Cauldroneyes took a pinch of dust off the shelf and sprinkled it into the hole as she said, "One should never open a hungry box if one can help it."

I nodded and fed the box a pinch of dust myself before the box burped and popped open. It appeared empty inside except for a couple of pairs of funny eyeglasses that looked as though a mad scientist had made them. They had odd screws that kept tightening and loosening themselves until coils popped out, and they had wide nailheads that were shaped like lightning bolts. But the oddest thing about the eyeglasses were the lenses, which were nearly a foot thick.

"Beautiful, aren't they?" Aunt Cauldroneyes said as she grabbed the pair that ticked like a clock. Once she put the glasses on, the lenses stuck out from her face farther than her nose.

She turned to me and blinked. I tried not to laugh. Her eyes were large without the glasses, but with them, they were downright gigantic.

"The lenses enlarge our eyes," she said. "So we can see

things we might normally not be able to. Go on, little dear. Put yours on."

I picked up the other pair, which creaked each time a screw tightened or loosened itself. Once I put them on, I expected them to be quite heavy because of how thick the lenses were, but they were as light as a feather.

"Wow!" I said, staring down into the box the glasses had come in. It wasn't empty after all. It was full of whispering threads, floating buttons, and enough charms to make several hats.

"My invisible collection," Aunt Cauldroneyes said, turning the box out on the sewing table. "Let's get started."

The ghosts had ordered three hats. We chose fabric that billowed and would hang down like veils over their faces.

"Because ghosts go *boo* for that sort of thing," Aunt Cauldroneyes said.

The bits and baubles we used were things like clusters of cobwebs and antique laces. Some of the buttons were called creaky buttons, because they creaked like old doors.

"Ghosts also like things that rattle and jangle and creak," Aunt Cauldroneyes said.

She put me in charge of the daughter's hat. I added extra charms to hers. I knew that's what I would like if I were getting a hat made. I also sewed on silver roses so they could rise up out of the fog we'd dipped the hats in.

We had just finished and taken off our glasses when there was a knock on the front door. I ran down to answer it while Aunt Cauldroneyes helped Egypt catch the hopping pincushions.

"Welcome to the magical hatmakers!" I said when I opened the door, because it's what I always said. Usually there'd be a creature or some magical folk on the doorstep with their order slip, ready to pick up their hat. But there was no one there.

I started to close the door. Then a woman's voice said, "We're here to pick up our hats, honey." Her voice had a little bit of a squeak in it. A delightful voice for a ghost.

"Oh," I said, "you're the ghosts! I'm sorry, I can't see you. I left my glasses up in the attic."

"We're the invisible ones," a man said. *"Boooooo!"* He sang a ghostly song, then laughed and asked, "Are the hats ready?"

"Stitch and sew, buttons and bats," I said. *"Come on in and get your hats!"* It was the rhyme me and Aunt Cauldroneyes always said to a customer. "Aunt Cauldroneyes will want you to go up to the attic to try them on," I added. "She'll want to make certain the hats fit."

I pointed the way up the staircase and waited for them to go first. Once I headed up, I nearly fell back down when a girl screamed, "You stepped on my foot!"

"Sorry," I quickly said. "I didn't see you there."

"I bet no one makes the mistake of not seeing you with those blue warts on your face." Her tone was just as sharp as the other kids' in the village who called my freckles goblin boogers or fairy spit.

"They're not warts," I said, frowning. "They're freckles."

"Well, if I had those hideous *spots*, I'd be glad I was a ghost," she said.

She stomped up the stairs while I made sure to stay a couple of feet behind. When I got into the attic, Aunt

Cauldroneyes was wearing her glasses. I quickly put my pair on. I thought ghosts might be a little scary-looking, but the mother and father were smiling at Aunt Cauldroneyes as she held up their hats and showed them the stitching and what she called "craftsmanship."

I could tell the ghosts had died several centuries ago because of all the ruffles in their clothing and all the lace in their cloaks. The mother had been beheaded and held her head in the crook of her arm. The head smiled at me, and I smiled back.

I was certain the father had died by drowning. His clothes were still wet and dripping with water that smelled like the sea. Best of all was that he had a rather funny-looking squid clinging to the back of his cloak.

"Would you put my hat on me?" the mother asked as she held her smiling head out toward Aunt Cauldroneyes.

"I most certainly will, my dear," Aunt Cauldroneyes said. She very carefully placed the hat on the severed head and made sure to hang the veil just right. The head smiled wider as a ghostly worm crawled from one nostril to the other. After Aunt Cauldroneyes stood back and examined every angle of the hat, she started to point out the charms on it and explain each to the ghosts.

"This dangly one is an upside-down squishy scab,[9*] and it's weighted," she said, "so if you find yourself in high

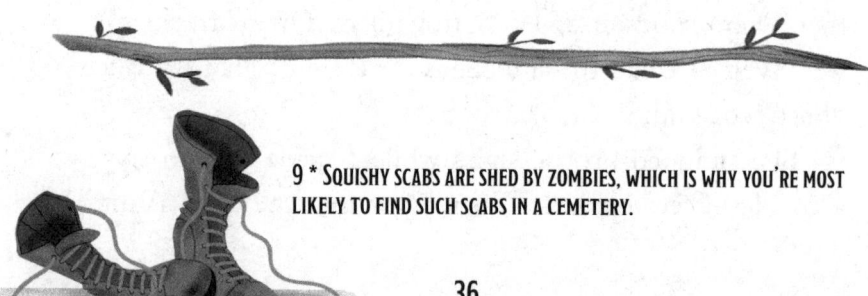

9 * SQUISHY SCABS ARE SHED BY ZOMBIES, WHICH IS WHY YOU'RE MOST LIKELY TO FIND SUCH SCABS IN A CEMETERY.

winds, you won't blow away. The charm is like an anchor."

The ghost girl was standing behind her parents. She had her arms crossed and was frowning at me. Her clothes were just as ruffled, and she wore the type of long dress that would snag on a branch whenever she climbed a tree. If not for the poisonous mushrooms filling her pockets, I might not have known how she'd become a ghost. I noticed right away that she had her mother's eyes and her father's hair. I couldn't help but wish I knew the color of my mother's eyes.

I turned away and saw the girl's hat was still sitting on the sewing table.

"Aunt Cauldroneyes?" I quickly picked the hat up. "I want to add one other charm to this, but I left it in my room. I'll go down and get it and bring the hat right back."

"Of course, little dear."

As I headed downstairs, I could hear Aunt Cauldroneyes telling the ghosts, "It was Spella's idea to add weighted charms. She's a wonderful hatmaker. Notice how straight her stitches are."

I ran into my room with the hat and stood in front of my dresser mirror.

"*Stitch and sew, buttons and bats,*" I whispered to my reflection. "*Come on in and get your hats.*"

I put the hat on, but it was too cold and too dark, and there was too much fog puffing out the top. My family weren't ghosts.

"What do you think you're doing?" the ghost girl shouted.

I turned around to see her in my doorway.

"That's my hat." She floated over and snatched it off

my head. "Your warts better not be contagious."

"I told you, they're not warts! They're freckles."

"You need to make me a new one." She shook the hat as if dusting off dirt. "Why were you wearing it? It's not yours!"

"I was just seeing if it fit me," I said.

"Why would it fit you?"

"I just thought that maybe your parents might be . . ." I looked down at the floor.

"Might be what?" She laughed. "Be yours? Are you, like, a stray or something?"

"Stop it." I looked up at her. "Stop laughing at me."

"You're just a silly hatmaker with blue warts. You could never be part of my family."

Her words hurt more than I thought they would. Not because I wasn't part of her family but because I wasn't part of anyone's.

"I wouldn't want to be part of your family!" I said.

I didn't know I was crying until she called me a blubbering baby.

I ran past her and down the stairs, throwing the eyeglasses off so I could no longer see her laughing.

"Spella?" Aunt Cauldroneyes was out of the attic and standing at the top of the steps. "What happened? Where are you going?"

But I didn't stop running until I was out of the house and in Hungry Snout Forest. I went to one of my favorite places. It was in the meadow of wild ooshberries. There I sat against one of the large boulders and stared out at the bright red berries, but they didn't make me feel better like they usually did. I stayed there until Aunt Cauldroneyes came out with a basket in her hand.

"Oh, here you are," she said.

"I want to be alone." I quickly wiped my eyes on my sleeves.

"Of course, little dear. Don't worry about me. I'm only out here to collect some Frobby tongues to wrap around the hatboxes."

But I knew she wasn't, because collecting Frobby tongues was what I did.

"You don't mind, do you?" she asked. "Oh, Frobby tongue, where are you?" she called into the forest, but stepped closer to me. "Here, Frobby tongue. Where are you?"

I wiped my eyes again and asked, "Are the ghosts gone, Aunt Cauldroneyes?"

"Oh, yes. They've taken their hats and floated away. I don't think their daughter was very nice, was she?" Aunt Cauldroneyes sat down beside me, laying her basket off to the side. "What did she say to you, little dear?"

"Nothing I haven't heard before." I started to rub my cheeks. "I wish I could wipe these freckles off."

"Don't say that, Spella."

"It's true! But they won't come off." I took a handful of mud and smeared it onto my cheeks, trying to cover my freckles. "So I'll just have to hide them."

"Spella, don't do that." Aunt Cauldroneyes tried to take my hands in hers, but I only grabbed more mud. I covered my face with it, then stuck leaves to my cheeks until it was like I was wearing a mask.

"There!" I cried out. "Now the world doesn't have to see how ugly I am."

I got up and ran through the field and farther into the trees, but I tripped, catching the hem of my shorts on a thorn. When I sat up, it tore the fabric in a long rip.

I shut my eyes, the tears falling down over the mud and leaves on my face.

"Don't cry, Spella," I whispered to myself, remembering the words of the ghost girl. "Stop being a blubbering baby. Stop it!"

"It's okay to cry, little dear."

I opened my eyes to see Aunt Cauldroneyes kneeling beside me, her knees creaking and cracking like an old wooden floor. She ran her fingers over the rip in my shorts made by the thorn as she said, "We'll have to patch this one up good."

She looked at the other patches already on my shorts.

"You are a strong girl," she said. "You've had many adventures. Look here." She pointed to the blue patch by my pocket. "How'd you get that one again, Spella?"

"I climbed a grumpy tumbler,"[10*] I said, and softly wiped my nose.

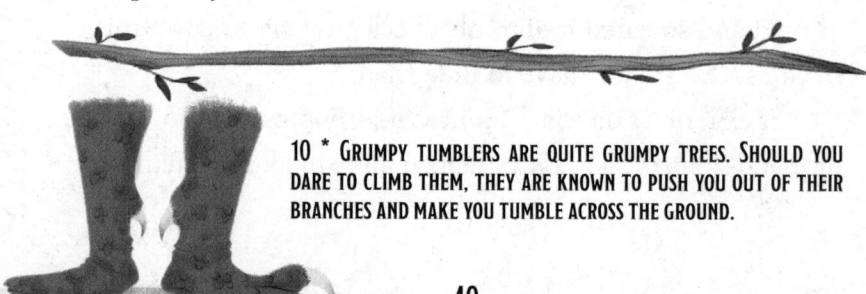

10 * Grumpy tumblers are quite grumpy trees. Should you dare to climb them, they are known to push you out of their branches and make you tumble across the ground.

"Oh, that's right." She smiled. "And what about that one?" She pointed to the yellow patch sewn with black thread and shaped like a heart.

"I raced the nine-legged cheetah around the house." I touched the patch, remembering.

"And this one?" She rubbed her fingers over the red fuzzy patch on the sleeve of my shirt.

"I got that when I arm-wrestled that cranky chugbug," I said a little louder.

"My, my, you've been as brave as a giant," she said. "As fast as a Pegasus. Even your boots speak of your wild life." She ran her fingers over the patches on them. "Toadfire." She whispered the one word like it was an entire spell.

"There's nothing brave about this one," I said, pulling at the new rip in my shorts. "It's only a thorn tear."

"It's not," Aunt Cauldroneyes said. "It's from the day you had to remember that you are perfect just the way you are. Blue freckles 'n' all."

"I don't feel perfect." One of the leaves dropped off my cheek to the forest floor.

"You know, when I was a little girl, folks laughed at me, too," Aunt Cauldroneyes said.

"No one would laugh at you," I said.

"Oh, they laughed at me something awful! They made fun of my hands so much, I started to wish I didn't have magical thread in them at all."

"But your thread is more amazing than a whole bowl of chocolate." I sat up taller. "How could you ever wish you didn't have it?"

"I just wanted to be like everybody else," she said. "So I started to wear gloves to try to hide my hands. But the thread kept spinning and piling up inside the gloves. I would snap the thread off and hide it in jars and old potion bottles and charm bags in my room. There was so much, the thread piled up all around me. Then one day an owl pecked at my window. He'd had all his feathers stolen by the moon when he flew too close to it. He had heard about me, he said. Heard there was a young witch with thread in her hands who could sew anything back on, including feathers."

The Star Spider came out of Aunt Cauldroneyes' hair to sit on her cheek and listen.

"The owl asked me if I would sew feathers back onto him," Aunt Cauldroneyes said. "I couldn't turn that poor bird away." She hooted like an old owl, then said, "That night, I took the gloves off my hands and started to sew. The moon is notorious for stealing feathers from birds who fly too close, and the moon never gives them back, so it was a good thing I had collected so many in my pockets over the years. I sewed on the fluff of bluebeaks and thunderbirds, of tweedlers and sparples. He became a quilt of feathers."

"He sounds beautiful." I imagined bright yellow tweedler feathers against the deep rich purple of a sparple's.

"He did look rather toadfire." She smiled. "I even made him a hat out of the bluest feathers from my pockets. He was so happy, he flapped his wings hard enough that all the windows in my room flew open and the piles of thread escaped out into the world, sewing the things that needed sewing and stitching the things that needed stitching."

She picked up the leaf that had fallen from my cheek and laid it over the thorn tear in my shorts. Blue thread came from her hands. She used it to sew the leaf on as it became a new patch.

"If I had kept wearing gloves and hiding my hands," she said, "I would have been hiding who I am." She touched the mud and leaves on my face. "Just like if you wear this mask hiding your blue freckles, you will be hiding who you are, Spella."

She started to search her pockets, pulling out whistling tea bags and half-eaten chocolate bars, even a startled but sleepy-looking mouse hat.

"Aha!" she finally said, pulling out the feather of the River Eagle. "Let's see what magic the old bird will give you."

She held the feather up and started to sweep it across my forehead. The water dripped from the feather and down my skin, causing the leaves and mud to slide off my cheeks.

"There's my Spella," she said, smiling at me. "And you are perfect just the way you are."

When I stared at my reflection in her large eyes, I could see that the feather had washed my face clean, revealing the bright blue freckles shining back at me.

"I bet your mother had freckles, too," Aunt Cauldron-eyes said.

I wrapped my arms around her and held her in a tight hug.

"I love you like a sky full of dragons, Aunt Cauldron-eyes," I said.

"And I you, little dear." She patted my back. "Now, how about we go and collect some Frobby tongues to tie around our hatboxes, eh?"

"I'd love to," I said as we stood up together. We didn't forage for long before I spotted a striped tongue on the ground by a bush.

"Ah, this is a good one," Aunt Cauldroneyes said as she picked up the tongue.

It flopped in her hand, and we laughed.

"There's always so much slobber on a Frobby tongue," she said.

"That's to be expected from a Frobby Beast." I smiled. "And they are perfect just the way they are."

CHAPTER 4
A Cauldron of Letters

WHEN YOU'RE RAISED BY A WITCH WHO IS ALWAYS looking into cauldrons, it means there's going to be plenty of cauldrons in the house. There were large iron ones in the kitchen for soups, and small copper ones for jams, jellies, and the boiling of milk for the chocolate curl. Hanging on the wall by the pantry was an oak rack of tiny cauldrons, each with a knobbed lid and labeled with spice names like "frog warts," "troll toenails,"[11*] and "gnome beard."

11 * Troll toenails are delightfully crunchy, but be warned, they will make your breath smell like feet.

Throughout the house were painted cauldrons that lit up and had shades over them like lamps. These cauldrons sat on tables by the sofas and chairs. The green cauldrons in the garden grew herbs and flowers and long twisting ivy. Sitting on Aunt Cauldroneyes' vanity were very tiny crystal cauldrons full of bright violet lotions and pale pink creams that she used for her rough feet and to soothe any pickle spots she got from the biting pixies in the bushes in the backyard.

In the attic sat the patchwork cauldron Aunt Cauldroneyes had quilted herself. It bubbled over with all the stuffing she would ever need to fill the hats with. There were plenty more cauldrons of all kinds and sizes that stored books and papers and little knickknacks. If you ever lost anything in our house, it would probably be found in a cauldron.

We even had one that delivered our mail. He was a big thing made of iron, and he walked on chicken legs. But he wasn't just *our* cauldron. He held all the letters and packages for everyone in Witches' Bells, which was the village we lived in.

It wasn't more than a week after I turned eight that the cauldron full of letters knocked on our door and delivered an invitation addressed to me. It had been sent from Dragon's Knob, a school for wand magic that was a journey to the west. The official school business came in a dark green envelope with a bright red wax seal.

The wax lay in heavy drips with gold flecks, and the seal was of the school's coat of arms, which was a whole sky's worth of dragons with a shield in the center that featured a dragon eye, claw, wing, and flame. On occasion a tiny fire would shoot from the seal, the dragons' breath coming out several inches before disappearing in puffs of smoke. The longer I went without opening the invitation, the more bursts of fire that came and the more the wax melted, spelling out the words OPEN AND DISCOVER.

I convinced myself that if I never opened the invitation, I would never have to go to Dragon's Knob. I'd read about it in some of Aunt Cauldroneyes' books on the history of wand magic. The school had once been the castle for the great Dragon King, who had been a well-loved leader in his day and had allowed everyone to come from all over to take books out of his castle library. He even allowed mudsters[12*] to take books, and everyone knows you never lend a book to a mudster. It'll come back half-eaten and covered in mud.

I thought the Dragon King sounded rather nice. One day he fell out of the sky while flying over a field full of spring flowers. He was several thousand years old by then, silvered in age. His wish was for his castle to become a school, open to anyone seeking the ways of the wand.

Every so often Aunt Cauldroneyes would ready her

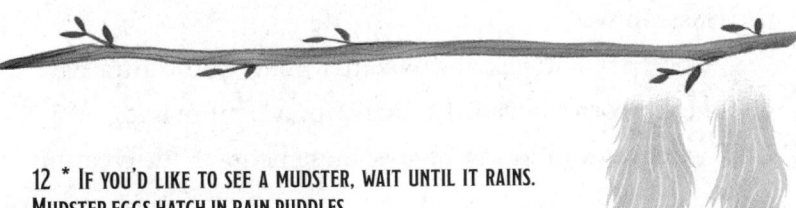

12 * IF YOU'D LIKE TO SEE A MUDSTER, WAIT UNTIL IT RAINS.
MUDSTER EGGS HATCH IN RAIN PUDDLES.

flying broom and go west to the school to repair the ancient castle, the way she would a worn hat. She mended the breaks and cracks in the brick with mismatched fabric patches while the old castle kept a close eye on her stitches.

"The castle will groan whenever the thread is too tight and it will sigh when it is too loose," Aunt Cauldroneyes would tell me when she returned home.

I never went to the castle with her. For as long as I could remember, Aunt Cauldroneyes had told me that when I turned eight years old, I would receive an invitation to the school. The more she talked about it, the more I started to worry. The other kids in the village spotted their cheeks with blue ink and laughed at me. There were going to be loads more kids at the school. And, despite having been found in a purple cauldron as a baby, I'd never felt particularly magical. I worried that if I picked up a wand, nothing but sparks would come out. I'd be known as the girl with blue freckles and no magic to tell of.

Aunt Cauldroneyes was excited when I received the invitation. She said Dragon's Knob was the finest school for wand magic. "And you will be among the first students to attend in this historical time," she told me.

It was a historical time because the school had become the first to completely do away with the use of creatures in the classrooms.

"The first witches and wizards knew you didn't have to cut a unicorn's horn off to make powerful magic," Aunt Cauldroneyes would say in speeches she gave for creature rights.

She was known far and wide for her activism against cruelty and her campaigns for laws that would ban the use of all creatures, including insects and reptiles, in magic. She held marches and protests and was one of the founders of the Sisterhood of the W.O.L.V.E.S., which stood for Witches' Oath to Love and Value the Environment for Spellwork. They were a group of witches who united for the cause.

At first they met in secret. They would leave messages for one another scratched into fern leaves or elf cups.[13*] They even left messages hidden in the flight patterns of migrating birds like geese and starlings. All the older members had lightning bolts tattooed around their left wrists like charms on a bracelet. I didn't have any because I was the youngest member of the sisterhood, but Aunt Cauldroneyes kept that secret from everyone who wasn't in the group, because not every witch and wizard was happy with her activism.

Aunt Cauldroneyes would get two types of letters in the mail. Some of the letters were from folks supporting her efforts to protect creatures, and some letters were from folks who promised to curse her if she continued. But Aunt Cauldroneyes didn't let threats stop her, and once Dragon's Knob committed to using only plants in their classrooms,

13 * ELF CUPS ARE VERY TINY MUSHROOMS SHAPED LIKE CUPS THAT ELVES FAVOR FOR DRINKING THEIR MILK OUT OF.

she said it was a victory for creatures everywhere.

Even though the school had changed, I still didn't want to leave my home in Hungry Snout Forest. I had read the history books on Dragon's Knob, trying to find something terrible about it that I could share with Aunt Cauldroneyes so she would say, "Of course you can't go to a horrid place like that. It wouldn't be nice at all."

But all I'd read about was how stars would float in through the arched openings of the bedchambers at night, which I thought sounded rather wonderful.

"And at certain times of the night," Aunt Cauldroneyes had told me, "the castle becomes so alive, it snores in its sleep."

Still I refused to open the invitation, and little puffs of fire shot out from the seal, melting the wax until it dripped off the parchment envelope and the words OPEN AND DISCOVER AT ONCE started to appear all over it, written in the melted wax.

"Will you make my hat for Dragon's Knob?" I asked Aunt Cauldroneyes one day as we were working in the attic on the hat we called Fleabag.

Fleabag was made of bright blue burlap with round patches that looked like spots. He wore bifocals, and the black frames of the glasses were wrapped with tape from all the times he had broken them. He was rather clumsy, which was why he was up on the sewing table again. We were trimming the fabric around his paws so he wouldn't trip so much.

"I have always made hats for the students of Dragon's

Knob," Aunt Cauldroneyes said. "I will be proud to make your hat, Spella."

"Even if I don't go?" I asked.

She turned to me, and her voice was gentle and patient as she asked, "Is that what you've decided, little dear?"

"I don't want to leave the hats or Egypt or the trees in the forest," I said. "I don't want to leave you. I love it here, Aunt Cauldroneyes."

"And this will always be your home." She laid her hand on the back of mine. "All the friends you have here will forever be your friends, even when you make other ones at Dragon's Knob. Sometimes in our lives we go to different places. We have new adventures. But none of that means we forget the old ones."

"Why don't you want me here anymore, Aunt Cauldroneyes? Why are you sending me away?" I looked up into her eyes, already filling with blue buttons.

"Is that what you think?" she asked as the buttons rolled down her old cheeks. "That I'm sending you away because I don't want you here? Oh, little dear. You're a wand witch. It's why you have that." She pointed at the shadow of the egg cast on the wall behind me. "A Wand Keeper must learn the wand so the egg can hatch."

"Why can't you teach me, Aunt Cauldroneyes?"

"You know why." She held her hands up in the air between us, the thread dangling from her palms. "I am a thread witch."

I jumped up from my chair and ran over to the wooden spools on the shelf.

"I can be like you," I said as I cut long strands of thread off and quickly taped them to my palms. "Now I'm a thread witch like you. I don't have to leave to learn about a stupid wand."

I shook my hands so the thread would dangle, but the tape fell off instead. We watched the thread float down to the floor.

"Why can't I be like you?" I asked.

"Oh, little dear." Aunt Cauldroneyes came over and wrapped her arms around me. "I come from Grandmother Spider, who passed the magic of the web down to me. You, Spella, come from the Wand Keepers. They are the ones who received the shadow eggs from the great thunderbird."

I turned my head to see the egg shadow.

"The creature in that egg is waiting," Aunt Cauldroneyes said. "Waiting for you to learn the ways of the wand so she may hatch into the world."

I walked out of Aunt Cauldroneyes' arms and stepped over to the wall. I laid my hand gently on the shadow. It was warm to the touch, like the belly of an animal turning over, and tiny bolts of lightning wrapped around my fingers.

"At Dragon's Knob you'll learn all the things I can't teach you about wand magic," Aunt Cauldroneyes said. "And when you get back home, I bet you'll find all the hats picking up sticks in the forest to be their wands, and you can teach them your magic, too."

The hats started to cry and gather around us as the blue buttons fell from Aunt Cauldroneyes' eyes and softly clacked against the wood floor. When Grandma's Boot began to cry, his tears were so big, they started to puddle at our feet, and Aunt Cauldroneyes said, "Come on now, everyone. Let's cheer up!"

As we walked back over to the sewing table, I looked down at my hands.

"I wish I had some of Grandmother Spider's magic like you, Aunt Cauldroneyes."

"Well, then let me give you some of her web," she said.

We all gathered around Aunt Cauldroneyes at the sewing table and watched her weave black thread into the pattern of a spiderweb. When she finished, she had a pair of fingerless gloves. After she slipped them onto my hands, she said, "Now you have a bit of Grandmother Spider's web."

Spell No. 13,457

**Kick a broom, break a bowl.
Keep an eye on a mean troll.
Count a witch's warts and moles.
Find out what the wizard stole.**

Note from the Before Long Witch

Have you lost your pet griffin's favorite toy? Or has a chimera been breaking into your greenhouse and stealing all the catnip and rosemary? This spell will allow you to find an object that has been lost, gone missing, or simply vanished. As you recite it, be sure to run in place, so when the path to the lost item is in front of you, you will have a head start. Because this spell takes a lot of energy, be sure to fill up on fairy cakes before attempting such an undertaking.

CHAPTER 5
A KNOCKITY-KNOCK AT THE DOOR

SOME PLACES HAVE BLUE SKIES. SOME HAVE PURPLE ones. But in Witches' Bells we had a sky the color of a witch's favorite potion.

"Everyone and their troll knows that color is bright green," Aunt Cauldroneyes would say.

Witches' Bells was a small village where you could find spices on creaky wooden shelves in the grocery store called Silver Bear, next to a cauldron-polishing shop.

I was always at the library, which was run by the most delightful of gnomes in their hollowed-out tree. I would check out all the books that weren't in Aunt Cauldroneyes' collection whenever she had to go into the village for another tin of mallowfluffs for our nightly chocolate curl, or to have her broom repaired. It was a hand-me-down from her mother and was often losing more bristles than the day had hours.

Nothing scary ever happened in the sleepy little village of Witches' Bells. That is, not until the night of the thunderstorm.

It was a couple of days before the first of October, and we had just gotten back from Witches' Bells with a fresh tin of mallowfluffs and a delightfully tall stack of books for me. I always loved coming in from the village and seeing the house at the end of the stone walk. No matter what side you stood on, you always saw the purple tentacles of the octopus hat, Mr. Sea Captain, hanging out the windows and wrapping around the tower of the attic.

"We're home," Aunt Cauldroneyes said as she smiled up at the wooden sign reading MATHILDA THE MAGICAL MILLINER nailed to the porch post.

We had new orders for hats, so after we put the groceries and books away, we headed up to the attic tower. Egypt was purring loudly. She had gone into the village with us and was particularly excited about the chocolate mice[14*] that

[14*] THE BEST CHOCOLATE MICE COME FROM CAT-OWNED BAKERIES AND ALWAYS HAVE JUST THE RIGHT AMOUNT OF CAT FUR IN THEM.

Aunt Cauldroneyes had picked up for her from the cat bakery Miss Fuzzlepaw's, which was beside Silver Bear.

"But you won't be getting any candy until after dinner," Aunt Cauldroneyes told Egypt with a twinkle in her eye. "I hid your mice in the kitchen. So don't try to find them."

Egypt frowned and said, "If I wanted a chocolate mouse now, I would have a chocolate mouse now. I only *agree* to wait, old one."

Egypt always called Aunt Cauldroneyes "old one," even though Egypt herself was older, by how many years, no one could be sure, except for the ancient cat herself.

"Yes, yes, I know you *agree* to wait." Aunt Cauldroneyes giggled and patted Egypt on the head. "Oh, for you, Spella. I got you some troll boogers. I used to trade them with my friends when I was a little bubble."

She reached into her pocket and pulled out eight bright green boogers.

"Wow, thanks, Aunt Cauldroneyes! They're toadfire." I quickly grabbed them and put them into a pocket.

When we got to the attic, she asked, "What's our next hat to be made, little dear?"

"It's for a baking witch," I said.

I pulled the hat order out from the top drawer of the sewing table.

"She wants a hat that will measure a cup of flour perfectly," I read from the order, "and a hat that will have a never-ending supply of sugar so she never has to go to her cupboards. She said she would like the hat to lay an egg at any time of the day with a gentle pat on the back."

"Oh, is that all?" Aunt Cauldroneyes chuckled.

"She also wants the hat to smell like chocolate in the morning and shortbread in the evening and have several pockets to keep all her recipes." I looked up from the parchment. "This seems like a lot."

"Just remember," Aunt Cauldroneyes said, "making a magical hat isn't much different than gathering ingredients like the baking witch does for a recipe. So, what will we need first?"

"Definitely some sparkly fabric." I reached up to the shiny pink roll floating above my head. "I'd say two yards to get us started."

Hearing that, the bat hats flew down from the rafters and used their fangs to cut a large flop of fabric, which then fell down onto my head.

"Thank you, batties," I said.

I pulled the fabric off my head and held it up to Aunt Cauldroneyes.

"Anytime this baking witch wants sugar," I said, "she just has to shake the hat."

I shook the fabric, causing sugar to rain down on top of Egypt, who immediately started to lick it off her linen. Getting the taste for something sweet, Egypt cleared her throat and said, "I'm going downstairs to make sure there aren't any cupboards and drawers left open in the kitchen." She looked up at Aunt Cauldroneyes. "I know how tidy you like everything to be, old one."

"Yes." Aunt Cauldroneyes smiled. "And I trust that

when I go down to see those drawers and cupboards you've checked on, I won't find any chocolate mice missing?"

"Oh, how dare you." Egypt held her head high. "I would never."

We watched her trot off, nearly tripping on the linen dangling off her legs more than once, before disappearing down the staircase. It wasn't but a few seconds later when we heard a crash from the kitchen.

"That'll be Egypt having found the chocolate mice on the top shelf behind the pots and pans." Aunt Cauldroneyes grinned. "Remind me to get at least two more boxes of those when we go back to Miss Fuzzlepaw's bakery, Spella."

I nodded and grinned as Aunt Cauldroneyes turned her eyes back to the fabric.

"A very wise choice to use sugar cloth, little dear." She clapped. "What else will we need?"

I laid the fabric on the table and said, "I think chocolate-covered thread to sew it all together."

As soon as I set a spool of the thread on the sewing table, the mice hats hopped up and chewed off strings of it to take back to their holes in the walls.

"And what should we sew onto the hat to make sure it will lay an egg with a gentle pat?" Aunt Cauldroneyes asked.

I ran my finger over the labels of the jars on the shelves until landing on one.

"Here's a feather from a cackling chicken," I said, grabbing the jar. "That'll lay an egg anytime she wants."

We spread out the charms and tools to get started.

"How about a spot of tea while we work?" Aunt Cauldroneyes asked.

"Most definitely." I nodded.

"Lady Lemongrass?" she called out. "Lady Lemongrass, care to pour us a cup?"

Answering was a hat who came climbing down from the shelf where she'd been tidying up china cups and saucers. She was made of fabric the color of copper, shiny in places, but water-stained in others, like an old kettle. She had a ribbon of tea bags that softly dragged on the floor behind her. Up close she smelled of lemonfrills and rosefuzzle, depending on the time of day.

Steam always rose from the top of her peak, but when she was stirring up a fresh pot of tea, the steam came in even bigger puffs.

"I have something lovely brewing today," Lady Lemongrass said, climbing up the leg of the sewing table to plop down in front of us.

She reached behind the big bow at her brim and pulled out two teacups, complete with saucers. She had the finest china in the house, printed with the flowers of the season.

"I'm calling today's brew Busy Me tea," she said. "Perfect for a busy day of sewing."

After she set the saucers and cups down, her spout started to whistle. Aunt Cauldroneyes picked her up by the wooden handle and tilted her, pouring out the fresh, steaming tea.

"Don't forget your sugar," Lady Lemongrass said,

reaching into one of her many pockets. She pulled out a couple of pink sugar cubes and dropped them into our cups with little splashes that giggled.

"Thank you, Lady Lemongrass." Aunt Cauldroneyes took a handkerchief from her pocket and wiped the dripping tea off the kettle's spout. Then Lady Lemongrass waited for us to take a sip.

"Go on," the hat said, her tea bags shaking in excitement. "Tell me if you like it."

I took a big sip. The tea was sweet and warm and reminded me of some of the best delights from Aunt Cauldroneyes' kitchen.

"Most delicious," Aunt Cauldroneyes said as I nodded in agreement and drank some more.

Lady Lemongrass smiled so big, she nearly popped a button. Aunt Cauldroneyes cackled as she picked the hat up and carried her back to her shelf.

"Just let me know if you need another cup," Lady Lemongrass said, her steam rising.

We sipped our tea and Aunt Cauldroneyes opened a tin of caramel buttons. Once the bat hats heard the lid pop off, they came swooping down from the rafters.

"All right, that's one for each of you," Aunt Cauldroneyes told them, handing out the buttons. "Go on, now. Let Spella and me work."

While the bats flew back to the rafters with sticky fangs covered in caramel, Aunt Cauldroneyes spread out the fabric and started the measurements. I smiled and watched her. There was still lots I had to learn, more stitches I needed to master, and I could be tighter with my knots. But I enjoyed knowing that one day I might be as good a magical hatmaker as she was.

"Thank you for teaching me all about chocolate thread and giggling thread and shy buttons and biting ones, Aunt Cauldroneyes," I said. "Thank you for teaching me how to be a magical hatmaker."

"Do you like it, little dear?" She smiled. "I mean, really?"

"I love it! I've gotten to meet all kinds of unicorns and wufflers and mooncalfs and other magical creatures that I might only have ever read about. They actually come to our house! You remember when we made that hat for the toad who lost an arm in the poacher's trap in the forest? He was so sad, but then when we gave him his hat, he smiled. And we were part of that. I especially like it when we make hats for the trees. The hats of mist with ribbons of rain."

I got up from the table and stepped over to the shelves, staring up at all the shining jars, boxes, and bottles of wonder.

"You know, Aunt Cauldroneyes, if anyone else had found me in that purple cauldron, I wouldn't have learned how to make hats, and I would never have known giant hats like to do puzzles."

I nodded toward Grandma's Boot. He was sitting in his poufy chair in the corner, his small gold glasses on the very end of his nose as he stared intently at the jigsaw pieces on the table in front of him.

"I also wouldn't have known that leaves on a hat change color with the seasons," I said, "like in a real forest."

I looked at the hat we called Green Toes. He was getting a book down from the shelf. He carried it over to one of the attic's plump reading chairs.

"Or that a hat can spin a web." I stared up at the spider hat hanging in the web woven in the corner of the attic. She had fangs that protruded from the edge of her brim. She waved at me with her eight legs as silk unrolled from her, adding more thread to her web.

When I turned back to Aunt Cauldroneyes, blue buttons were sliding down her cheeks.

"Why are you crying, Aunt Cauldroneyes?" I asked.

"They are happy tears, little dear." She ran over and grabbed me into a hug.

I could feel the buttons falling onto my head, until she sniffled and said, "If Egypt were here—instead of eating all the chocolate mice in the kitchen—she'd say, 'Stop your crying, old one.'" Aunt Cauldroneyes laughed and wiped her eyes. "Let's get this baker's hat finished, shall we?"

I nodded with a smile. "It's going to be toadfire."

We spent the rest of the afternoon working. By early evening, a thunderstorm was brewing just outside the windows.

"Looks like there'll be some good thunder tonight," Aunt Cauldroneyes said. "I'll be able to collect quite a few lightning bolts. Our stock is getting low." She nodded over to the jars on the shelves where bolts of lightning flashed in bright purples and pinks.

I was eager to watch her catch more lightning, so it was a good thing we only had a few details left to finish on the hat, like deciding between the burgundy ribbon printed with whisks and the blue ribbon printed with bags of flour.

"Baking witches do love their whisks," Aunt Cauldroneyes said, holding both ribbons up. "But they also love their bags of flour."

Before I could say I preferred the blue ribbon, a loud knock came from downstairs.

"Someone's at the front door," I said.

"Must be another hat order." Aunt Cauldroneyes started to get up, but I told her I'd go.

"I always like it when a new order comes in," I said, before running down the stairs. I wondered who it would be at the door. A delightful troll requesting a new hat made of moss and twigs, with a drop of hocus-pocus and a hobgoblin's howl? Or a dragon wanting a flameproof hat?

Just before I opened the door, the knock came again.

Knockity-knock, knock, knock!

It was the loudest knocking I'd ever heard. It rattled the paintings on the walls and shook the crystal of the cauldron chandelier hanging above my head.

KNOCK, KNOCKITY-KNOCK!

I watched the fat raindrops slide down the windows as the wind howled and lightning flashed outside.

I took hold of the doorknob and slowly started to turn it.

CHAPTER 6
The Magical Hatmaker Disappears

AS THE FRONT DOOR CREAKED OPEN, A BOLT OF lightning shot down, illuminating a wizard in a cloak. I knew he was a wizard because of the wizard's knot on his cloak. A knot that looked like wands entangled around a shiny red stone. The only difference between it and a witch's knot was the color of the stone. For witches, it was bright green.

He wore his hood up, hiding his face but not the small octopus he wore as a bow tie. The octopus was electric purple with orange tentacles that waved through the air.

"Where's the hatmaker?" The wizard's voice was

deep and booming, like the thunder of the storm.

He held a burlap sack tied with frayed rope. There was something moving and growling inside the bag, nearly jerking free from his tight grip.

"I said, where is the hatmaker?" he shouted, a quick flash of lightning striking behind him.

"Aunt Cauldroneyes is upstairs in the attic," I said.

I had answered the knocks of dragons and slithering slurps[15*] and plenty of ogres, but I had never been frightened of any of them. This wizard was different. When the next gust of wind came, it picked up the back of his cloak and I realized it wasn't made of fabric at all. He was wearing a dragon's wing as a cloak. The wing flapped in the wind before falling back to the ground behind him. Whatever was inside the burlap bag growled louder.

"What's in there?" I asked.

"A beastly thing," he said.

"Beastly or not, you shouldn't keep them in a bag." I frowned. "That's cruel."

I stomped my boot for good measure. Aunt Cauldroneyes always stomped her foot at her meetings and protests.

"*Cruuuuel?*" The strange wizard repeated the word. "Maybe I'll let this beast out and put you in the bag instead."

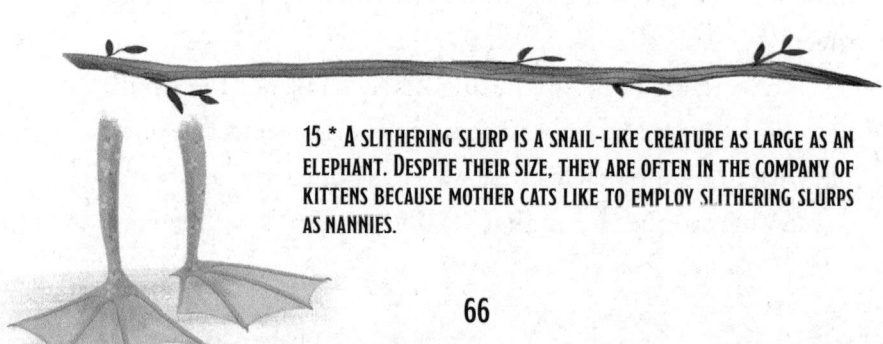

15 * A SLITHERING SLURP IS A SNAIL-LIKE CREATURE AS LARGE AS AN ELEPHANT. DESPITE THEIR SIZE, THEY ARE OFTEN IN THE COMPANY OF KITTENS BECAUSE MOTHER CATS LIKE TO EMPLOY SLITHERING SLURPS AS NANNIES.

"I'm not scared of you," I said, even though my voice was shaking.

"Oh, no? Why not?"

"Because there's a giant hat upstairs in the attic who will stomp you if you do anything. And there are bat hats who will bite you and owl hats who will chase you and mice hats who will find your name in your pockets so that they can tell the whole world who you are."

The wizard grunted and snarled, then quickly held the bag out to me. It swung from side to side in his grip.

"Give this to the hatmaker, blue-freckled girl."

"I'm not taking that bag until you tell me what's inside it." I crossed my arms.

"Wouldn't you suppose it might very well be a hat?"

"I've never heard one growl so much," I said.

The wizard shook the bag and told it, "Shut up, you." The bag jerked one last time before hanging limp in the wizard's hand.

"He's in need of some repair," the wizard said. "You do repair hats, correct?"

"Yes, we repair hats," I said. "But I'm not sure about that one."

"Even if it's a hat from Herbalia Folklock?" he asked as he held up the yellowed parchment tag tied to the rope. Scribbled on the tag in black ink was:

Property of Herbalia Folklock

Herbalia Folklock was someone I knew by name only. She and Aunt Cauldroneyes had grown up together. They stayed in touch through the years with letters. Folklock was one of the other founding members of the Sisterhood of the W.O.L.V.E.S., but she never seemed to attend the meetings. Aunt Cauldroneyes said it was because Folklock spent a great deal of time researching plants. She was a scientist and wrote books about the importance of the environment. She was also set to begin her first year as headwander at Dragon's Knob, leading the school through the change to plant magic.

"If the hat is from Folklock, then I'll take it," I said, grabbing hold of the bag.

"I thought you might." The wizard smiled as I set the bag on the floor by my feet and started to untie the rope.

"No!" he said. "Wait until you're in the attic with the hatmaker. I wouldn't want such a hat getting loose in this storm. We'd likely never be able to find him again. Worse yet, he's quite hungry. He'll feed on the thunder. Then there's no telling what he'll do."

"What's the hat's name?" I asked.

The wizard paused, then said, "He growls quite a bit. Just call him Growling Hat."

As the wizard turned to leave, I saw he wore black ankle boots with long silver-clad claws lining the toe.

"I need him repaired tonight!" he shouted over his shoulder.

Lightning flashed and lit up enough of his face for me to see shaggy red sideburns growing down his cheeks, and wild hair sticking out from under the hood. His bushy red eyebrows hung heavy over his eyes, which glowed like fire above his raised and wrinkled nose.

I quickly closed the door and peeked out the window just in time to see the wizard disappear into the darkness.

"Ow!" I cried as the bag at my feet threw itself into my leg. I looked down at the yellow parchment tag again. The words on the tag started to move until they read:

You have just been fooled,

you have just brought in a ghoul.

He'll take your thread and your spools,

he follows only a monster's rules.

The rope unknotted itself before the bag quickly rolled away from me and down the hall.

"Hey," I said. "Come back!"

The bag kept rolling until it hit the grandfather clock. Growling Hat shot out. He was scruffy with patches of matted gray fur and a bushy tail that was so long, it flopped behind him several feet and shed clouds of hair as he jumped up and started to knock cauldrons off tables and pull books off shelves.

"Stop it!" I tried to grab him, but he moved too fast.

"*Grrrr,*" he growled, and ran into the living room. I tried to keep up with him as he shredded the fabric on the walls with his claws and spit on the leaves of the houseplants. When he saw the cabinet full of Aunt Cauldroneyes' ceramic gnome collection, he picked up the figurines and threw them back into my path one by one. It was a good thing Aunt Cauldroneyes had enchanted the sofas and chairs to be mindful of the breakable items. The sofa came first, running on its wooden legs to catch the figurines on its soft pillows and cushions. I caught one figurine myself before it broke against the floor.

"*Grrrrr!*" Growling Hat growled louder as he ran down the hall and into the kitchen. I chased him and nearly tripped over Egypt lying on the floor in a pile of pots and pans she'd knocked over while getting to the chocolate mice on the top shelf. The foil wrappers from the candy were scattered, and chocolate was smeared across the linen around her mouth. The hat was nowhere in sight.

"Egypt!" I tried to wake her up. "Egypt, c'mon, you ate too many chocolate mice again."

"What?" She yawned but only turned over, her belly full. "What is it, young one?"

"There's a wild hat loose in the house. He came in here. Did you see where he went?"

"Oh, those hats are all wild," she said, her voice drawn out and lazy.

She laid her head down on the handle of one of the copper pots and fell back asleep, her belly too full for her to do anything more.

I heard something fall behind me in the pantry. I ran over, but found only a box on the floor. The cookies that had been inside it were leading in a trail of crumbs back toward the front of the house. I followed them and found freshly made claw marks on the staircase.

"Spella!"

I jumped at Aunt Cauldroneyes' scream. It had come from the attic. I ran upstairs to find her trying to yank one of her long braids out of the mouth of Growling Hat, who had since grown bright red tentacles that filled the attic. The tentacles were large and plump and were dotted with big eyes. The eyes stared at me, their wrinkly eyelids bunching up with each blink.

"Spella," Aunt Cauldroneyes cried out. "Get out of here!"

A tentacle quickly slithered across the floor and grabbed me by the boot, while another latched itself around my waist and picked me up high into the air.

"Let me go!" I banged my fists on the flesh of the tentacle. The only thing that happened was it slobbered more slime.

I wasn't the only one trapped. I saw the owl hats above me. No matter how hard they flapped their wings, they could not fly free of the tentacles wrapping around them in the rafters. The spider hat had been caught in her corner, a tentacle breaking the strands of her web. I turned to the whimpering of the forest hats. Tentacles were squeezing them so tightly, their leaves were falling down to land on Grandma's Boot. He was not big enough to break free from the largest of the tentacles, which swung him from one side of the room to the other, causing several jigsaw pieces to fall out of his pockets along the way.

"Let them go!" Aunt Cauldroneyes yelled at Growling Hat as she tried her best to yank her braid free from his mouth.

Not even Mr. Sea Captain, whose own tentacles were trying to fight back, was able to escape. Everywhere I looked, there was a hat that was trapped. I even saw the fiery hat from the fireplace burning in between the two tentacles that held him. I thought all the hats had been trapped, but then I saw the little mice hats, who were scurrying across the floor. They were quicker than the tentacles chasing them. The fairy hats were fast, too, but when they tried to dart out the attic door, a tentacle came and slammed it shut.

"I said, let them go!" Aunt Cauldroneyes shouted again. Growling Hat only grinned and yanked her toward him by her braids.

"No!" I tried with all my might to squeeze out, but I couldn't. Then a bat hat landed on one of the eyeballs on the tentacle wrapped around my waist.

"Bite 'im, batty," I said. The bat hat smiled before sinking his fangs down into the eyeball. The tentacle screamed out and dropped me to the floor with a thud.

The other bat hats dived down from the rafters and bit the tentacles, helping to free the hats while I ran to the shelves and grabbed the jar of lightning. Once I opened the silver lid, it became a silver glove that slipped onto my hand and protected it as I reached inside the jar and grabbed the lightning bolts. I threw them one by one at the tentacles, the electricity sizzling across their lumpy flesh until they dropped the rest of the hats.

"Well done, Spella." Aunt Cauldroneyes laughed as the tentacles started to curl up and slither back toward Growling Hat.

"You let go of my aunt's braid." I threw the remaining lightning bolt at the hat himself. He released Aunt Cauldroneyes' braid to catch the bolt in his mouth. He growled as he chewed and chomped on it just as the last of the tentacles disappeared under his brim.

"Where did this hat come from, Spella?" Aunt Cauldroneyes asked. Her nose was twitching. It always did when she was nervous.

"A wizard dropped him off to be repaired," I said. "Whoever made him didn't make him very well. Do you see his stitches? They're all uneven. And the fabric has never been patched. He doesn't even have any charms, unless you count his fangs and claws."

"Yes," she said. "Whoever made him did so without love."

The hat swallowed the last of the lightning bolt, then started to spin so fast that he rose high above our heads.

"Why is he doing this, Aunt Cauldroneyes?" I grabbed on to her as she grabbed on to me.

"I don't know, little dear."

His spinning created a wind that knocked all the jars off the shelves. It sent the floating fabric and lace crashing through the windows and into Mr. Sea Captain. He wrapped his tentacles around the fabric. Together they were blown out into the night.

The force of the spinning flung the bat hats back up into the rafters. The other hats were thrown so hard into the walls that their buttons popped off and their fabric tore. Fleabag's glasses cracked and broke, while the spider hat tumbled through the air and into the shelves. She fell down to the floor, one of her eight legs now limp.

Me and Aunt Cauldroneyes were pulled apart. I tried to reach for her but I was sent barreling toward the far wall of the room. If not for Grandma's Boot catching me, I would have been cast out through the windows.

The wind whirled around us. The feathered hats were losing their feathers. The fairy hats were losing their tulle. The warty hats were losing their warts. All the bits and baubles were torn off. Thread was yanked and snapped, and fabric was ripped to shreds. Blue buttons started to fill the air. I knew they were the tears of Aunt Cauldroneyes. She was being spun around the room and lifted upside down by the force of the wind. Her braids swung toward the floor as her feet disappeared into the dark shadows under the brim of Growling Hat. He was taking her.

She looked at me one last time and said, "I love you like a sky full of dragons."

"No!" I screamed.

The ends of her braids were the last things I saw of her before she was sucked up inside Growling Hat.

The wind finally stopped, and the hat burped loudly, then vanished in a puff of green smoke. A single red tentacle whipped across the air before it, too, sparkled and fizzled itself out.

"Aunt Cauldroneyes, please come back," I cried as Grandma's Boot held me tight and the hats wobbled around the attic. They were still dizzy from the force of the wind.

"Wait!" Grandma's Boot said. "I hear something at the door."

We all turned to the sound of scratching against the wood of the attic's door. It was still slammed shut.

"Aunt Cauldroneyes?" I quickly ran out of Grandma's Boot's arms and to the door to open it, but Aunt Cauldroneyes wasn't there. It was Egypt.

"What happened here?" She walked in. "I heard all the racket from down in the kitchen. Did one of the hats open a jar of twirlblasts again?" She looked around at the mess and stepped over the stuffing spilled out from the patchwork cauldron now lying on its side. "Where is the old one?"

After I dropped down to the floor, Egypt leapt over and put her paws on each side of my face and shook it. "Where is the old one?"

"She was taken," I cried. "By a hat!"

Spell No. 942

Rain, rain, let it pour.
Scare the toad back through the door.

Note from the Before Long Witch
This spell is for those who love thunder too much, and when you simply just have to have a good storm to write poems by. This should be whispered into the ear of a sleeping pixie. And it should be said with a wet wandle. You will, of course, have to worry about rain in your pockets.

CHAPTER 7
ANOTHER KNOCKITY-KNOCK

EGYPT LOOKED AROUND AT THE HATS. THEY HAD gotten wounded in the force of the spinning wind. Some were dragging themselves across the floor, trying to collect their own buttons and thread. Some were even attempting to push stuffing back in that had popped out through tears and rips in their fabric. Others, like the spider hat, were trying to pull themselves back into corners to hide their injuries.

I quickly wiped my eyes and stood up. In the mess around me, I spotted Fleabag's eyeglasses on the floor. I headed to the sewing table and grabbed the roll of tape. The lenses on his eyeglasses were cracked, but not as badly as the frames. I taped them back together as best I could, then found Fleabag. He was whimpering behind a curtain.

"It's okay, Fleabag."

After I put the glasses on him, he gave me a lick on the cheek with his warm, flat tongue.

"None of you worry," I said to all of them. "I'm going to find Aunt Cauldroneyes. But first I'm going to repair you."

I gently picked up the spider hat. She didn't want anyone to see she was crying, so I let her bury her face in my arm as I carried her over to the table where my sewing box sat. I reached inside it and pulled out a mending needle that was carved from snoffle bark.[16] I looked at the spools of thread and chose one that was woven with healing charms. I began to work on the tear in the spider's back leg until she could walk again.

As she returned to the rafters to make a new web, I went around with my needle and thread, sewing the buttons and baubles back onto each of the hats. The fabric and laces came floating into the attic from the dark of the night, having found their way home. No doubt because of Mr. Sea Captain's directions. He was riding the floating fabric, his tentacles steering as if navigating a great ship on the sea. As the fabric floated over my head, I reached up and cut off patches to sew onto every hat that needed them.

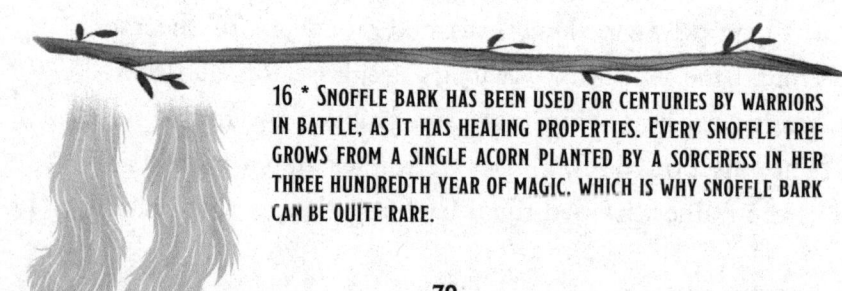

16 * SNOFFLE BARK HAS BEEN USED FOR CENTURIES BY WARRIORS IN BATTLE, AS IT HAS HEALING PROPERTIES. EVERY SNOFFLE TREE GROWS FROM A SINGLE ACORN PLANTED BY A SORCERESS IN HER THREE HUNDREDTH YEAR OF MAGIC. WHICH IS WHY SNOFFLE BARK CAN BE QUITE RARE.

Egypt helped to collect all the charms. She also picked up the hats too wounded to move, draping the larger ones across her back. She carried them to me at the sewing table. I fixed them just the way Aunt Cauldroneyes had taught me how to. I hoped that by the time I finished sewing and patching, Aunt Cauldroneyes would appear in a great wind as suddenly as she had disappeared in one. But once the last button was sewn on, I laid the thread and needle down, and she was still gone.

"What will we do?" Grandma's Boot asked. His puzzle table had gotten knocked over, and he stood in the place it had once been. Egypt and me helped him pick the table back up.

"You all wait here," I said. "I'll go down to the library and check Aunt Cauldroneyes' desk. Maybe I can find something that will help."

The hats started to put the attic back together by standing the shelves up and collecting the jars and boxes that had fallen off them.

"It's a good thing the old one enchanted the glass jars and bottles in the attic with anti-breaking charms," Egypt said as we headed down the stairs.

The library was in the back of the house, next to the kitchen. It was lined with oak shelves and was full of more than just Aunt Cauldroneyes' flying books. There were whispering mushrooms under glass bell jars, ships in bottles that rocked as if on the sea, bowls of wild warts, and Aunt Cauldroneyes' own watercolor paintings, which hung on the patchwork-covered walls.

In the corner was her rolltop desk, with enough drawers to file all the hat orders from the past few centuries. I ducked beneath a book flying by and ran over to her desk. In the top drawer I discovered her bluebird quill lying on a letter that had been started but not finished. The letter was written in lightning language, where the words were drawn lightning bolts. It was the secret language used amongst members in the Sisterhood of the W.O.L.V.E.S. One word might be three bolts crossed together, or another might be a bolt split in half. Because I was a member of the sisterhood, I could read it easily.

My dear Herbalia, a sister of the wolves,

I have been dreaming of cauldrons. Of big ones and little ones. Of fiery ones and watery ones. As you know, anytime a witch dreams of cauldrons, it means something is brewing in the winds. My grandmother would lay her old wooden spoon on her pillow at night so her dreams could be stirred with good things. I have started to lay my old wooden spoon on my pillowcase with a sprinkle of blue spice to match Spella's blue freckles, for I hope what is brewing in the winds is something beautiful for her.

Spella does not want to go to Dragon's Knob. I will continue to encourage her, but this must be her decision. What is it we used to say when we were young and still had tender warts, Herbalia? That we would walk out into the world and sing? We could only hope our voices would be kind and wise and enough of a river in a world of fire. I know now that Spella is my song, my river, my hope for a better world.

I look forward to your first year as headwander of Dragon's Knob.
I hope

The letter stopped at that one word. I looked up and saw Aunt Cauldroneyes' mauve shawl draped across her poufy desk chair. I wrapped the shawl around me and sat down with the letter.

"What do I do without you, Aunt Cauldroneyes?"

"Maybe you shouldn't be asking what *you* should do without her," Egypt said. "Maybe you should be asking what *she* would do."

Egypt pointed at the cauldron sitting in front of the windows. It was Aunt Cauldroneyes' midnight cauldron, and it was stirred by moonlight.

"I know what she would do," I said, letting the letter float out of my hand and back over to the desk. "She would look into a cauldron."

Keeping Aunt Cauldroneyes' shawl wrapped around me, I got up out of the chair and walked over to the cauldron. The moon that night was called the Werewolf's Eye, a name given to the brightest moon of the year. Not even the storm was going to stop the light from shining in the windows and stirring the old wooden spoon inside the cauldron as if by an imaginary hand.

The last potion brewed in the cauldron had been made out of Aunt Cauldroneyes' sleeping herbs and dream roots. A shallow puddle of it remained in the bottom.

"What do you see?" Egypt asked as I looked into the cauldron.

"Nothing," I said. "I only see the reflection of myself."

Egypt tilted her head, her linen hanging off to the side.

"Maybe that is the answer, young one," she said.

I raised my eyes to the windows and stared out. I knew the hats and Egypt were counting on me to find Aunt Cauldroneyes.

"I could fly on Aunt Cauldroneyes' broom and go into the village for help," I said.

"Yes." Egypt nodded. "But you've never driven a flying broom by yourself. You're likely to end up in a tree."

Lightning flashed outside. The storm wasn't letting up, and the rain was falling hard, like rocks against the window glass. Suddenly a loud boom echoed through the house.

"The thunder is so loud tonight," I said, shivering beneath the shawl.

"That's not thunder." Egypt looked over her shoulder. "That's a knock." She turned her yellow eyes back to me. "There's someone at the door."

The two of us crept out of the library. The hats had come down from the attic and were staring with wide eyes toward the front door.

"I don't know if we should open it," Wormella said. She was shaking so hard that dirt was falling off into puffs of clouds around her.

"I have built the mighty pyramids in the desert," Egypt said. "And she has climbed the tallest tree in the forest." She pointed at me. "And all of you have survived the whirlwinds of a most dangerous hat. I think we should now be brave enough to answer a knock at the door."

Her yellow eyes shone brightly up at me.

"Yes," I said. "We have to be brave. But also smart."

I looked at the vase on the table by the door. It was full of curling sticks, leafy twigs, and wildflowers that me and Aunt Cauldroneyes had collected in the forest. I grabbed the shortest of the curling sticks. Holding the straight end out, I pulled Aunt Cauldroneyes' shawl farther down over my shoulders, covering the stick so it looked like a wand.

"Very smart indeed, young one," Egypt said, followed by a long meow.

The fairy hats flew into my hair and peeked out. The others stayed close behind as I slowly reached toward the doorknob, my hand shaking.

"*Grrrrrr.*" Egypt started to growl and stood up on her toes, ready to pounce on whoever was behind the door.

KNOCK, KNOCK, KNOCKITY-KNOCK!

I turned the doorknob.

"*Meooooowwwwwww!*" Egypt hissed as I swung the door open.

"I have my wand!" I shouted, pressing the end of the stick against the shawl.

A blast of lightning illuminated the short, plump bird standing on the doorstep.

"Let me in, let me in," he said. "It's a downright shiver out here. Don't you have the decency to open a door on the first knock?"

He pushed past us, the rain dripping off his feathers. He stood about three feet tall, with a large fat beak that curved down, and a bushy tail of electric-blue feathers. His small wings stayed close to his sides. The left wing was artificial. It was like a wonderful sail on an old pirate ship, the wooden mast ribbed like a bat wing, and the sailcloth ragged and frayed.

"You're a dodo!"[17] I said. "I've read about you in one of Aunt Cauldroneyes' books."

"You've read about us dodos? Lucky me." He rolled his small round eyes. "I guess you know everything there is to know about us strange birds, then, huh? Can you tell me how long my wings are?" He shook his wings angrily in the air. "Or how about my favorite color? Hmm?" He stomped his foot, and I noticed he had silver scars on both ankles.

"He has the temper of a thousand Egyptian hornets," Egypt said. "I like him."

17 * IF YOU EVER INVITE A DODO TO YOUR HOUSE, YOU SHOULD HAVE A PANTRY STOCKED WITH TEA BAGS AND LOST SHOES. BOTH ARE A DODO'S FAVORITE THINGS TO EAT.

"I didn't mean to be rude," I said.

He slapped the rain off his beak. "Oh, I know. It's just all those books always say dodos are dumb, which isn't true."

"The book I read didn't say that," I said. "It did say that dodos were extinct, though."

"Oh, yes. That." He shook more of the rain off. "I don't like to talk about that so much."

He took a step toward us, and all I could think about was Growling Hat. I pressed the stick harder into the shawl.

"You stay back," I said. "I have my wand, and I'll use magic on you."

I shook the stick because I wasn't sure what else to do with it.

"Oh, you have a wand, do you?" The dodo stared at the shawl. "You, who are eight years old and have not even learned the ways of the wand, have one already?"

"How do you know how old I am?" I asked.

"I'm here on official Dragon's Knob business."

"I don't believe you." I jabbed the stick so hard into the shawl, it poked a hole through the fabric, exposing the wood.

The dodo stared at the stick, then said, "Nice wand." He shook his head. "You got your invitation in the mail, didn't you? You should know why I'm here."

"Yes, I got it." I handed the stick to Fleabag, who chewed on it at my feet. "But I didn't exactly open it."

"You what?" The dodo nearly fell back as he laid

a wing across his chest. "Most can't wait to tear open their invitation to the greatest school of wand magic ever. I've been a Dragon's Knob dodo for years, and I have never heard of such a thing. Goblin's gackles! No wonder you don't know who I am. Where's your invitation now?"

"It doesn't matter," I said. "I have more important things to worry about. My aunt—"

"More important things!" the dodo shouted. "What could possibly be more important than opening your invitation to Dragon's Knob?" He took a deep breath, then spoke loudly to the house, "Invitation? Come here right this second!"

From upstairs we heard something knock over. We looked up to see the invitation whooshing out of my bedroom, tossing off the dirty laundry I had covered it up with. As shirts and blankets flew through the air, the invitation came zooming down the stairs and stopped in the air in front of the dodo.

"Been waiting a long time to be opened, eh?" the dodo asked the envelope, who eagerly nodded. "Well, go on. Open up."

The flap of the envelope seemed to smile as the wax seal broke itself and the letter lifted out. The paper was the same green shade as the envelope. The words had been written in gold ink and flickered in the light.

The dodo cleared his throat before reading the little poem at the top of the letter.

"*Where dragons take flight, through the dark of the night.*

Where the fire ignites, you will find the light."

He looked up at me and said, "Those are the school's watchwords."

Dropping his eyes back to the letter, he began to read aloud:

Dear Wand Keeper Spella,

I am using my quill with the longest feather to write this because I only use it for the best of letters. I am delighted, excited, downright tickled, and thrilled to inform you that you are accepted to Dragon's Knob, school of wand witchery and magic. Wand Keeper Spella, your dodo will arrive soon in order to make sure you are ready to start classes on the first of October. Or, as I like to call it, Octoburrrrrrr.

I would write a longer letter, but it is the season of the last berries, and there are birds flying in and out of my hat as we speak. Their wings are whispering to me that I have many more letters yet to write to your fellow classmates. Please have everything packed and ready to go upon your dodo's arrival. They will escort you to Dragon's Knob, where I will be so eager to welcome you that I just might break out in hives.

And remember, today belongs to you. Do something wonderful with it,

Deputy Headwander Rose Harriet Candlehour

P.S. I have already broken out in hives.

In the margins, Candlehour had drawn little hearts and dodos.

"The new deputy headwander is *really* looking forward to the start of the school year," the dodo said. "And now you know why I'm here."

"Maybe he can help us find the old one," Egypt said, looking up at me.

"Who is this 'old one' that the mummified rat speaks of?" the dodo asked. He seemed particularly interested in the hodgepodge pattern of the rug as he wiped the mud from his feet on it.

"I, for your information," Egypt said as she flung some loose linen out of her face, "am a cat. Not a rat. I have built the pyramids and—"

"The old one," I said, interrupting what I knew would be a long speech from Egypt, "is my aunt. That's what I've been trying to tell you. She's gone."

The dodo looked up from the rug. "Is that why you've been crying?" He waved a wing toward my face. "Your eyes are red, but I didn't want to pry. Who did you say she was again?" He looked at the magical hats behind me.

"My aunt Cauldroneyes."

"*Mathilda* Cauldroneyes?" His short wings started to flutter. "The hatmaker for Dragon's Knob?"

"Yes! A hat has taken her." I wiped away the new tears that had started to come. "She has disappeared completely."

"Oh warty wobbles!" The dodo flapped his wings and paced the hall, the hats backing up to clear a path for him. "This is not good news."

He stopped and flipped onto his head, his feet waving in the air.

"This is how a dodo thinks," he said as he spun around on his head.

He suddenly stopped, and turned back over to his feet. "I've got it." He looked up at me. "I'll take you to the school. If anyone will know what to do, it will be Headwander Folklock."

"The dodo is right," Egypt said. "Folklock will be able to help us."

"You heard the mummified rat." The dodo flapped his wings at me. "Hurry up and get packed! I will fly you to Dragon's Knob as fast as I have ever flown anyone."

"You're flying me?" I looked at his small wings. "You?"

"Who else do you think is gonna do it, you silly Wand Keeper? Now go!"

CHAPTER 8
THE MAGIC OF A DODO

I RAN UP THE STAIRS WITH EGYPT ON MY HEELS. THE hats followed us and squeezed into my bedroom. I quickly closed the door so the dodo couldn't hear from downstairs.

"Egypt, I have to tell you something about Folklock," I said. "Growling Hat had a tag that had her name on it."

"The hat belonged to Folklock?" Egypt's linen pinched across her forehead as she frowned.

"I think that maybe the wizard put Folklock's name on the tag," I said, "so I'd bring the hat inside the house. I don't think the hat was hers. But maybe she knows something about the wizard who brought it. Maybe it all has something to do with the start of the new school year. This is Folklock's first year as headwander, after all."

Egypt's whiskers curled up at the thought. "If this has something to do with the school," she said, "I'm not sure you should go to Dragon's Knob."

The hats nodded in agreement.

"If I don't go," I told them, "I might never find Aunt Cauldroneyes. I have to know how Dragon's Knob fits into all this."

"Then I will go with you," Egypt said, sitting taller. "The old one would want me to make sure you are safe. And I have built the pyramids and—"

"We will go, too," Grandma's Boot said. He seemed to delight in interrupting Egypt.

"You absolutely will not," Egypt told him. "All of you hats will stay here at the house."

"Can't they go, Egypt?" I asked.

"We have business to take care of," she said. "We will do it much faster if we are not babysitting hats. Some of which, I might add, are not potty-trained."

She turned her yellow eyes to the bat hats, who blew raspberries at her and flew out of sight behind Grandma's Boot.

"One hat, however, may go," she said. "Moonsplash, where are you?"

A fuchsia velvet hat stepped forward. His ribbon was a black belt with a big silver buckle. Small pale moths fluttered around the purple flowers growing along his brim, and around the point of his hat, which curled into a spiral. It held a rolled parchment map of the stars.

Moonsplash wasn't very big, but because he had been splashed with moonlight while Aunt Cauldroneyes had made him, he had a huge pocket on the inside that was as vast as a crater in the moon. It made him an excellent suitcase.

I went over to my dresser and quickly started to pull out clothes to pack, while Egypt ran to the corner of the room where she kept her mummy box[18*]. It was carved like her, though the colors had faded since it was first painted more years ago than most could count.

She dragged the mummy box across the floor and waited for Grandma's Boot to lift it up and pack it into Moonsplash's never-ending pocket.

Egypt started to pack my blankets, but I didn't want to take too many things. I worried that if Aunt Cauldroneyes did come back to the house and saw my room empty, she would think I left her. I knew the hats would tell her what had happened, but I also wanted to leave something in my own words.

I ran over to my desk in the corner and quickly grabbed a piece of parchment and a quill.

18 * THIS BOX WAS GIVEN TO EGYPT WHEN SHE WAS MUMMIFIED. THOUGH SOME MUMMIES LIKE TO SLEEP IN THEIR BOXES, EGYPT ONLY USES HERS TO KEEP HER YARN IN FOR HER KNITTING PROJECTS.

Dear Aunt Cauldroneyes,

I've gone to Dragon's Knob to see Headwander Folklock. I hope she might be able to help me find you. In case you come back while I'm gone, I want you to know that I haven't left you. Wherever I go, I love you like a sky full of dragons,

Spella

I perched the letter on top of a stack of books on the desk and told the hats to give it to Aunt Cauldroneyes if she came back. The hats were whimpering and slumped together. Grandma's Boot was trying to wipe the tears away from the fairy hats' eyes, but his finger was too large to do anything more than ruffle their hair.

"I will be back as soon as I can. I promise." I grabbed them into a hug.

"What if you don't find Aunt Cauldroneyes, Spella?" the spider hat asked.

I knelt in front of them all and said, "You remember the great fog last summer? It was so thick, we couldn't see our way out of the forest. Aunt Cauldroneyes ran in after us and didn't stop until we were all safe and together in the house. She was in the fog for so long, she got a fog beard. She had to shave the beard off with a piece of giggling tree bark, and it kept giggling at her beard."

The hats laughed.

"Oh, I remember," Mr. Sea Captain bellowed, his tentacles waving around him.

"I'm going to do the same thing," I said. "I won't stop looking for Aunt Cauldroneyes until we are all together again."

"We best go now, young one." Egypt was standing by the door.

She reached up and grabbed the knob, before turning back to the hats and adding, "I've counted the chocolate mice that I left in the kitchen. I will count them again when I return. I will know if a single one is missing and I will mummify you if you eat them."

The hats nodded, but I knew none of the chocolate in the house was safe left alone with them. I thought it was nice that they would have each other, their poufy chairs, and their chocolate while I was gone.

"Let me just get Moonsplash," I said to Egypt.

I started to pick up the hat, but Grandma's Boot asked me not to.

"If you don't mind, Spella," he said, "we'd like to say goodbye to Moonsplash and wish him well on his journey. You go on downstairs, and we'll send him down after."

"Just don't take too long, giant one," Egypt said, walking out the door.

I hugged all the hats one last time, then followed her down the stairs.

"Finally," the dodo said when he saw us. He had been pacing so hard, he'd nearly worn the rug out. "Are you ready, Wand Keeper?"

He had a tin from the kitchen. It had been full of tea bags, but he was eating the last one.

"I hope you don't mind," he said. "A dodo cannot resist a tea bag, and we have a long flight in front of us." He burped and a cloud of dried herbs hit the air.

"I don't mind," I said. "If you don't mind that Egypt is going to come with me."

"Fine, fine." He stomped toward the front door, setting the now empty tin on a table. "The storm has stopped, so at least we will have a calm takeoff."

"Moonsplash," I called up the stairs. "It's time to go."

The hat came walking out of my room. He wobbled from one leg to the other down the stairs. I picked him up and put him on my head. He was enchanted, so none of the things inside him ever fell out.

"We're leaving now." I spoke loud enough for the other hats to hear, but no one came out of my room.

"It's too hard for them to see you leave," Egypt said. "Best that we go now."

I hoped at least one of the bat hats would fly out, but when they didn't, I followed Egypt and the dodo out to the yard.

I looked at the dodo's short back and said, "I don't mean to be rude again, but how is it that you're going to fly us to Dragon's Knob?"

"Did your book on dodos not tell you the most important thing about us, Wand Keeper?" He flapped his short wings until they started to grow. "Our mothers were dragons."

I quickly stepped back with Egypt as the dodo's feathers disappeared and his skin became covered in hard reptile scales that shimmered like the crystals in Aunt Cauldroneyes' jewelry box.

He grew taller and wider within seconds as his neck stretched long and sprouted spikes. A bushy yellow beard popped out from his chin at the same time that a pair of purple-and-white-striped horns twisted up out of his head. He still looked like a dodo in the face, only the beak was larger and spotted with yellow dots. The electric-blue feathers he had had as a bird returned in a fluffy collar around his neck that matched the feathers on his tail. He was now a dragon.

Unlike other breeds, his legs were rather short and his claws were rather tiny. When he shook his head, a mane of bright orange hair grew from the top of his head and down his back.

"Am I big enough to fly you now?" he asked, flapping his wings. They were the biggest I had ever seen. The pirate sail on his artificial wing had grown with him and flapped through the air, the wooden mast of it creaking like an old ship.

"Did your book say dodos can turn into dragons, young one?" Egypt asked, staring up at him.

"No," I said with a smile, wishing Aunt Cauldroneyes was there to see him. "It didn't."

"Ah, so there is some mystery to us dodos yet," he said, laughing.

When he took a step, I saw he still had the silver scars on his ankles.

"If you're a dragon, does that mean you can breathe fire?" I asked.

He stopped laughing, and his voice grew quiet. "No. That I can no longer do."

He held his short arm out for us. As Egypt started to climb up it, I asked the dodo, "What's your name?"

He lowered his eyes to me. They were no longer small and green as they had been when he was a dodo. They were now large, with each iris split by a black lightning bolt.

"My name?" He paused before finally saying, "My name is Hartshorn."

"Nice to meet you, Hartshorn." I stepped up onto his paw and climbed across his wide back. I sat down beside Egypt, who was rubbing her paw against his hard reptile scales.

"What are we supposed to hold on to?" she asked.

"That's what the long hair is for." He shook his orange mane. "Are you both ready?"

I'd only ever flown with Aunt Cauldroneyes on her broom, my arms wrapped around her waist. When her broom got really high, I sometimes held my arms out, with the owl hats flying beside us. That close to the stars, my freckles would begin to shine and Aunt Cauldroneyes would look back and say, "You have stars on your face, little dear." Then she would sing a song, and I was never afraid to be that high up in the clouds.

I wrapped my fingers around the ends of Hartshorn's hair and said, "We're ready."

"Hold on tight, Wand Keeper and cat of ancient

pyramids." He lifted up into the air, which still felt damp from the storm earlier, and Egypt howled at how quickly we soared.

I looked down at the house, expecting to see the hats perhaps on the porch or at the windows, waving us off. But there was no sign of them. And even though the lamps were still burning, the house seemed darker without Aunt Cauldroneyes. I felt more alone than I ever had in my life. But once Hartshorn flew high enough that Egypt said, "Your freckles are shining, young one," I smiled and heard the memory of Aunt Cauldroneyes' voice singing, *"Cauldron fire and cauldrons of old, listen to what the stories have told. Of glittering stars and glittering gold, but none more shiny than the love I hold."*

Spell No. 79

A dragon's cough, a mermaid's sneeze,
Fever in a kraken's knees.
A cauldron of medicine, if you please.

Note from the Before Long Witch

This spell will heal you from sea slug sniffles, snapdragon pox, and mermaid worms. It will not, however, cure you from the notorious dinosaur cough unless you flutter your wandle while running like mad toward a blazing asteroid.

CHAPTER 9
Dragon's Knob

"WE HAVE ARRIVED." HARTSHORN'S BOOMING VOICE echoed far and wide. "Welcome to Dragon's Knob!"

He swooped down, cutting through the white clouds of the purple sky that was so different from the green sky back home in Witches' Bells. The morning light revealed large forested mountains. The tallest peaks hung in a mist as Hartshorn flew over a long stone bridge lined with statues of witches and wizards, their wands held high. The bridge crossed a wide river, bordered by dark green pines and silver ferns that led up a winding path to the school.

The castle was just as Aunt Cauldroneyes told me it would be.

"Made of brick in the same fiery red and orange shades of a dragon's fire," she had said.

There were more towers on the castle than I could count. None of them were straight. They reached like crooked arms with bent elbows, and wild legs with knobby knees. Some of the towers were thin and scraggly, others were wide and bulgy, each with a roof that reminded me of a lopsided hat.

Aunt Cauldroneyes had repaired cracks in the castle's brick by laying patches of mismatched fabric over them. Some of the patches had stripes and others had polka dots. There were patterns like houndstooth, flamestitch, and troll tweed. She had used several patches of corduroy and velvet fabric, but my favorite was the floral printed with flowers like cackling carnations and toadflax. I could see where Aunt Cauldroneyes had sewn the patches to the brick with thick black thread, held together like a grandmother's quilt. Growing in the cracks of the bricks not yet repaired was fluffy moss. It popped out like stuffing.

"The old one has done good work here," Egypt said as her eyes filled with her own memories of Aunt Cauldroneyes.

I looked up at the iron weather vanes. They dangled and coiled like loose threads sprung from the elbows and knees of the towers. They whirled in different winds, churning up sparkling dust in deep pink hues that rose in front of the glowing cauldron-shaped windows.

"Hang on!" Hartshorn said as he flew in between the towers and took a quick dive at the front of the castle, where the brick was built like a large nose. As we flew beneath it, I saw green bats hanging upside down inside the caverns of the nostrils.

"Like boogers," Aunt Cauldroneyes had said when she told me about the little green bats.

Hartshorn flew us past several greenhouses surrounding the castle and over gardens where large cabbage heads grew with leafy ears and noses. Ripening on dark green vines were pumpkins shaped as poufy chairs large enough to seat giants.

After we circled the entire castle, Hartshorn flew down to land in the tall witchgrass^{19*}. It was hopping with fuchsia frogs. Egypt laid her paw on my arm and said, "There's a rumor the castle has fleas. That you can hear the brick scratching itself. Do you think that's true, young one? It took me over a thousand years to shake off the sand fleas I got building all those pyramids. Fleabag likes to keep his fleas to himself, thank the witches, but I'd hate to think about how long it takes to shake off castle fleas."

"Aunt Cauldroneyes has been here plenty of times repairing the castle," I said. "And she never got fleas."

"She never *got* fleas," Egypt said, "because she already had them." Egypt showed me all her yellow teeth. She always did whenever she smiled.

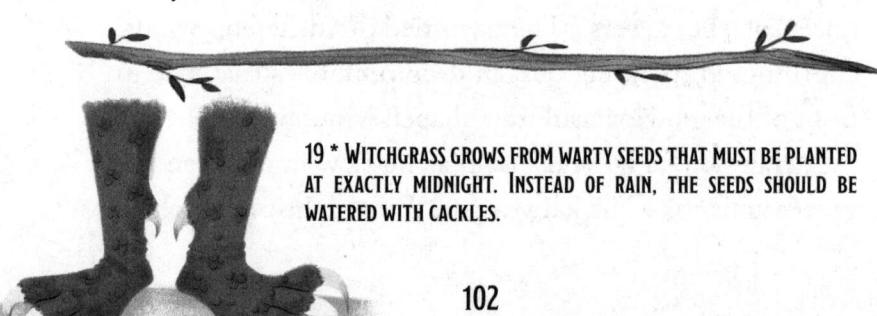

19 * Witchgrass grows from warty seeds that must be planted at exactly midnight. Instead of rain, the seeds should be watered with cackles.

"Have you just made a joke?" I asked.

She nodded, still showing all her teeth. "Remind me to tell it to the old one when she is back," she said. "I have a feeling she will like it."

Egypt slid down the dragon's arm, then waited at the bottom with both arms out as if she had to catch me. I kept one hand on Moonsplash so he wouldn't fall off my head on the way down.

"If you will just give me a moment," Hartshorn said, "I will change back into a dodo and show you inside the castle."

Hartshorn waved his giant tail and started to grow smaller. His reptile skin softened and was replaced by feathers. He squawked as his wings shrank and he was a short, plump bird once more, except for the purple-and-white-striped horns left on top of his head.

"Oh, there's always something that takes a little longer to change back," he said, before shaking his head until the horns disappeared.

He led us to the front of the castle and under the large brick nose. Egypt meowed up at the green bats hanging above our heads as we stopped in front of the castle's door. It was cut with a smaller fairy door. Both were made of dark wood with large hinges of black iron shaped as feathers. At the bottom of the door were two huge hairy feet.

"To open the door," Hartshorn said, "you must repeat the school's watchwords. *Where dragons take flight, through the dark of the night. Where the fire ignites, you will find the light.*"

The feet walked the door open, and we stepped into what Hartshorn called the grand entrance hall, which was a greenhouse. It had diamonds of both clear and bright yellow glass. Sunlight filled the room, beaming in on the plants and trees that grew inside.

"The Dragon King built many greenhouses in his castle," Hartshorn said. "But for the past several years, heavy tapestries have been laid over the glass and no plants were grown. This is one of the things Headwander Folklock has changed. She took down the tapestries, and I helped her move in the plants along with the other dodos."

We took a large step over the dark green vine slithering across the stone floor.

"This is the biggest place I've ever been in," I said, staring up at jewel-colored beetles walking across the glass.

"It's just as big underground," Hartshorn said. "As many towers as you saw above us, there are even more dungeons below us. I don't like the dungeons," he added quickly. "They are colder than any other part of the castle. No one goes down there anymore."

He stopped walking and stood with his feet close enough for the silver scars on his ankles to touch.

"Are you okay, Hartshorn?" I reached toward him, but he backed up.

"Of course I'm okay," he said, frowning. "Let's keep moving."

Egypt and me followed him through the rooms ahead. They were brightly lit with upside-down candles made of green wax with purple flames. The rooms were cozy for a castle, with tufted velvet chairs that had blankets over the arms. The wallpaper was printed with images of owls and big flowers like yelly mums and lazy daisies. There were shelves in nearly every room, full of thick encyclopedias or rolled parchments, and plenty of small crystal cauldrons holding hard candy and sitting on doilies on the tables.

I knew the mice hats would have loved to scurry across the lopsided shelves while Mr. Sea Captain stretched his tentacles through the twisted towers. I surprised myself by imagining how fun it might be to run through the maze of hallways to class, where bubbling cauldrons waited.

"Where are the other students?" I asked.

"I flew you so fast, we've arrived one day early," Hartshorn said. "The students are always scheduled to arrive exactly on time to prepare for the first day of classes on October first. Only the staff and a few of the teachers will be here now."

"But Folklock is here, right?" I asked.

"Yes." He nodded. "She's been here since the middle of summer, moving into her new office. She had quite a few plants to bring with her. It's her first year as headwander, you know. She was selected based on her work as a botanist. Are you familiar with her books on endangered plants? She's won quite a few awards. I think she'll make for a rather nice headwander. Not like the last one."

"What was she like?" I asked, staring up at the

upside-down candles waving down at me with their purple flames and lighting our way.

"*He*," Hartshorn said. "I've already told you about the dungeons. How they're colder than the rest of the castle. I know how cold they are because it is where the previous headwander forced us dodos to sleep."

"He sounds terrible," I said.

"He was more than terrible." Hartshorn picked up his pace.

We soon entered what he called Enchanter's Hall. There were troll tapestries and chandeliers made out of empty potion bottles. At the center was a wide staircase. It was the first of many that led us to the tallest tower of the castle, where Headwander Folklock's office was. Her door was closed. Above it was a window where a potted plant sat. The long vines hung down on either side of the door and grew large blue flowers.

"Headwander Folklock?" Hartshorn knocked. "I've brought one of the Wand Keepers. She must speak to you right away. It's urgent."

"Folklock is not here," a small voice said. The voice then whispered in a language that sounded like ivy creeping across stone.

"Hello?" Hartshorn spoke though the door. "Why are you in the headwander's office?"

"We are not in the office," a different voice said. "We are outside her office. We are here. *Leafy does, leafy do, leafy boo.*"

The vines of the plant lifted up and gently draped themselves across Hartshorn.

"Do you see us now?" the leaves asked. "We are Folklock's chatty clematis. She left this morning to collect some more of our sisters."

"When will she back?" I asked. "I have to talk to her right away."

A vine reached out toward me. The littlest leaf on it opened a very tiny mouth and said, "She'll be back tomorrow."

The vines returned to hang by the door.

"I do apologize, Wand Keeper Spella," Hartshorn said. "I thought she would be here. I think it's best that I show you to your room now."

I slowly nodded and picked up Egypt. I held her close to my chest. It felt nice to have something from home.

As we passed the windows, I looked out at the river snaking around the castle, and at the gardens surrounded by more greenhouses, which reminded me of gnome cottages.

"The previous headwander used all those greenhouses for housing the creatures used as ingredients for potions in the classrooms," Hartshorn said.

"I'm glad I've never met the old headwander." I shivered just thinking about him.

"You will like Folklock," Hartshorn said. "She moved all of us dodos out of the dungeons. And she's the one who gave me my wing." He raised the artificial one.

I knew Aunt Cauldroneyes would say it was rude to ask how he'd lost his wing, but Egypt didn't care.

"What happened to it?" she asked him.

"I don't like to talk about it," was all he said.

When we got to a hallway that sounded as though

it was full of snakes and owls, Hartshorn said, "This is Hisses and Hoots Hall. It is the tower that houses the first wands, like you."

Lizards hopped from sconce to sconce, while snakes slithered up the paintings and owls swooped from one end of the hall to the other before perching on the tall bookshelves.

Egypt jumped out of my arms and started to chase after a frog, until Hartshorn shouted in a firm voice, "There will be no chasing of the creatures."

"*Meeeeeeow,*" said Egypt with a shrug.

"You don't have to worry about her," I told Hartshorn. "She doesn't even eat real mice. Hers are always chocolate." I waited for a two-headed turtle to cross in front of me. "Do the creatures live here in the hall?"

"Yes," Hartshorn said, "ever since Folklock freed them from the greenhouses. The smaller creatures were kept in boxes and jars. All of them had once been destined to be ingredients in spells. But thankfully, not anymore."

He touched the tip of his wing to the head of a toad smiling at his feet.

Hisses and Hoots Hall was lined with doors that had knobs in different sizes, some large enough for giants, others small enough for fairies, but all with bat-shaped keyholes. My room was at the end of the hallway. Egypt ran to open the door. Inside, all the paintings on the walls hung perfectly crooked, and the wood paneling had the most fantastic carvings of pumpkins and gourds, which made me feel like I was in a field of them. I ran my hands over the dark green wallpaper. It had images of bright white unicorns. They made me think about all the hats me and Aunt Cauldroneyes had made for unicorns over the years.

Egypt tripped on her linen while walking over to the fireplace. It was carved like a dragon's head coming out of the wall. She passed by it and headed toward the pile of socks on the floor.

"I wouldn't do that if I were you," Hartshorn told her.

Egypt got close enough to smell the socks, but she hissed when the socks suddenly jumped up and barked at her. She ran to hide behind me as the socks chased her.

"His name is Socky," Hartshorn said. "He's harmless. He's like a floppy dog, only made entirely of socks."

Socky looked up at me, his mouth open with a red sock lapping about like his tongue. There were brown socks and gray socks and plenty of white ones. He had one sock with a red toe for his right ear and a blue sock with a green toe for his left. I knew he was nice because he started to wag the yellow sock that was his tail.

"He's created out of every sock any student at Dragon's Knob has ever lost," Hartshorn said. "Be sure to feed him a sock each night, or he'll tear through your dresser looking for one."

As Egypt came out from behind my legs to touch noses with Socky, I turned to see a poufy chair facing the windows. The chair was tufted with buttons and had a ruffled skirt just short enough for the dark wooden claw feet to show. There were doilies on the arms and tassels on the top. It reminded me of the chairs we had back home. Then I saw someone was sitting in it. Someone with silver hair.

"Aunt Cauldroneyes?" I quickly ran around to the front of the chair, only to find a silver-colored blanket folded across the top and nothing more.

I walked over to the windows. I didn't know in what direction Aunt Cauldroneyes was, but I wished she would suddenly appear, flying through the clouds on her old broomstick.

"I know of something that might make you feel better," Hartshorn said, stepping over to the window's velvet drapes. "The curtains used to taste all dusty and old. But Folklock enchanted them. She thought it would be nice for the students to have a curtain they could snack on if they got hungry in the middle of the night, or simply felt a little homesick."

He picked up the edge of a curtain and took a bite out of it. The fabric broke off like a candy bar.

"They taste like chocolate," he said.

At the mention of chocolate, Moonsplash started to rock back and forth on top of my head, before suddenly hopping to the floor, where he turned over, spilling out all the hats from home. The bat hats made a mad dash toward the chocolate curtains, where they started to nibble them, all the way up to the rods.

"Stop that this instant!" Hartshorn tried to catch them.

More hats were still spilling out. The burping ones burped, and the farting ones farted. The hats with the brims of mist filled the room with it while Grandma's Boot made his way over to a table by the bookshelves.

"This will do for my puzzles." He emptied his pockets of jigsaw pieces and scattered them across the tabletop.

"This is a madhouse!" Hartshorn shouted, but was barely heard over the cackles of the warty hats and the grumblings of the ogre ones, all while the owl hats went flying by.

Balls of fabric started to fall down to the floor, and Hartshorn made a face when I laughed and said, "Those are the owl hats' droppings."

"No, we cannot have this!" he shouted.

He was interrupted by Lady Lemongrass as she passed by. "About time we got out," she said as she dusted off her tea bags in Hartshorn's face. "How can I be expected to brew a nice cup under these conditions?"

The dragon hat was the last to come out. He saluted me with his ribbon before walking over to the fireplace. He climbed inside it, his flames casting a warm glow across the room.

"I'm so happy to see all of you!" I patted the heads of the mice hats and held my hands out to the fairy hats.

"You didn't expect us to let you go looking for Aunt Cauldroneyes all by yourself, now, did you?" the spider hat asked as she crawled up the wall to find a cozy corner in which to spin a new web.

"They cannot be here!" Hartshorn puffed his cheeks out. He had pieces of chocolate curtains dropped on his head, and a herd of bat hats circling him to grab them. "They're making a mess!"

He watched the hats with claws climb up and shred the wallpaper. His eyes widened as he stared at the leafy green hats swinging on vines from the chandelier, while the fairy hats buzzed about and knocked jars off the shelves that Egypt had to try to catch before they broke.

"This is a school, and there are rules," Hartshorn said. "If we don't follow them, we will be sent to the dungeons."

"The dungeons?" I looked down at the scars on his ankles.

"Yes!" He took a deep breath. "At least, that's how it used to be. If we didn't follow the rules of the school, the former headwander could be quite stern."

Hartshorn was nearly knocked over by Socky, who was being chased by the bat hats. I thought at first Hartshorn would yell at them, but instead he started to laugh, his beak flopping open with deep bellows. He picked the chocolate pieces off his head and started to hand them out to the bat hats. As he watched them fly around the room, he said, "They remind me of the small bats my mother had in her garden back home."

"So you'll let them stay?" I asked.

"Yes," he said, stepping out of the way of a hat rolling by. "But they have to remain in this room. Could you imagine if they got loose in the castle?"

As the hats ran around us, they redecorated the room by throwing pillows off the poufy chairs and turning the collection of ogre figurines upside down in the cabinet by the fireplace. When I looked up to watch one of the hats go sailing by our heads, I spotted a floating four-poster bed[20]*.

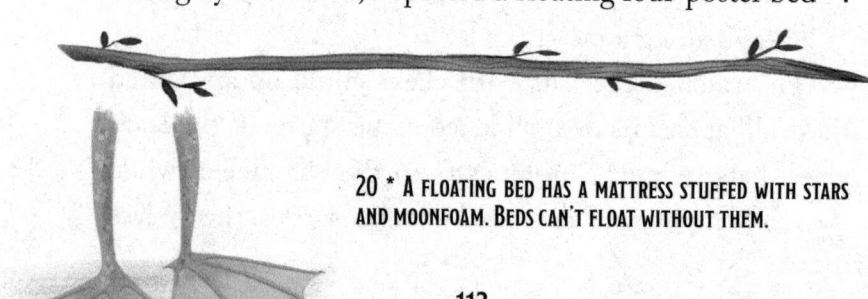

20 * A FLOATING BED HAS A MATTRESS STUFFED WITH STARS AND MOONFOAM. BEDS CAN'T FLOAT WITHOUT THEM.

It was hovering up toward the dome of the tall ceiling. The bed had a canopy of billowy curtains on it that were printed in dragon's plaid. The same plaid was on the bed skirt. I was very familiar with the plaid because me and Aunt Cauldroneyes had used it on some of the hats. It was a fabric that at night would light up with glowing yellow dragon eyes and shimmer in the moonlight. It was said that fire was weaved in to make the fabric warm to the touch.

Floating beside the large bed was an identical one, though much smaller. It was the perfect size for a dodo.

"Folklock thought it would be nice for us dodos to share rooms with the students," Hartshorn said. "I like it much better than sleeping in the dungeons. You know, it used to be that we would only fly the students in. Before this year, if you had asked me my name, I wouldn't have been allowed to tell you. The former headwander thought it best that we only be known as dodos. It felt nice to be able to tell you my name when you asked."

He smiled just before a fabric ball landed on the floor at his feet. He looked up to see an owl hat flying by.

That first night, I put the hats to bed the way me and Aunt Cauldroneyes always did back home. Some slept in teacups or pockets. Others preferred to go to bed on the plump chairs or on a blanket in front of the fireplace. I wished I had some chocolate curl to give them. Especially to the little ones, who whimpered Aunt Cauldroneyes' name. I did have some cinnamon sticks in one of my pockets, so I sprinkled the cinnamon into the fire so the room smelled like home.

"How do we get up there?" Egypt asked, staring up at the floating beds.

"All you have to do is yawn extra big," Hartshorn said. He opened his beak wide in a yawn and vanished.

When we looked up, he was staring down at us from his bed.

"To get out of the bed, just pull that." He pointed to a tassel hanging by the curtains.

I picked up Egypt, and together we yawned until we were in the large bed. It was full of pumpkin-shaped pillows, comfy quilts, and a nest of crocheted afghans.

"The afghans were made for the school by the Great Witches Crochet Club," Hartshorn said, pulling his afghan up to his chin. "As you know, your aunt is a member of that club."

While Egypt stretched out beside me, I stared up at the stars floating in the arched openings of the dome, just like I'd read about in the books about the school back home. It wasn't long before Egypt started to snore. I thought for a moment I heard the clack of a spoon against the side of a mug. I raised up as if I might see Aunt Cauldroneyes standing down below the floating bed, a mug of chocolate curl in her hand, the steam rising up to her smile, but all I saw was Socky pulling on the tail of a small silver dragon figurine on one of the shelves, the dragon's wings clacking against one another.

"Aunt Cauldroneyes," I whispered, "I miss you."

I turned over in the bed and shut my eyes as more stars drifted in.

CHAPTER 10
A Sky Full of Dragons

"THE OTHER STUDENTS ARE ARRIVING, YOUNG ONE."

Egypt's voice woke me. She was already out of the floating bed and at the windows down below. "Come and see. It's a sky full of dragons."

I quickly threw my blankets off and pulled the tassel. I disappeared, only to reappear a second later beside Egypt at the windows.

"I've never seen so many dragons before," I said just as a large dragon flew by so close to the windows, we could have reached out to touch his scales.

"Toadfire!" Grandma's Boot said as he and the other hats rushed over from their beds to see for themselves.

The dragons were flying in from every direction. I could tell that the ones with mountain mist on their wings had flown in students from the highest peaks. And that the dragons with tall grass caught in their talons carried students from fields and meadows. There were dragons that had sea-foam on the ends of their tails, which they had dipped into the seas they flew over, and there were even dragons who glistened with the slime of the swamp.

"Dragons are so big," one of the fairy hats said as she flew over and landed on one of the windows.

Egypt looked at the hats, who had their faces pressed up against the windows, looking out. "I know you are all excited to see the dragons of the school," she said, "but you are to stay in this room."

"But I want to see the dragons up close," one of the mice hats said in a very small voice.

"Certainly not!" Egypt said. "Dragons stomp and they thomp and they thump, and you're likely to get smashed. At the very least you'll lose more buttons than we have time to replace."

"I have to agree with Egypt," I told them. "I don't want any of you getting hurt."

"I'll make sure everyone stays in the room," Grandma's Boot said, even though the bat hats were blowing raspberries at him.

I looked for Hartshorn, but his bed was already empty and neatly made.

"He's gone outside to collect the names of the incoming students," Egypt said, tying up the loose ends of her linen.

I knew she was concerned about getting stomped, too.

We had not yet learned the castle, and though Egypt tried to pretend she knew the way, it was a few wrong turns later before we found ourselves outside in the tall witchgrass in front of the school. I looked up at the sky. If I had been a giantess, the dragons might have looked small enough to me to be sparrows coming in from a long journey. But to me as an eight-year-old girl, the dragons were larger than the largest storm cloud, the largest comet, the largest swirl at the end of Aunt Cauldroneyes' telescope.

Though they all looked like dodos in the face and had tails made of feathers, each dragon was colored differently. There was one as yellow as a gourd-gosh[21*] with bright purple feathers. Another was red with lightning bolts of pale pink. There were blue dragons and green ones and a few that were as gray as old owls.

"There's a turquoise-colored one," Egypt said.

The ones that were all white were brightest on the ground, while the marbled ones reminded me of the wooden beads on Aunt Cauldroneyes' necklaces.

"Their wings are huge," I said.

I thought it would take an hour to count a single dragon's

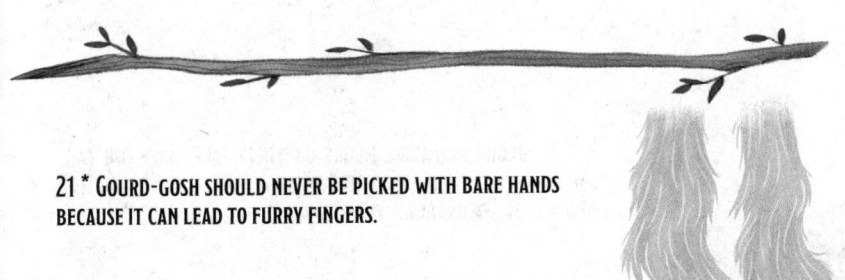

21 * GOURD-GOSH SHOULD NEVER BE PICKED WITH BARE HANDS BECAUSE IT CAN LEAD TO FURRY FINGERS.

horns,[22*] there were so many. Take a century to count their scales. Take a lifetime to count their thoughts. There have been many things said about dragons. That they can see in deep water. That they eat the stones of ancient ruins. That their hearts are made of stardust. That they are nothing more than haunted birds.

I don't suppose there have been as many myths and legends made up about any other creature. It has even been said that stars are the eyes of dragons, staring down upon the world.

"Here they come!" Egypt meowed loudly and held tight to the ends of her linen.

As the dragons landed on the ground, the earth shook and tiny pebbles exploded up around their feet.

"So this is where earthquakes come from," Egypt said as the dragons laid their giant wings down, bending the tall blades of grass.

"Hartshorn is over there," I said, finally spotting him. He looked so small as a dodo surrounded by dragons. He had a piece of parchment clipped to a board and was writing with a double-feathered quill.

We stepped carefully as we walked in between the dragons. They were out of breath from their long flights, and their bellies heaved in and out. Egypt kept an eye on them

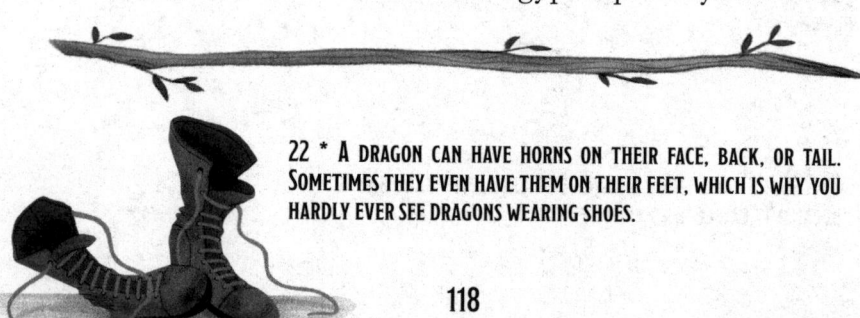

22 * A DRAGON CAN HAVE HORNS ON THEIR FACE, BACK, OR TAIL. SOMETIMES THEY EVEN HAVE THEM ON THEIR FEET, WHICH IS WHY YOU HARDLY EVER SEE DRAGONS WEARING SHOES.

as she said, "I worked with a dragon once while building a pyramid. We had just finished placing the last stone, when the dragon burped. The gust of it was so strong, it knocked the pyramid down. We had to start all over again. He was very sorry about it, but when it happened three more times, we came to the conclusion that dragons don't make the best pyramid builders."

I couldn't help but laugh as Egypt made sure to watch out for any burping dragons.

"Good morning, Wand Keeper Spella." Hartshorn looked up from his clipboard when he saw us. "I have not seen Headwander Folklock yet. But I told the chatty clematis to tell her that I need to see her as soon as she's back in her office. For the time being, there are some of the other teachers." He used his wing to point to a group by the castle. "You will call them 'wanders.' Some of them have taught here for a long time, like Wander Acidelia Mummyheart, who has the shadow of a sphinx. And Wander Fortuna Fairycrumb. She's that tiny one flying."

I had been around wand witches and wizards before, when they'd come to our house for hats, but no matter how many times I saw a Wand Keeper, I always got excited to see their wand shadows crackling with bolts of lightning.

"You know, many have said that I should be a teacher," Egypt said, standing taller. "I am rather wise, if I say so myself."

Hartshorn looked at her before scratching his beak slowly and saying, "I'll let you know if any positions open up."

As I watched the group of teachers, one stepped

forward. Wander Mummyheart. She was staring at the stone bridge that connected the castle to the other side of the river. I just then noticed a crowd of people on the bridge. They stood up against the iron gates that closed the entrance to the school.

"Who are all those people?" I asked Hartshorn.

"Protestors," he said. "We expected there might be some for the students' arrival. But we didn't anticipate there would be so many."

Signs and banners had been enchanted to float above the protestors' heads. The signs were written with things like NO TO PLANT MAGIC and DON'T RUIN DRAGON'S KNOB. Some of the signs had images of plants and herbs crossed out in big black *X*s with WE DON'T WANT YOUR PLANT MUD, KEEP OUR MAGIC PURE BLOOD written beneath.

A few of the protestors held unicorn horns in their hands and chanted, "Leave our cauldrons alone. Our spells are not yours to own!"

I looked back at Wander Mummyheart. She was frowning at the protestors. Then she held up her hand and her sphinx shadow jumped into it with a blaze of lightning, instantly turning into a wand that had the sphinx's face. I knew from seeing wands before that they always looked like the creature that had made them. One time I'd seen a wand that was as winding as a snake's body with a little tongue that hissed on the end, and another time I saw a wand with enough tentacles to be at home in the sea. When the creatures were shadows, they were silhouettes, so you saw their features whenever the lightning bolts cut through. But once they turned into wands, you got to discover their feathers, talons, scales, or eyes in vibrant colors.

"She's casting a spell," I said as I watched Mummyheart's lips moving. We were too far away to know what the spell was, but I knew it must have been an old one, because she spit onto her wand, then touched it to her right elbow. You only spit on your wand and touch your elbow when you're casting the oldest of the old spells. Then she held her wand high, and sand fell from the tip of it. The sand flew in a swirling cloud over to the bridge and knocked the protestors' signs down.

As the signs fell, some of the protestors grew angrier and tried to climb over the gate to the school, but like the front door of the castle, the gate had feet and would use them to encourage those who got too close to move back. Wander Mummyheart laughed as her wand became a shadow once more.

"Even though they may be protesting the start of our school year," Hartshorn said, "we have a record-breaking enrollment of first wands. I am optimistic that there will be many who find hope in what we're trying to do here."

He looked up at me, his small dodo eyes searching my face.

"Wand Keeper Spella, if I may be so bold," he said, "was the reason you didn't open your invitation because you don't approve of Dragon's Knob being a school for plant magic only?"

"No," I said quickly. "That wasn't why at all. I didn't want to come here because I didn't want to leave Aunt Cauldroneyes and all my friends, like the hats. And Egypt, of course."

She purred against my leg.

"I'm sure you'll make lots of new friends here," Hartshorn said, returning to his clipboard.

He might have been sure about that, but I wasn't. I looked around at the other kids sliding off their dragons. Some of the students already knew each other. They collected in groups and started to talk excitedly about the ride there. A few who passed by stared at my freckles. I picked up Egypt and held her in front of my face so I could peek out above her linen.

I knew which students were ten years and older. They, like the wanders, had their wand shadows, already hatched from the eggs. These students also came dressed in their cloaks from the previous years. They had fabric badges sewn onto them. Some also had badges sewn onto their scarves, hats, and bags. The badges were brightly colored and in different shapes and sizes. I saw one that looked like a long-necked dinosaur. Another was in the shape of a toad that had a star on his back. One student had a badge that looked like a cauldron boiling over, and there were several that were like potion bottles.

A few of the students carried albums under their arms that were titled *Badge Book*.

"Students who perform well during the school year are rewarded with them," Hartshorn said once he noticed me staring at the badges. "Whenever you collect a badge, you can put it on your cloak or scarf, or even your hat. You can also put them in an album and trade them with your fellow classmates. In the past, students who received the most badges were allowed to do special things. Sometimes it was a field trip to the mountains to watch a herd of Pegasuses fly by, or you could ride a pirate boat down the river."

He looked up at a dragon flying crookedly over our heads, then quickly wrote something down on his clipboard.

"But that's all changed this year," he said. "Though the badges will still be handed out, there will be no special field trips that only a few will be allowed to go on. Now the badges can be turned in at the Wrinkled Pumpkin. It's a little store Headwander Folklock has started. Everyone will have the opportunity to exchange badges for things like candies or little potions. One might even earn enough for a new flying broom or cauldron. I quite like the change. I always thought it was a little unfair that some of the students got to see and do things that others did not, because in the past, the badges weren't always handed out fairly. The former headwander had favorite students and he would make sure they got the most badges, even if they didn't earn them."

He pointed toward the cloak of a passing student. "See those lumpy green badges?" he asked. "Those are called troll boogers. They're usually the first badges a student can earn. They're quite easy to get, for things like showing up to class on time. Kids like to trade them the most."

"Troll boogers?" I remembered the boogers Aunt Cauldroneyes had given me the day she disappeared. I quickly reached into the pocket I had put them in, but when I pulled them out, I discovered they weren't boogers anymore. They were badges. Aunt Cauldroneyes had given me my first ones for the new school year.

"Thanks, Aunt Cauldroneyes," I whispered to her, wherever she was. I tucked the badges safely back into my pocket just as I heard a boy shouting.

"This stupid dodo kept getting lost like he hasn't been here a million and one times by now," the boy said. He had just landed on a silver dragon who had a tiny pair of wire-rimmed eyeglasses slipping off his nose. When the dragon transformed back into a dodo, I saw he had silver feathers and a beak that was a bit droopy. His aged eyes squinted behind the glasses.

"That's Magis," Hartshorn said to me. "He's the oldest dodo working here."

Like Hartshorn, Magis had silver scars around his ankles. I quickly noticed that all the dodos did.

"The school really should retire them once they're old enough to forget where the dang castle is," the boy said. He was dressed formally in a blazer that had a crest with the image of a cliff against a night sky. Being a magical hatmaker, I recognized the fabric of the sky as being night cloth.[23*]

I knew the boy had elves in his lineage because of the slight point in his right ear. I also knew he had one of the

---

23 * NIGHT CLOTH IS A FABRIC CUT FROM THE EVENING SKY. BECAUSE OF THIS, THE FABRIC MOVES WITH IMAGES OF THE STARS AND MOONS.

latest hairstyles. It was called the wolf snout because the hair was curled high into a tunnel on top of the head until it looked like a snout. Shorter pieces of hair were spiked into fangs. A sprinkle of howling dust meant the hair could howl at night. I'd only learned about the style when a couple of werewolf hairdressers had come in to get new hats.

"I've heard there's a waiting list for those shoes," Egypt whispered to me as she used her paw to point at the boy's sneakers.

The shoes had squishy balls on the sides that, when you pumped them, inflated the bat wings on the heels. The shoes were called Bat Blasters and didn't do magic, except let everyone know that you had something they didn't. Worst of all, they were said to be made from unicorn leather.

"Who is that mean boy?" I asked Hartshorn.

"Grackle Nightcliff," he said. "His family is old money. Their factory manufactures ingredients."

"What do you mean by ingredients?" I asked. "Like cinnamon and stuff?"

"No, Wand Keeper Spella," Hartshorn said. "Ingredients like unicorn horn, dragon hearts, and troll eyes. The types of ingredients we no longer use here at Dragon's Knob, thank goodness."

I wasn't surprised to hear Grackle's family bottled creature parts once I saw Grackle's dragon-eye ring on his right hand. The shimmering green-and-black hide of the dragon's skin made the ring band. The eye itself was large with a wrinkled eyelid. I knew the eye had come from a cave dragon because of the red pupil that glowed in the middle of the yellow and orange iris. The eye stared back at me.

"Anyone who wears a cave dragon's eye is keeping secrets," Egypt said in her most mysterious voice.

"It's true," Hartshorn added. "Cave dragons are notorious for collecting secrets in their caves. If you pluck an eye from a cave dragon, you have an eye that will always be on the lookout for hidden things, and it will gather them for you."

Hartshorn turned to the sound of another dodo calling his name.

"Wand Keeper Spella," he said. "I've got to go around and check off the last arrivals. I will let you know as soon as I hear of Headwander Folklock's return."

He wobbled off into the crowd with his clipboard.

"Oh, you stupid, stupid bird," Grackle shouted at Magis, who struggled with the clothing trunk. Unable to bear the weight, Magis dropped it, causing clothes to spill out. "You're pathetic!" Grackle yelled, and stomped his foot, causing the laser lights in the sole of the shoe to flash. The lights were another thing that made the shoes popular, though they were also said to attract moths if the shoes were worn at night, which always made me giggle at the thought.

"I'm sorry, Wand Keeper Grackle." Magis started to pick up the clothes.

I quickly put Egypt down and ran over to help the old dodo.

"Stop being mean to him," I said to Grackle.

I picked up a large pile of his clothes and shoved them into his hands.

"Don't you know who I am?" Grackle dropped the pile back down to the ground.

"Who are you?" I asked. "A toad's wart? A unicorn's fart? A goblin's spitball?"

He snarled at me as another boy appeared. He had an equally popular hairstyle called the centaur flip. It was named for the mound of hair that sat high on his head and was curled back with jelly until it was shiny and slick. This boy wore his hooded cloak on one shoulder so that it fell to the side of him. The cloak looked like a tiger, and it roared anytime the boy flipped it up. It was just as expensive as the bat sneakers.

"I see you've been making new friends, Grackle," the boy said with a smirk.

As I handed Magis a shirt to put in the trunk, the old dodo said to me, "Thank you for helping me, Wand Keeper."

Before I could say you're welcome, Grackle grabbed the shirt out of Magis' hand and held it up toward the other boy.

"Look at this," he said. "They've gotten mud all over my new clothes." Grackle shook the shirt in Magis' face.

"I'm sorry, Wand Keeper Grackle," Magis said.

"What did you say?" Grackle loomed over the bird.

"He said he was sorry." I stepped forward to stand between him and the old dodo.

Grackle threw the shirt back down into the mud and said, "If it wasn't my family's tradition to graduate from Dragon's Knob, I would not be here. Both my father and I agree, this new plant magic and Folklock are going to ruin the school."

The boy beside him nodded and tossed his cloak so it growled. "I'd like to be out there with them," he said, nodding toward the protestors on the bridge. "I wouldn't be here at Dragon's Knob either if my parents hadn't made me come. They think plant magic is a good thing."

I returned to helping Magis pick up the clothes and whispered to him, "Who is the boy with Grackle?"

But the old bird didn't hear so well. When I repeated it, I had to say it loud enough that the boy heard.

"I'm Slithe Wolfice." He raised his cloak, causing it to roar again. "My family owns Wolfice Media. We publish the newspapers *The Daily Cackle* and *The Midnight Cackle*. I'm sure you've heard of them."

He looked at my clothes. Instead of expensive sneakers, I had old boots crusted with mud that grew fuzzy ferns and were full of creatures like blast worms and pixies that kept peeking out. He looked at my shorts and T-shirt, both of which had patches over old rips. Added to that, my vest and pockets were overflowing with things I had collected, which I'm sure to him looked like nothing more than throwaway baubles. Certainly nothing as new as the cloak he wore.

"What do your parents do?" he asked, then smiled as if he already knew. "Let me guess. They repair brooms or polish cauldrons, something like that, right?"

"I was raised by Mathilda Cauldroneyes," I said. "The greatest magical hatmaker ever."

"Magical hatmaker?" Grackle said before leaning over to whisper something to Slithe. Together they laughed.

You're brave, Spella, Aunt Cauldroneyes' voice echoed in my ears. *You've climbed the tallest tree in the forest. You've outrun the fastest cheetah.*

I took a deep breath, her words fueling me as I said, "You two sound like a couple of chortling buffyfish."

Grackle stopped laughing. "Yeah, well, at least we don't have blue freckles."

"Yeah." Slithe grinned. "Did some fairy sneeze in your face or something? And where did you get those hand-me-down clothes? Out of some gnome's trash can?"

Egypt growled and hissed. I had to quickly pick her up and hold her, or she would have showed them what a pyramid pinch was.

"Since when are they allowing raccoons wrapped in rags at the school?" Grackle made a face at Egypt, who hissed even louder. "Yuck." He stood back. "Her breath reeks."

"I have been mummified for thousands of years," Egypt said. "Do you think it's going to smell like roses and perfume?"

"C'mon, Egypt." I held her closer. "They're not worth it." I turned my back to the two boys as they walked off, laughing.

"They were a couple of rotten pumpkin seeds," Egypt said. "Just like them." She nodded to the protestors on the bridge. They had grown louder as the last of the students slid off their dragons.

"Those protesters really don't like Dragon's Knob changing to plants," I said before lowering my head. I couldn't help but think about Aunt Cauldroneyes and all the work she had done to make things better for creatures.

Egypt laid her paw on my arm, then looked out at the dragons. "You know," she said, "I bet if I think really hard about it, I can turn into a dragon."

She held her breath and tensed her arms, but the only thing that happened was that her yellow eyes bulged. I couldn't help but laugh.

She smiled up at me. "Feel better, young one?" she asked.

"You always make me feel better." I hugged her tight as the dragons around us started to change back into dodos.

Just like what had happened with Hartshorn and his purple-and-white-striped horns remaining on his head after his transformation, the dodos were all left with something that didn't change back right away. For some it was their long dragon tail. For others it was their eyes, or a single talon. They all shook their heads and bodies until the last of the dragon parts disappeared. At the same time a voice spoke loud enough for us all to hear.

"If you find yourself reaching for gold, think instead of the magic of old. For the true treasures to be told are within the wand that you hold."

Spell No. 8,323

I bet you know a fairy,
Small, blue, and hairy.
But the one I got I carry,
And she is big, blue, and scary.

Note from the Before Long Witch

If you ever find yourself in a fight with a four-eyed toad, a hairy-tongued wildcat, or a farting piebutt, use this spell. Remember to say these words loud, so your voice echoes. The echoes should last for at least seven seconds. This spell is also useful for running dirtfingers out of your garden and keeping sticky-footed ants out of the sugar pot.

CHAPTER 11
CANDLEHOUR

THE VOICE CAME FROM A TALL WOMAN WHO WORE A bright red blouse that rose in ruffles of black feathers around her neck. The feathers matched the ones covering her sleeves. Her shoulder pads reminded me of the plump velvet pincushions we had back in the attic. Tinkling from each of her shoulder pads was a fringe of small skeleton keys that matched the buttons on the side of her very long skirt, which was covered in rows of real roses. A pair of large stone legs showed from under her skirt. The legs looked as though they belonged to a giant.

"Everyone gather around," she said, waving us over into a group around her.

"Her hair blows," Egypt whispered to me. "Even though there is no wind."

The woman's hair moved as if she was in a whirlwind. It smeared the red lipstick she wore into whiskery lines around her mouth. Only when her hair whipped up could you see her dark bushy eyebrows and her green eyes shining like the gooseberry jam Aunt Cauldroneyes would jar at home.

She wore a stovepipe hat that was three feet tall, at least. It leaned to the left, and the loose crown flapped up every once in a while. In the tall pipe were several round holes through which nesting material like leaves and twigs poked out. Birds were flying in and out of the holes. It was the reason for the rainbow-colored splatters of bird droppings on the brim of the hat.

"Welcome to Dragon's Knob!" The woman tossed her cloak back toward the griffin[24] shadow behind her. Lightning cracked across the griffin's beak.

The woman had a rope around her waist. Hanging from it was a small wicker basket that started to shake. I knew there was something inside it.

"Are you Headwander Folklock?" I asked.

"Goodness, no." She giggled. "I am Deputy Headwander Candlehour. Not candle *minute*. Not candle *second*. But Candle*hour*." The group remained quiet. "I'll have you

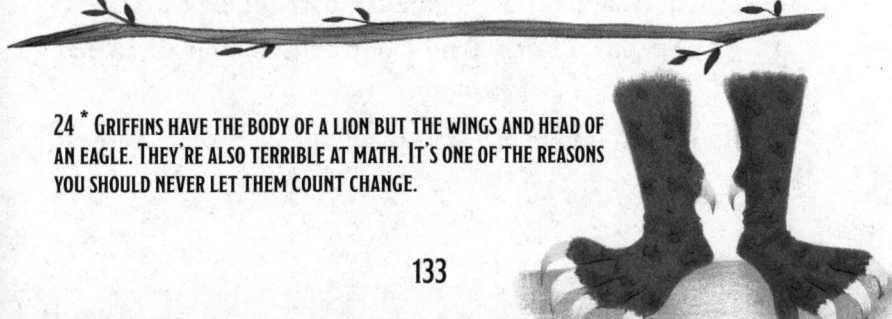

[24] * GRIFFINS HAVE THE BODY OF A LION BUT THE WINGS AND HEAD OF AN EAGLE. THEY'RE ALSO TERRIBLE AT MATH. IT'S ONE OF THE REASONS YOU SHOULD NEVER LET THEM COUNT CHANGE.

know, that joke usually gets quite a few cackles."

Candlehour hiccupped, and a bubble came out of her mouth. It had a bright blue frog inside it. Once the bubble popped, the frog fell down to the ground. We watched him hop away.

"I have a terrible case of the frog hiccups," Candlehour said. "Of course, that's what you get when you eat a stale popcorn ball, and that's exactly what I did. The only cure is to be frightened, nearly to death, by a tree wart troll. Just about the worst thing to be frightened by. I am not looking forward to that."

As Candlehour continued to talk about the school and what to expect, the boy beside me gently elbowed my side and whispered, "She's my aunt, if you can believe it."

He had shaggy hair and was rather small, which made the bright orange corduroy tie he wore seem even bigger.

"She's the one who made me wear it." He flipped the tie up. "She said, '*You want to make a good impression on your first day.*' But no one else is wearing a tie. Except for that goat over there in that field."

He pointed toward the bucktoothed goat chomping on the tall grass. The goat was wearing the same orange corduroy tie. I tried not to laugh.

"I bet she made him wear his tie, too." The boy shook his head and sighed. "My name is Burrland, by the way."

"I'm Spella," I said. "And I don't think your tie is that bad."

He looked down at it and made a face. "Yeah, I guess not."

We turned back to Candlehour, who was still talking about how exciting she thought this school year would be.

"Oh boy." Grackle spoke loudly. "Where'd they find this nut? Under a goblin's booger?"

Slithe laughed. The two of them were getting the whole group's attention.

"I'll have you know," an owl said as he popped up from the wicker basket hanging from Candlehour's waist, "they found her in the attic, where all the best things are found."

The owl just so happened to be wearing a bright orange tie around his neck, too.

"Oh, great." Burrland crossed his arms. "So it's me and the goat and the owl all matching for the day, I see."

Unlike Burrland, the owl seemed to enjoy wearing the tie as he flopped it forward over the basket for all to see. He had a wonderful round head and two pairs of eyes, each of which was wearing gold oval spectacles. He was blinking his four eyes at different times, making it hard to see in which direction he was even looking. His ears were long and tufted. They were the tallest part of him, as he was no more than a few inches high.

"This is my book owl." Wander Candlehour patted the owl's head. "It's said that every time you flip a page in a book, the egg of an owl falls out. That's another reason why it's so important to read. We create the most remarkable of owls when we do. Of course, some will say that's only a myth and that such little owls are made in nests, the same as any other. But I say, what's the harm in believing?"

The students started to whisper to each other. Some

whispers were about her owl, others were about her hat. But most were about her hair and why it blew in a wind that did not exist.

Hearing the whispers, Candlehour smiled.

"I enchanted my hair," she said, "because eighty-eight years ago I ate a very spicy pepper and have been hot ever since. Having my hair whip about keeps me quite cool."

Egypt raised her paw.

"Do you have a question, mummy cat?" Candlehour asked.

"Are you part giant?" Egypt asked.

"I wish I were. Why do you ask, little kitty?"

"Because of your stone legs," Egypt said.

Candlehour looked down and said, "Oh, these aren't mine." She pulled her skirt up just enough to reveal a pair of dark green shoes with curled toes standing on top of the stone legs.

She hopped down and landed on the grass. We saw that what she had been standing on was a statue of legs, the top part of the statue having eroded long ago.

"I just thought I'd stand up there to welcome you all to Dragon's Knob," she said. "And I really hope you do feel welcome." She started to knead her hands against one another so much that the spider rings that had been on her right fingers were now on her left. "I know I'm forgetting something."

"You must separate the students by their grades," her griffin shadow said to her just as a flash of lightning lit up his wings.

"Oh yes!" she said with a hiccup. The hiccup created another bubble that floated from her mouth and popped almost immediately, releasing a blue frog that hopped across her feet. "All of you first wands are to stay here with me. The rest of you, please follow your dodo, who will take you to the wander assigned to your grade."

She pointed to the other wanders. They were waiting by the castle's doors but were still staring at the protestors on the bridge.

"And remember." Candlehour held up her finger as the group started to break up. "Today belongs to you. Do something *wonderful* with it."

The older students followed their dodos and were led into the castle by the wanders.

I stayed with Candlehour and the rest of the first wands, including Burrland, who was showing off his tie to the others. I hoped Grackle and Slithe would be with the second wands, but I wasn't so lucky. The three of us frowned at one another.

"I'm so happy to be in charge of you first wands," Candlehour said. "It's such a magnificent thing to be at the beginning of something."

She shook her sleeve, and seeds fell into the owl's basket. He blinked all four eyes and grinned up at her, before pecking the seeds up and chomping loudly.

"I teach the classes about birds, wings, and all the ancient Fuzzlefeatherfoop," she said. "My lessons also include a history of Fuzzlefeatherfoop—"

At the word "Fuzzlefeatherfoop" a boy with a big smile began clapping. He wore square black eyeglasses that were too large for his face. When he saw us staring at him, he quickly dropped his hands and his cheeks grew red. I noticed there was a tiny dragon hanging off his right ear. At first I thought it was an earring, but then the dragon hopped down and hid beneath the collar of the boy's red cardigan. He stepped out of sight behind a tall girl.

"Curious creature," Egypt whispered. I didn't know if she was talking about the small dragon or the boy himself.

"Excuse me, Wander Candlehour?" I held up my hand. "Do you know when Headwander Folklock will be back to Dragon's Knob?"

Before she could answer, a loud, rumbling snore came from a tree behind her. The tree had dark, swirling bark, and the leaves were as large as the quilts on Aunt Cauldroneyes' bed back home.

What I thought was odd about the tree was that there seemed to be no creatures near it. I'd never seen a branch without at least one dragon squirrel on it.

"This is what is known as a slumber tree," Candlehour said as her griffin shadow walked behind her. "Anyone who dares to sleep in the shade of its branches will never wake back up."

The snores grew louder. When we got to the other side of the tree, we saw a woman sleeping in the only sunny spot, up against the tree's trunk.

"Can't you make her stop that horrible racket?" Slithe moaned.

"What would you have me do, young man?" Wander Candlehour asked, her griffin shadow squawking toward Grackle.

"Get rid of her," Gackle said. "Along with this dumb dodo." He pushed Magis, who fell over.

"Don't do that!" I yelled at Grackle as I quickly helped Magis up.

Some of the old dodo's feathers had gotten bent. I gently tried to straighten them.

"Why am I not surprised you're a bleeding heart for the weak?" Grackle made a face.

"You think that just because you can push someone down, that makes you strong?" I said. "It doesn't! It makes *you* the weak one."

"I don't care if you take that worthless bird," Grackle snarled. "You two belong together."

"That is enough!" The voice came from the woman beneath the tree. She was now awake and standing up.

"But how?" I asked Wander Candlehour. "I thought you said that anyone who sleeps under the tree will be there forever?"

"You did not listen carefully, Wand Keeper." Candlehour smiled. "What I said was that anyone who falls asleep in the slumber tree's *shade* never wakes again. You can clearly see that she had been sleeping in the only sunny spot."

The woman's eyes were purple. Her lips a midnight hue. I knew she was wise because she had a wonderful hump in her nose, which is always a sign of wisdom. The thinnest of unicorn hair could have been threaded through the end of her nose, it was so pointed. She had a haircut that resembled a cauldron, with glass barrettes that were like the bubbles of a most delicious potion.

"She looks wonderful," I whispered to Egypt, who nodded.

The woman had fresh herbs fastened to her blouse like a brooch. The flannel skirt of her dress, printed with golden acorns, was pinned up, revealing a black cotton slip and striped leggings rolled up to her calves. The patches on her cloak all seemed to be plaid. I recognized the fabric from the floating rolls in the attic back home. Like Aunt Cauldroneyes, she walked barefoot.

"She pays close attention to the ticking of time," Egypt said to me as she stared at the silver pocket watch. Its chain was wrapped around the balloon sleeve of the woman's blouse while the bright blue watch face dangled at her wrist.

"She looks like a hag," Grackle muttered to Slithe.

Egypt growled at the two of them as the woman walked past us. She smelled like crisp autumn leaves. It reminded me of Aunt Cauldroneyes' perfume. She would crush leaves every October and distill them in a bottle with a cork that she would then dab her neck and wrists with.

"Wow!" Burrland said. "Her shadow is a Pegasus."

The great horse galloped around us, her hooves crackling with lightning, while the woman stopped to stand in front of Grackle.

"I believe you have insulted my dear friend Magis," she said to Grackle as Magis came over to stand by her side. He looked up at her and smiled a toothless grin.

"Ugh, he doesn't even have teeth!" Grackle made a face.

"You don't like old things, do you, young man?" the woman said to him. "Don't you know that our wrinkles are the ripples of magic? Our hands have held a million spells. The cracks in our feet hold the secrets of the stars. Our silver hair is the silver web of the spider of time."

When Grackle only rolled his eyes, she said to him, "You are not deserving of Magis or any dodo and therefore will have none for the year. You must learn that you do not push others down at Dragon's Knob. Am I as clear as crystal?"

Grackle started to speak, but the woman said, "Before you ask me if I know who you are, I do indeed. You are the one and only Grackle Nightcliff, son of Armory Nightcliff. But being his son will be no golden ticket at Dragon's Knob, no matter what your father has told you."

Her Pegasus shadow galloped up behind her and leapt into her hand. Gasps came from the students as we watched the winged horse transform into a slender wand carved as the Pegasus and capped in moonstone. She pointed it at me.

"Your kindness in defending Magis deserves a reward," she said.

The wand started to neigh. She spun it in fast circles as she stomped her feet. I knew she was conjuring something small, because she held her other hand in one of her pockets.[25*]

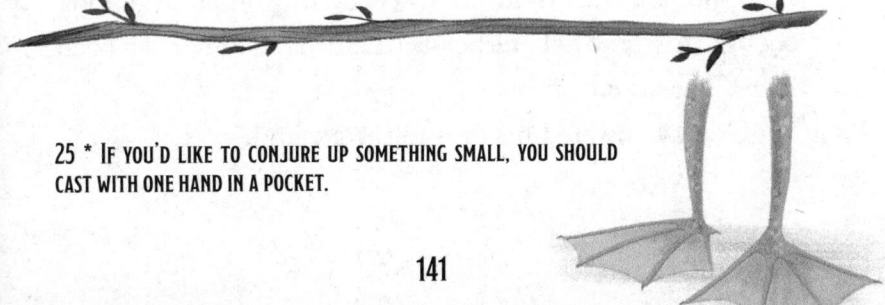

25 * IF YOU'D LIKE TO CONJURE UP SOMETHING SMALL, YOU SHOULD CAST WITH ONE HAND IN A POCKET.

"*I'll give you a candy full of delight,*" she said, starting to cast her spell, "*something sweet and crunchy in every bite.*"

The wand neighed again as a piece of candy appeared in the air between us. It floated toward me. By the time it landed in my hand, it had flatted into a fabric badge that smelled and looked like peppermint candy.

"You've earned the first badge of the new school year," she said, her wand jumping out of her hand and returning to her side once more as a Pegasus. "That badge will be good for one free bag of peppermint elves from the Wrinkled Pumpkin."

She smiled and looked at my blue freckles.

"Welcome to Dragon's Knob, Spella," she said. "As the stars come to tell it."

"How do you know my name?" I looked at her just as Hartshorn came running up, out of breath.

"That is Headwander Folklock," he said.

"Headwander Folklock?" Grackle asked. "But I thought Folklock would be a man. The school's headwander has always been a man. It's tradition. You can't change that. You've already driven this school into the mud with all this plant garbage."

Headwander Folklock turned to Grackle with a smile.

"You are surprised to discover a woman is strong enough to stand where before there have only ever been men?" she asked.

Grackle lowered his eyes to the ground.

"And you thought I was just an old woman you could—What were the words you used, young man?" she asked. "'Get rid of'? Me and my old friend Magis?"

"Headwander Folklock!" I said. "I have to tell you something."

I was so excited to finally meet her, I didn't realize I was squeezing Egypt so tightly until a piece of linen popped out with a cloud of dust. But Egypt didn't mind. She was excited, too, and said, "We have to speak to you about Mathilda Cauldroneyes. It's very important."

"I left you a note with the chatty clematis," Hartshorn was quick to add.

"I haven't been up to my office yet," Folklock said. "What's happened to Mathilda?"

"My aunt was taken," I said. "By a hat."

The other students started to whisper.

"Did that girl with the blue freckles just say a hat stole her aunt?"

"Isn't that strange?"

"I've never heard of a hat kidnapping a person before."

"Do you think she's lying?"

"She does have blue freckles. Maybe she just likes attention."

"I bet she just ran away to get away from you," Grackle said as he stared at me.

Slithe laughed but stopped when Headwander Folklock laid her eyes on the both of them.

"She didn't run away!" I shouted at him. "I swear. The hat took her."

"Good goblins!" Wander Candlehour said. Her hair had started to blow even harder. "The magical hatmaker kidnapped by a hat."

"What type of hat was it, Spella?" Folklock asked.

"It wasn't a hat she made," I said. "Someone brought it to her."

Folklock's Pegasus paced behind her, while Wander Candlehour's griffin did the same.

"Who brought it?" Folklock asked quickly.

"He was a stranger," I said. "He had a dragon's wing for a cloak."

Hartshorn nearly fell off his feet at the mention of the cloak. Folklock shared a glance with him, before asking, "What else can you tell me about this stranger, Spella?"

"He had bushy sideburns and wild hair, and his eyes blazed like fire."

"Herbalia." Wander Candlehour leaned in to whisper into Folklock's ear. "It's him."

"Who?" I asked.

Folklock turned her violet eyes back to me. "Have you had any other strangers stopping by recently, Spella?"

"Just folks coming by for hats," I said.

"There have been letters," Egypt added.

"Letters?" Candlehour's eyes flickered.

I looked over toward the shouting protestors on the bridge.

"From witches and wizards angry with Aunt Cauldron-eyes," I said. "They blame her for Dragon's Knob changing to plant magic."

"Plant magic," Grackle groaned as he faced Slithe. "People who do plant magic eat dirt."

"We know about such letters ourselves," Folklock said as she looked at Candlehour. "We've gotten several bins full of them, too, haven't we, Rose Harriet?"

Candlehour slowly nodded.

"I wouldn't have taken the bag," I said, "but there was a parchment label on it that said the hat belonged to you, Headwander Folklock. I didn't realize it was a trick until I took the hat inside the house."

"None of what happened to your aunt is your fault, Spella," Folklock said before she and Candlehour stepped away. They whispered amongst themselves as their wand shadows did the same. The Pegasus turned to look at me, her eyes lit up by lightning.

When Folklock came back, she took my cheeks in her hands. They smelled of green leaves and the earth.

"I will leave for your house in Hungry Snout Forest today," she said. "There might be something left behind that will tell us a little more."

"I want to go, too," I said.

"No, you will stay here at the school, where you are safe." Folklock's voice was firm.

Egypt purred and her glowing yellow eyes met mine. I had known the old cat long enough to know what she was saying without her speaking a single word. She was saying that we had to believe Folklock was right. At least for now.

I looked back up at the headwander and stared into her violet eyes.

"Aunt Cauldroneyes trusted you," I said. "So I will, too."

"And I will honor that trust," Folklock said. "As the stars come to tell it." Her Pegasus rose up on her back legs and tossed her mane. Her loud neigh echoed across the land.

CHAPTER 12
ONE FANG COMES TO THE RESCUE

THE CASTLE WAS FILLED WITH SOUNDS OF STUDENTS' feet on the staircases and their voices in the halls. As I watched Headwander Folklock disappear around the corner, headed to her office, Egypt said, "It's good that she is returning to the house. Maybe she will find something."

I held Egypt close and fell in line with the other first wands as Candlehour led us through the castle.

"All the doors have knobs of different sizes and shapes," she said. "The big ones are gifts from the giant kings. The very tiny ones are from the empire of the fairies. There are doorknobs from trolls, goblins, and creatures such as the unicorns and centaurs, for every realm has a door. The

Dragon King wanted his to be open to all. So that no matter who you were or where you came from, you could have a way in, and no matter the size of your hand or the shape of your hoof, you could feel welcome knowing that you, too, can open the door to step inside."

The heels of her curled-toed shoes clacked against the floor as she pointed up at the paintings on the wall and asked, "What do you notice about each of them, Wand Keepers?"

The paintings were framed in dark woods carved with leaves and old flora. I could tell they were oil paintings from the way the light reflected off the textures, and because of the hairline cracks that looked like tiny spiderwebs.

What I noticed about all the paintings was that they were of nests. There was a twiggy nest that held bright green eggs. Above that was a nest made out of white leaves that cradled tiny red eggs. The nest made out of ice had started to thaw. Water dripped out of the painting and down the frame. Students ducked from tiny pebbles falling from a nest of them higher up on the wall, while chirps from eggs that had already hatched could be heard coming from a nest made out of seashells. Even though they were paintings, the nests were real. You could touch the eggs and feel the warmth of one, or the cool dew on another.

"Why do all the paintings have nests in them?" I asked.

Candlehour smiled as she said, "It was my idea. I've always loved birds." She patted the owl in her basket. "Not only am I deputy headwander, but I'm also a Fuzzlefeatherfoop. In more scholarly terms, a Fuzzlefeatherfoop is a scientist who studies all flying creatures. Some of you might have read my book." She hiccupped and a blue frog dropped down to the staircase. She ignored the frog and asked, "Anyone here read my book, *Endangered Feathers?*"[26*]

Burrland reluctantly raised his hand, causing Grackle and Slithe to snicker.

"My little Burrland." Candlehour patted her nephew on the head. "I know you've read it. For all of you who haven't, the book is about birds who are endangered. One of the reasons they become endangered is because they've lost their nesting homeland. During the course of my research I've collected many nests. I've hidden them in the paintings so the eggs will have a safe place to hatch."

She stood in front of a painting with a phoenix nest made of fire in it. She reached above the flames and picked up one of the black eggs. It was lined with orange veins, and smoke was rising from it.

"I hope that one day they can all return to their homes in the wild," she said, placing the egg back into the painting, "where they truly belong."

Her griffin laid his wing on her shoulder and patted it.

"Right," she said. "Off to the rest of the tour. After

26 * *ENDANGERED FEATHERS* IS A BOOK THAT HAS A HABIT OF LAYING AN EGG IF LEFT IN ONE PLACE FOR TOO LONG.

all, today belongs to us. We shall do something wonderful with it."

When we got to the staircase leading up to Hisses and Hoots Hall, the boy in the square black glasses asked Candlehour why the school was named Dragon's Knob.

"Once the ancient king died," she said, "a bell tolled for each year of his long life. There were so many years, and the bell tolled for so long, banging into the sides of the tower, that the bell got a bump in its brass. Those who saw it called it the knob of the Dragon King."

Candlehour stopped on the staircase to tell us that if we rubbed our hands against the wooden rail, it would create a smell of pumpkin and spice.

"The faster you run up the stairs, and the more your hands rubs against the wood, the stronger the scent," she said, giggling as she ran up the stairs, the hood on her cloak bouncing up and down and her owl hooting in delight.

As the other students rubbed their hands on the railing and ran up after her, I walked up slowly, remembering the pumpkins that Aunt Cauldroneyes grew, and the pies she made from them, smelling of the same spices.

"I'm sorry about your missing aunt." The boy in the square black glasses had stopped on the step in front of me. I saw the tiny dragon moving just beneath the collar of his red cardigan.

"Thanks," I said.

He was a lanky boy with a belt tied into a knot to hold up his loose pants.

"I didn't know a hat could steal anybody." He ran his

hand through his floppy hair as if he didn't know what else to do with it. He looked ready to say something more, but instead only smiled before following the rest up the stairs.

When we got to Hisses and Hoots Hall, Candlehour spoke about the creatures who lived there. She explained, just as Hartshorn had, that the creatures had previously been caged in the greenhouses. I noticed as she spoke that Grackle had his arms crossed, while his dragon-eye ring watched Candlehour very closely. The red pupil of the eye glowed a little brighter. I remembered what Hartshorn had said about cave dragons collecting secrets.

"Your dodos will now show you to your rooms," Candlehour said.

Thankfully, Grackle and Slithe had rooms that were closer to the staircase. The boy with the square glasses and red cardigan had a room that was next to mine. He smiled at the welcome wreath and waited patiently for his dodo to open his door.

Once I was in my room, I found the hats passed out from too much play. They were piled in front of the fireplace, snoring.

"I see they've been chewing on the chocolate curtains again." Hartshorn looked down at the chocolate smeared across the rug. "It's a good thing the curtains are enchanted to grow back."

There was a hat still up. One Fang. He was named for the single tooth hanging from his brim. He was using his fang to move around the jigsaw pieces in Grandma's

Boot's puzzle when we heard loud voices from down the hall.

"Mr. Hartshorn!" A dodo came running into the room. "We need your help. Hurry!"

Me and Egypt ran after them into the next room, which belonged to the boy in the square glasses. Slithe was holding one of the boy's arms behind his back. Grackle was there, too.

"I want this room," Grackle said to the boy. "Give it to me."

"But this is my room," the boy said quietly, wincing and trying to wiggle his arm free.

"Don't care." Slithe tightened his grip, causing the boy to cry out. "Ain't your room no more. Say it ain't your room no more. Say you're nothing but a puddle of goblin vomit."

"Stop!" I shouted.

The boy looked up at me. His square black glasses had been knocked off his face and were on the floor at his feet.

"You again!" Grackle glared at me. "Why do you keep following me?"

"Let him go, Wand Keeper Slithe," Hartshorn said.

"Are you gonna make me?" Slithe asked.

"I am one of the senior dodos." Hartshorn held his beak high. "I report directly to the headwander. Would you like me to find her now?"

"I'm not going to listen to some bird," Grackle said, before nodding toward Slithe, who twisted the boy's arm even harder, making a hole in his cardigan.

"One Fang!" I shouted before whistling. We heard a

loud bang from out in the hall, then One Fang came running in so fast, he slid into the wall before catching his footing and galloping to me.

One Fang's language was spoken in slobbers and grunts, which to the untrained ear sounded like growls. Exactly what I wanted. But it also meant you had to speak back to him in the same language. I made my feet wide and hunched my back, just as Aunt Cauldroneyes would do when she spoke to One Fang. Then I waved my arms around like a woodland troll as I growled and bared my teeth. To everyone else in the room, I knew I looked like a wild animal, but to One Fang, I was telling him in his own language to make Slithe stop hurting the boy. One Fang understood me perfectly. He slobbered loudly and started to lurch toward Slithe, his fang looking extra sharp.

"What is that thing?" Grackle took a step back.

"You should know," I said. "He lives in this room."

"It lives in here?" Slithe let go of the boy's arm.

"That's right," Hartshorn added. "So if you really want this room, he'll be your roommate."

One Fang slobbered and grinned.

"I'm outta here." Grackle made a dash for the door, Slithe not far behind.

One Fang started to chase them, but I quickly grabbed him.

"I better get you back to my room," I said in a few more growls to him.

Hartshorn stepped over to the boy and asked, "Are you okay, Wand Keeper?"

The boy quickly picked up his glasses and turned his back to us. I could see in the reflection of the mirror hanging on the wall that he was wiping his eyes.

"Leave me alone, please." His voice wasn't much louder than a whisper.

I didn't expect him to say anything more, but just before we left, I heard, "Thank you for helping me."

Spell No. 203

Unicorn bones and monster stones.
You will never take the wild one's throne.

Note from the Before Long Witch
This spell works when you have to urgently safeguard against a doomboom, or a giant lizardspit, among other such fearsome monsters. This spell must be prepared well in advance because it requires you to allow a fairy to bite the back of your wandle-wielding hand. You must wait for that wound to heal, because you can only speak this spell with success if you have a fairy scar. Be sure to feed your scar with stardust. It keeps the scar looking quite shiny and splendid.

CHAPTER 13
THE BOY WITH THE DRAGON

THE SCHOOL HELD A WELCOME DINNER THAT EVENING. I didn't feel like eating, so I stayed in my room. I told the hats about meeting Folklock and how she was going to return to the house. I tried to sound hopeful, especially for the younger hats.

"I'm sure Folklock will find something," Grandma's Boot said as he sat down at the table in the corner. Though his puzzle was in front of him, he only stared at the pieces.

The hats were especially quiet that evening, so when the knock came at the door, it startled all of us.

"Who is it?" I asked through the door.

Hartshorn had gone down to the dinner to help the other dodos. I wasn't expecting him back for some time.

"It's me," came a voice.

I opened the door to the boy with the square glasses. He was still wearing his red cardigan and was holding a basket with a napkin draped over it.

"Your dodo . . ." He looked down, trying to remember his name.

"Hartshorn," I said.

"Yeah. Hartshorn." The boy cleared his throat. "He said you weren't coming down. So I asked him if it would be okay if I brought you some food."

He pulled the napkin back and revealed several dishes of food. There were baked pot-a-noses, cheesy noodles, and plenty of owl-shaped bread rolls. Bowls of winter savory stems were steaming alongside toasty cinnamon bark and mashed potatoes. Beside those were some strange-looking candy balls.

"What are they?" I asked.

"Hartshorn called them gooey fur balls," the boy said. "That's not really fur on them. It's just sugar. He said that on the inside there's a fruit goo or jelly or something. I've never had them either. I guess they're supposed to look like fur balls of a sphinx." The boy scratched his head. "I'm not sure why that's supposed to be appetizing, but Hartshorn said they're one of his favorite desserts. I didn't want to be rude by turning them down."

He paused before adding, "They have all kinds of food down there. Different stuffings. Oh, and gravy boats[27*] are just sailing around everywhere. And there's a ton of pudding." He pointed into the basket at a bowl. "That's nervous pudding. See how it's shaking? I know Hartshorn said you're not hungry, but sometimes when I say that, I really am."

He held the basket out.

"Thanks," I said, taking it by the handle. He was about to turn to leave, but I asked, "Do you want to meet the hats?"

They were all looking at him from the fireplace as if he were more of a curious creature than they.

"You've already met One Fang," I said just as the hat came over, reaching for the basket. I let him carry it to the fireplace, where he and the others started to grab the food.

"Wow!" the boy said. "I didn't know there were other hats besides that one. They're amazing. How many do you have?"

Wormella passed by his feet and sneezed. Out came a cloud of dirt that landed on his shoes.

"A lot." I smiled.

We went over and sat down on the rug in front of the fireplace as the hats dunked their faces into mashed

27 * MOST GRAVY BOATS ARE MANNED BY AT LEAST TWO PIRATES.

potatoes and threw owl rolls across the room into each other's mouths.

"I don't know how you're all still hungry," I told them. "You already ate the huge dinner Hartshorn brought up for you earlier."

The boy laughed when the bat hats came over and started to pull at his hair.

"They're checking to see if it's chocolate," I said.

"Is that what they eat?" he asked.

"They eat all kinds of things, but chocolate is their favorite."

I looked down at the large hole in the sleeve of his cardigan.

"Slithe did that when he twisted your arm," I said.

The boy nodded as the bat hats darted into the basket. "It's my grumps' cardigan, too," he said.

"Grumps?" I asked.

"My grandfather," the boy said. "He gave it to me before I left to come here."

I could tell the cardigan had once belonged to his grumps. It was as old as anything, with lopsided patches on the elbows. It was also about two sizes too big for the boy. But I knew the cardigan was something he would always wear, like me with my vest.

"If I had my sewing box, I could fix that hole for you," I said. "It looks like your glasses are broken, too." There was a small crack in the left lens.

"It's okay," he said, taking them off. "I can see just fine without them."

"Then why do you wear them?" I asked.

"They belonged to my dad." He put them back on, blinking behind the crack. "He's a whale scientist. He went out to swim with them one day and never came back. I'm pretty sure he's living in the belly of one of them. I'm just not sure which one yet."

He pushed his floppy hair out of his eyes and stared at the basket of food.

"If you don't like anything in there," he said, "I can give you one of my grams' sandwiches." He held the pocket of his cardigan open.

"You keep sandwiches in your pocket?" I asked.

"My grams enchanted the pocket to have a never-ending supply of her sandwiches so that when I got homesick, all I'd have to do is reach inside and pull out a piece of home." He reached into the pocket and pulled out a lettuce sandwich on soft white bread. "The sandwich is different every time. Sometimes it's peanut butter and jelly, sometimes it's melted cheese. That's my favorite."

As he held the pocket open, I could hear seagulls.

"Grams enchanted it to sound like home, too," he said. "We live by the sea."

He offered the sandwich to me. Even though it looked a bit limp, I took a bite. I quickly spit it back out.

"That'll be the taste of Grams' perfume," he said, trying not to laugh. "She also enchanted the pocket with it, which means all the sandwiches taste like perfume."

Egypt came over and sniffed at the sandwich.

"Smells good to me," she said. She grabbed it out of my hand and started to gulp it down.

"She likes them," the boy said, reaching into his pocket and getting another for her. "Is she really mummified?"

"Oh, she's definitely mummified," I said. "We always have to go to Mummy City to get new linen wrappings for her whenever the old ones get too ratty."

He laughed as he watched her eat the sandwiches.

"So you live with your grandparents?" I asked.

He nodded and looked down at his cardigan.

"I think that's cool," I said. I took a deep breath, then added, "I was found in a cauldron—"

"Ewww." Grackle's laugh filled the room. He was standing in the open doorway with Slithe.

"You're a cauldron baby?" Slithe laughed even louder. "A blue-freckled cauldron baby!"

One Fang, who had crawled into the basket to get to the food on the bottom, leapt out of it and ran toward them.

"Get away, you beast!" Slithe screamed as he and Grackle took off running.

One Fang chased them all the way down the stairs. After he returned, he smiled up at me. I thanked him with a growl, then made sure to close the door after him.

"Sorry," the boy said, his cheeks red. "Grackle and Slithe must have followed me up. I didn't see them. I'm really sorry."

"It's okay. It's not your fault." I sat back down and stared into the fire.

"I think it's cool," he said. "To have been born in a cauldron."

"I wasn't born in one," I said quietly. "I was left there."

"Oh." He looked down. "Your aunt who disappeared, she's the one who found you in the cauldron, then?"

I nodded and said, "She's the best. We live in a house in the forest. It's got laughing stones, and the doors are enchanted to smell like chocolate. She must have told Headwander Folklock about it. I bet it's why the curtains at Dragon's Knob are enchanted."

"I'd love to see some chocolate doors," he said. "We just have regular ones back home."

"You'd also love all the patchwork fabric." I smiled. "Being a magical hatmaker, Aunt Cauldroneyes loves sewing all the loose scraps together. She's made patchwork lampshades and sofas and footstools. There's even patchwork fabric on the walls. The kitchen cabinets are wood, but they have patches to cover the scratches from the hats. We make the hats in the attic tower."

"They're wonderful," he said, staring up at the spider hat making her web in the corner of the room.

"The forest we live in is called Hungry Snout," I said. "You ever hear of it?"

"Hungry Snout!" He sat up on his knees. "Oh, I've heard of it. Ice-fang dragons live there. Well, they used to. They hibernated in the summer and came out in the winter. But now the winters are too warm. Their fangs are melting. They're rarely seen anymore."

"You like dragons?" I asked.

"I love dragons." He said it so loud, he startled a fairy hat flying by. She poked him with her pine-needle sword until he laughed and apologized. As she flew off, he turned to me and asked, "Wanna see my dragonackers collection?"

He pulled a small album out of his pants pocket and started to flip through the pages, showing the dragon stickers he had collected. He started to list every dragon by name and breed, ranking them from worst to best, before saying, "That's why I wanted to go to school here. Because this was once the castle of the Dragon King himself."

Peeking out from the boy's collar and staring at me was a pair of tiny eyes.

"Who's that?" I asked.

When he saw the creature, he gently put her back inside his collar. "Nothing," he said. "That's—that's nothing."

"I won't tell anybody if you've brought a dragon." I held out my pinkie and waited for him to hook it with his. "Promise on a pinkie," I said. "If I tell, I'll lose a spell, and be forever stinky." We laughed as I said, "Aunt Cauldron-eyes taught me that."

He smiled, then reached into his collar and pulled out the dragon. She was small enough to fit in his palm. She had a paunchy pink belly and thin blue legs that she crossed at the ankles. She looked up at me with a dopey smile, then stuck her tongue out and blew a raspberry.

"Her name is Softfang,"[28*] he said as he let the dragon

28 * Dragons with soft fangs eat only one thing. Mallowfluffs!

climb back into his collar. I could tell that was where she felt safest of all.

"She's toadfire." I spoke softly because I didn't want to scare her. I noticed how she stayed close to his ear and whispered into it.

"Toadfire?" he asked. "What's that mean?"

"It means she's not just cool but supercool," I said. "My Aunt Cauldroneyes says 'awesome 'possum' all the time. If she was here, that's what she would say."

Softfang stayed close to his ear and seemed to whisper to him every time I did.

"Where'd you get her from?" I asked.

He listened to her whispers before saying, "My grumps gave her to me. She helps me hear. People think I wear glasses because I can't see good. But I see just fine. It's hearing that I'm not great at. Softfang whispers to me so I can hear everything. Grumps gave me her as a hearing aid."

He lowered his eyes.

"It's okay if you don't wanna hang out with me, now that you know I can't hear very good," he said. "I'd think I was a loser."

"You're *not* a loser," I said. "You have dragon hearing. That's super-witch stuff."

He looked back up and smiled as he said, "I don't have many friends. To be honest, other than Softfang, I don't have any."

I pointed to the bright blue freckles on my cheeks. "The

other kids make fun of them," I said. "They say I've got dragon cooties or fairy pox. They can never decide which."

"I thought with freckles like that you'd be the most popular person around," he said.

"You like my freckles?" I asked.

"I was wishing I had some."

"I'll share some with you." I pretended to pluck my freckles off and hand them to him until we both laughed.

"My name's Tolden, by the way," he said. "Tolden Tutters."

"I'm Spella De-Broom Cauldroneyes." I grabbed his hand and shook it above our heads the way I'd seen Aunt Cauldroneyes greet her friends, while Egypt slipped her paw into his pocket and pulled out another sandwich.

"She really likes those," I said. "If you had chocolate mice in your pocket, you'd really be in trouble. Those are her favorites. Aunt Cauldroneyes always has to stock up on them." I fell silent, thinking about her.

"You really miss her, don't you?" Tolden asked.

"I don't know if I'll ever find her." I pulled my knees up and wrapped my arms around them.

"One time, I lost my dad's glasses," he said. "I looked everywhere. I thought I'd never find them."

"How did you?" I asked.

"I never stopped looking," he said. "I'll help you look for her, if you want."

"I'd like that," I said.

He pulled the basket over and reached inside. He

pulled out the one gooey fur ball the hats hadn't found. He tore it in half and gave me the bigger piece. After he took a bite of his, he wiped the raspberry jelly off his chin and said, "Hey, these aren't bad."

I smiled as we ate in the warmth of the crackling fire.

CHAPTER 14
A Funny Sort of Beard

THE NEXT MORNING A FRANTIC BAT FLEW INTO MY ROOM THROUGH the large, bat-shaped keyhole in my door and woke me up.

"Get up, get up, Wand Keeper! There's a firefart loose in the castle!" The bat flapped his wings in my face until I nearly rolled out of the floating bed with Egypt.

"A firefart!" I said. "What on earth is that?"

"It's nothing." Hartshorn slowly sat up in his bed with a yawn. "That dang bat does the same thing every morning to get everyone up. Sometimes it's a belchhound, or a wrestling worm. You name it, he's said it. He's the worst alarm clock. He scares you awake."

The bat grinned, showing an overbite of fangs, as he chewed on a wad of bubble gum.

"Here's your list, Wand Keeper." He dropped a piece of rolled parchment. I caught it as he flew back out through the keyhole.

"What's it say, young one?" Egypt asked as I unrolled the parchment.

The School List for First Wands

Although many books will be assigned by individual wanders for their specific classes, the following books will be required foundational reading for all first wands:

The Wand Keepers—A history of the magic of the wand and of those who wield it

Born with the Stardust—A journey through magical philosophy and wand lore

3,650 Days—Cultivating the shadow of your wand, from egg to creature

The Last Flying Leopard—The importance of conservation and protection of all magical creatures

Mr. Wigglebean's Key to Elf's Wort and Enchanter's Ivy—An illustrated guide to ancient plants and their magical uses

On a Butterfly's Wing—An encyclopedia of insects, fairies, and other life from the tiny world

When Twilight Bubbles—A guide to beginner potions[29*]

A Sky Full of Brooms—Handbook for the recently winged

REQUIRED BITS AND BAUBLES

One hooded, velvet cloak to be worn at all times while in class. The cloak will be the color of your birthstone, matching the cloak-brooch that will be set in a brass fitting. Each cloak will be lined with spider silk.

One spell-book hat, made by the world-renowned magical hatmaker Mathilda Cauldroneyes. Hat is to be worn during class and study.

One vial of dragon spit to flameproof your clothes and skin for your potions lessons.

One pair of broom-riding gloves. All first wands will use the standard school flying brooms provided in Wander Wuthering Winds class. No first wand will be allowed to ride their own flying broom on school grounds for safety purposes.

One conjure satchel, lined with witchgrass. Your conjure satchel will hold all your supplies and books.

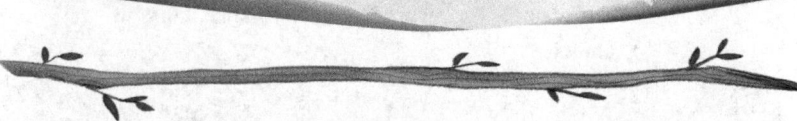

29 * IF YOU FIND YOURSELF IN NEED OF A TEMPORARY CAULDRON, TURN TO PAGE 983 IN *WHEN TWILIGHT BUBBLES*. THE PAGE IS ENCHANTED AND YOU CAN STIR IT LIKE A CAULDRON, BUT BE WARNED, THERE WILL BE MORE BUBBLES THAN YOU'LL KNOW WHAT TO DO WITH.

FOUR CAULDRONS

One pocket-sized, for most basic spells. The cauldron will shrink to fit a pocket, but will expand to average size when ready for a spell. Comes with stir counter and timer.

One flying cauldron. Can choose between feathered or bat-winged.

One dragon cauldron, lined with scales for hot potions. The scales used inside the cauldron have been naturally shed by dragons.

One frost cauldron, lined with moonlight, best for cold potions.

INK

Fairy spit

Giant green

Bat black

Boiled blue

Wide ruled parchment, beige #2

QUILLS

One number 8 for everyday use, feather of your choice.

One fairy-sized quill specific to Wander Fairycrumb's class.

One quiz quill with built-in alarm that will blare if it senses any cheating whatsoever.

Note: If selecting a phoenix feather as a quill, you must have the companion tray to catch all ashes once the feather burns, since a phoenix feather will burn once a day. On average it takes about two minutes and fifteen seconds for the phoenix feather to rise from the ashes, so it is not a good quill to have when taking tests.

Pick up supplies from the Wrinkled Pumpkin. All students will receive supplies free of charge, no badges or payment required.

I couldn't help but be excited about what spells I might stir in a flying cauldron or what I might write with a fairy-sized quill. But then I thought about the school hats made by Aunt Cauldroneyes. I worried that wherever she was, she was cold without her shawl, hungry without her copper cauldron full of soup, and lonely without the hats. I didn't dare think anything worse.

As I got ready for the first day of classes, I put on the fingerless spiderweb gloves that Aunt Cauldroneyes had made me, and the T-shirt she had given me for my eighth birthday. It had the Venom Spitters on it. They were an all-girl unicorn rock band that Aunt Cauldroneyes knew I liked. They had rainbow-dyed manes and tails and piercings in their ears and snouts.

When Aunt Cauldroneyes had given me the shirt, she showed me how she had enchanted it so the unicorns were constantly headbanging as they rocked on their guitars and drums. If you tugged on the right sleeve, it was like turning a volume knob, and sound blasted out.

"A forager is a girl of many pockets," I said, as Aunt Cauldroneyes would have, as I put my vest on over the T-shirt.

When I grabbed my boots, I said hello to the critters who lived inside them, like the tiny chugbutt lizards and slughugs who peeked out from the holes in the toes.

All Egypt had to do to get ready was tie up her loose pieces of linen and dust herself off. Mummified cats are rather dusty. Before we left, I told the hats to stay out of trouble, even though I knew all the books would be knocked off the shelves and the curtains would be eaten to the rods by the time I got back. I also knew the hats would tire themselves out in about an hour. I made sure to lay a quilt on the floor in front of the fireplace for their nap, just like Aunt Cauldroneyes always did.

Hartshorn was waiting impatiently at the door. He didn't like to be tardy for anything.

"You still have to eat breakfast, you know," he said.

Down the hall we stopped to knock on Tolden's door. His dodo answered. Tolden had told me his name was Rainrattles.

"Morning, Rainrattles. Is Tolden up yet?" I asked.

"I'm up," Tolden said from the back of the room. He was tucking Softfang down into the collar of his red cardigan. "That crazy bat scared us to death. Did you see the school list? It's amazing! I'm glad we get new cauldrons. I thought I might have to use the one Grams and Grumps sent me here with. It's rusty."

He saw the unicorns on my shirt.

"The Venom Spitters! I love their music." He played an air guitar and banged his head the entire walk down to breakfast, his dodo playing backup drums.

Breakfast was served in the morning hall, which was also the rose greenhouse. Decorative panels of clear and rose-stained glass were separated by black iron grids. There were tons of rosebushes bursting with red, white, and pink roses, their petals scattered across the brick floor. At times a drizzle of rain would fall gently down onto the plants.

"The room is built with rain glass," Hartshorn said. "It senses when the plants are dry, and rain will fall from the glass in the ceiling whenever it's needed."

The entrance to the kitchen was through an archway. I expected to see copper cauldrons and kettles steaming and boiling on stoves. What I saw instead were large feet passing by. The laces on the shoes were twenty feet long at least. I tried to see the stoves, but all I saw were their gigantic iron legs. There was a stack of brass pots on the floor. They were large enough to make soup for thousands, while the rolling pin leaning up against the wall could roll out dough as wide as any field.

"Everything in the kitchen is ten times larger than you can imagine," Hartshorn said. "Giants are the best cooks around, after all."

A whisk, covered in batter, dropped to the floor and rolled out in front of us.

"Whoa!" Tolden stared up at the handle casting a shadow over him. "That thing's as big as Grams and Grumps' whole kitchen back home."

"Pardon me, little man," a voice said just before a very large hand reached out from the kitchen and picked the whisk up. A towel dropped down next to wipe up the batter on the floor.

"If giants cook the food," I said, "does that mean the food itself is giant?"

"Not at all," Hartshorn said. "They use tweezers to portion the food for us wee folk."

Plates were walking in and out of the kitchen. They were as dainty and as mismatched as any of Aunt Cauldroneyes' transferware back home. Some of the plates carried fairy fruit salad. Others were loaded down with at least nine different types of breads.

"Hmm." Tolden rubbed his belly. "There's biscuits and gravy. Grams makes that."

"Those are delicious." Hartshorn pointed toward a platter walking with a stack of pancakes. "They're called hungry burpjacks, because after you burp, you're hungry for 'em again."

The plates walked to the tables where the students were served. Following the plates were glasses sloshing with loopy woopy berry juice.[30] One of Aunt Cauldron-eyes' favorites.

The cafeteria was already full of students.

"You can sit here!" Burrland waved us over.

Tolden picked up a plate of biscuits and gravy before quickly grabbing a braided roll off another plate walking by, while I dived into some grumbling cereal. I learned why it was called grumbling cereal as soon as I put my spoon in.

Egypt hopped up onto the table and started to chase a plate that had chocolate balls, while Hartshorn and Rainrattles ate several stacks of burpjacks. Just as I was pushing my bowl of cereal away, tired of its grumbling, Tolden took a bite out of the bread roll he'd grabbed. He instantly grew a fluffy gray beard.

"Oh, that'll be beard bread," Rainrattles told him.

"Beard bread?" Tolden lifted up the end of the long beard and nearly went cross-eyed staring at it. "I look like Grumps."

He wasn't alone. There were several students growing beards after eating the bread.

"Don't worry," Hartshorn said. "The beard doesn't last that long."

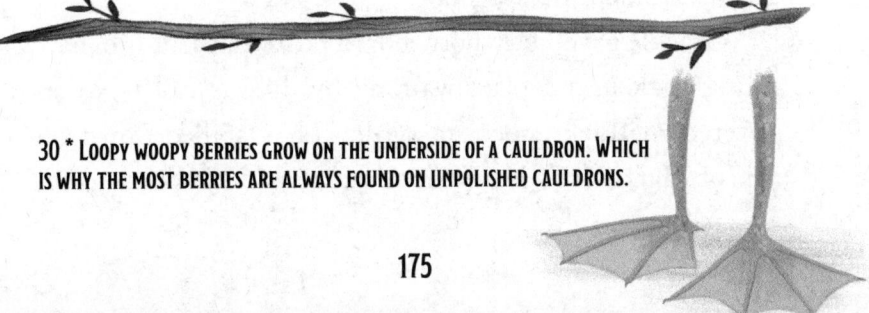

30 * LOOPY WOOPY BERRIES GROW ON THE UNDERSIDE OF A CAULDRON. WHICH IS WHY THE MOST BERRIES ARE ALWAYS FOUND ON UNPOLISHED CAULDRONS.

Tolden watched as the beard suddenly started to disappear.

"Now, that is toadfire," I said, picking up the rest of his roll. "I'll take this back to the hats. They'll love growing beards."

The bubblegum-chewing bat flew in and announced that breakfast was over. The plates started to walk back to the kitchen as we all got up and followed our dodos. On the way, Tolden tripped and fell with a hard thump against the floor. Grackle had stuck his leg out and was now laughing with Slithe.

"Better watch where you're going," Grackle said, before seeing Softfang. She had tumbled out of Tolden's collar. Grackle quickly grabbed her.

"Give her back!" Tolden said.

Grackle squeezed Softfang, causing her paunchy belly to bulge in his grip. "This sure is an ugly rat," he said.

"What did you say?" Tolden asked.

"What did you say?" Grackle repeated after Tolden.

"Why are you so mean?" I shouted at Grackle.

"I'm not mean to people who matter," Grackle said.

"Everyone matters," I said.

"All right, all right." Hartshorn stepped between us. "That is enough now. Wand Keeper Grackle, give Wand Keeper Tolden the dragon."

Grackle gave Hartshorn a hard push that sent him barreling back into a plate walking by. It was full of cakes covered in thick chocolate syrup. They spilled down on top of Hartshorn's head. As Grackle and Slithe laughed,

Hartshorn's wings started to grow and his tail shot out across the room, knocking over tables and chairs. He was turning into a dragon as the students around gasped.

"You think I'm scared of you?" Grackle said. "None of you dodo dragons can even breathe fire anymore. My dad told me."

Hartshorn's chest heaved with his heavy breathing as his eyes started to fill with tears.

"We might get to see a dragon cry," Grackle said with a mean grin.

"Candlehour's here!" one of the students said.

Her hair blew as hard as I'd ever seen it, while birds flew in and out of her stovepipe hat.

"What has happened here?" she asked as her griffin shadow hopped up onto the overturned table behind her. "Hartshorn, did you do all this?"

"I'm sorry, Deputy Headwander." Hartshorn quickly transformed back into a dodo, wiping his eyes.

"It wasn't his fault, Wander Candlehour," I said. "Grackle stole Tolden's hearing aid—"

"Hearing aid?" Grackle laughed louder. "This school really has gone to the trolls."

Grackle stopped once Wander Candlehour's griffin shadow fell over his face.

"I will not stand for cruelty." She held her hand out to Grackle. "Give me what you've taken, Grackle Nightcliff. Or I will give your name to the Migrating Scholars. Do you know about them?"

He shook his head.

"You will learn about them in my class," she said. "The Migrating Scholars are birds who always fly in a group of no less than a hundred. It is said if you give them a name, they will fly the name for so long and for so far that it will be flown from the minds and mouths of the world, until no one remembers how to speak it ever again. Do you want to be the boy who lost the great Nightcliff name to the birds?"

"Birds don't have such power," Grackle said, even though he quickly put Softfang into Wander Candlehour's hand.

He and Slithe started to sneak away, until her griffin shadow spread his flashing wings behind Candlehour, making her look as though she were the mighty bird herself.

She gave Grackle and Slithe a stern look, then held Softfang up to her eyes, her hair whipping in between them.

"Ah, I know this species," she said. "A *Gentilus paucharella*. A very intelligent dragon who will only spend their time with exceptional individuals."

She gently handed the dragon to Tolden. Softfang ran and hid inside his collar, tripping on her way in.

"Thank you, Wander Candlehour," Tolden said softly as he looked down.

"I once knew a wizard who could hear a thistle fairy from one hundred stars away," Candlehour said, her hair blowing across her smile. "And do you know what? That wizard would stuff mud up your nose just for the heck of it. It's not what you can hear with your ears that makes you a great person. It's what you hear with your heart." She pressed her finger gently into his chest.

"They're trying to get away again." The owl in Candlehour's basket was pointing his small wing at Grackle and Slithe. They groaned and stopped in their tracks.

Candlehour circled around to stand in front of them.

"What you two have done is most wrongous," she said.

"'Wrongous' isn't even a word," Slithe said.

"When something is so wrong, young man, it is a whole new word," she said. "Now follow me to my office. I will be making a call to each of your parents. The day belongs to you. But you have not done something wonderful with it."

As Wander Candlehour escorted Grackle and Slithe out, the tables and chairs righted themselves.

Tolden didn't look up at the other students as they walked past, even though most were smiling at him and talking about how mean Grackle and Slithe were.

"*They're the worst,*" someone said.

"*Nothing but bullies,*" another person added.

Burrland stopped to say to Tolden, "I think it's cool to have a small dragon."

"Yeah," a girl added as she walked by. "She's supercute."

When they had all left, Tolden muttered, "They're just saying that to be nice."

He sat down on one of the chairs after it righted itself. Hartshorn and Egypt walked out to the hall with their heads down, as I sat beside Tolden. Rainrattles patted him with his wing before wobbling after Hartshorn.

As Tolden wiped his eyes on his sleeve, I tried to think

of something to say. Then I remembered the bread roll in my pocket. I grabbed it out and held it with a smile. As soon as I took a bite, my chin felt scratchy. I reached up to feel the wad of hair. I was growing a beard. I took more bites. Only when the beard had grown down to my shoulders did Tolden notice.

"I don't think it's long enough, do you?" I said, taking yet another bite. He started to giggle as the big bushy beard grew down to my belly.

"What do you think?" I asked.

"Now you look like Grumps." He laughed.

"Watch this," I said, tugging on the sleeve of my shirt and turning up the volume of the Venom Spitters. The unicorn rock band strummed their guitars and banged their drums as their rainbow-colored spit landed on the cafeteria floor. I banged my head right along with the band, my beard flopping up and down as I strummed an air guitar.

Tolden started to laugh so hard, he nearly fell out of the chair.

"Thanks, Spella," he said, just as the beard started to fade and disappear.

Spell No. 3,078

Warty, warty wizard, run to the moon.
The spider will come out with her web soon.

Note from the Before Long Witch
Suffering from lazy rat boils? The dragon pox? Fairy bumps? Then this is the spell for you. It should be spoken while holding pink sand and letting that sand fall through your fingers. If you cannot get such pink sand, then as a replacement you may make a pink eagle laugh, and pink sand will fall out of her feathers. While the sand is falling, you should point your wandle at the boils, pox, bumps, or whatever it is that ails you and say the spell before the sand hits the ground.

CHAPTER 15
A Discovery of Wandles

WE GOT OUR SUPPLIES ON THE SCHOOL LIST FROM the Wrinkled Pumpkin, a delightful store that was actually in a wrinkled pumpkin. It grew in the castle's garden, in between a couple of the greenhouses. It was the largest pumpkin I'd ever seen, and the most wrinkled. You had to be careful not to trip on any vines while walking through the door.

The store was cheery inside, with huge pumpkin seeds sticking out of the pumpkin flesh that made the walls. The store had displays of cauldrons the way a grocery store would display canned soup. There was even a fireplace carved into the pumpkin. The glow from the fire burning on pumpkin-seed logs was reflected in the funny-shaped glass jars, crystal eyes, and telescopes on the shelves.

"This place is toadfire," Tolden said as we ran excitedly through the aisles. For the older students, there were two aisles dedicated exclusively to flying brooms, like the Thunder Chaser and the Sky Hound. In the aisle of inks, there were feathered quills floating just above our heads. There was a special display that had bright pink potion bottles labeled HOMESICK TEA. Written on the labels was NO MATTER IF YOU LIVE IN THE MOUNTAINS, FORESTS, SWAMPS, OR SEAS, A SIP OF THIS AND HOME YOU'LL BE. It was right next to a display of edible wands made of crackling candy.

Egypt had grabbed our conjure satchels. She handed Tolden's to him. The satchels were made of what I knew was cauldron cotton[31]. The bags had tall pockets for potion bottles, and even a compartment to keep quills. The satchel already had a small telescope inside it, and a pair of tweezers hung on a string from the side.

While Hartshorn and Rainrattles went to join the other dodos chatting in the corner, me and Tolden pulled out our parchment lists. Egypt helped find the books and dropped them into our satchels. When she found *A Sky Full of Brooms*, she sneezed and said, "It smells like old broom bristles."

---

31 • CAULDRON COTTON IS GROWN FROM CAULDRONS PLANTED IN FIELDS WATERED WITH DUST AND FERTILIZED WITH WARTS.

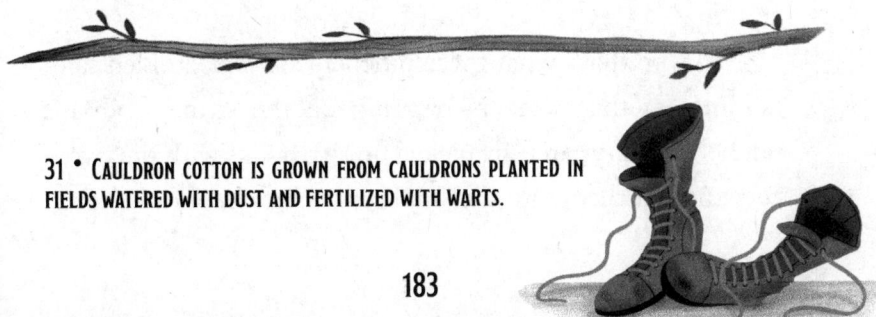

"All that's left is the book titled *On a Butterfly's Wing*," I said.

"It's the book on fairies," Tolden added.

"Hmm." Egypt climbed up the shelves, before circling back around and saying, "I can't find it, young one."

"Excuse me," I called out to a woman passing by.

She had a face that looked like a wrinkled pumpkin, and her jewelry was made out of gourd seeds, with the largest ones on her necklace and bracelets.

"I am Ms. Gourd Vines. How may I help you?" She smiled big. Her teeth were seeds, too.

"I can't find the encyclopedia for fairies," I said. "It's on the list for first wands?"

She stepped over to a tiny bookcase floating next to the wall. She reached out to grab the magnifying glass floating by it. She handed it to me and said, "They're on the top shelf of that tiny bookcase."

I held the magnifying glass up to my eye but saw only tiny centipedes walking through dust on the shelf. Then I discovered the tiniest of books stacked up in between a couple of acorns.

I was going to ask Ms. Gourd Vines how to pick up such a tiny book, but she had already left to help another student get a flying cauldron down from the beams in the ceiling.

"Maybe that's what these pinchers are for?" Tolden said, holding up the tweezers hanging on the string from his satchel. He very carefully picked up two books with the tweezers and put them into the smallest pockets in our satchels.

"Hey, look at those quills," Tolden said as two flew by us. They had bright orange feathers with red stripes on them.

"Those are phoenix feather quills," I said. We chased them into the ink aisle, where the feathers flew to a shelf already covered in ashes. There, the feathers caught fire, the fresh ashes collecting in a pile.

"Oh, I'm definitely getting one of these," Tolden said.

"Remember what the parchment list warned about phoenix quills," Egypt made sure to tell him. "It takes them two minutes and fifteen seconds to rise from the ashes."

"I know," Tolden said with a big smile. "They're so cool."

While we were in the aisle, we collected our inks and parchment. Then we excitedly ran through the rest of the store, grabbing the other items from the list. When we got to the cloak aisle, we found a rather short woman frantically circling students. A measuring tape, flying on its own, followed her dutifully. With a point of her finger, it would measure the length of a student's arms or their shoulders.

"You're a size garnet," she shouted. "You're a short, you're a tall, you're an in-between, you're an everything and all!"

She called out sizes that were in the colors of birthstones and pulled velvet cloaks off wooden hangers with such speed, the aisle became full of them flipping through the air. No matter what size a student was, the cloak fit them perfectly.

Grackle already had his cloak on. It was as black as his birthstone, onyx. Slithe had the same color. He was putting his on over his tiger one. When he flipped up both, a roar filled the aisle.

When she got to me, she said, "You're a size sapphire. A September girl. The strongest gemstone of all."

She tossed a bright blue cloak into my hands. The tag inside the hood read, LINED WITH GENUINE SPIDER SILK, HUMANELY HARVESTED FROM CAST-OFF WEBS.

"I like that the silk is humanely harvested now," Tolden said, running his hand over the lining. "The new school rules are one of the reasons why Grams and Grumps wanted me to come to Dragon's Knob. They love animals. Grams always puts out dry kibble for the stray dragons that come to the house."

The woman's measuring tape flew over to swirl around Tolden's arms as he held them up for her.

"Oh, you're an August boy," she said. "Size peridot for you. A stone formed in the lava of the earth."

A green cloak came flying into his hands. After he put it on, Softfang peeked out of the collar with a little dragon sneeze.

"Do I get a cloak?" Egypt asked. I didn't think the woman had heard her, not with all the commotion of students flocking to get measured, but she turned around with a smile.

"Ah, a cat in a cloak?" Her measuring tape shot over to Egypt and measured everything from her ears to her tail. "You are a size— Oh, you were born in a time when the calendar had thirteen months. They don't have a name for yours anymore, but luckily for you, I still remember the stone for it. You are a size wesa, a rock of the times."

An opal-colored cloak flew toward Egypt. It was velvet, like the others, but small enough to fit her narrow shoulders. I helped her put it on, securing the cloak with the large opal brooch set in a brass fitting. We all had the brooches, the color of our birthstones. I heard some of the older students saying the brooches could be used as telescopes, and even made good spell-splash guards.

"Don't forget your hats, Wand Keepers," Hartshorn said. He had returned with Rainrattles. They elbowed their way through the crowd to a spiraling staircase that led up into the stem of the pumpkin. There were already several students inside the stem and standing around a long table stacked with books.

I picked one up. The books were several inches thick but enchanted so they weren't heavier than a feather. The cover was sewn in diamonds of shaggy fabric. I recognized the fabric as being from our attic. I also knew that the thread had come from Aunt Cauldroneyes' hands. I flipped through the book and found pages full of spells, illustrated in full color. There were also diagrams of wand movements with the instruction, *Using a wand is not just a whish and flick.* On the back of the cover was a bio of the book's author:

> These spells have been collected by the Before Long Witch. The Before Long Witch was born in a dragon's

footprint but raised by a most wild herd of unicorns. She was named "Before Long" because she knew that before long there would be a whirling, there would be a storm, there would be a wind that blows the old ways away. She gathered these incantations, enchantments, sorcery sonnets, and cauldron prayers throughout her long life so that the ancient magic would never be lost, much less forgotten to the tides of time.

Please practice these spells responsibly.

"Go on," Hartshorn said. "Put the book on your head."

Both me and Tolden looked around at the older students. We watched how they opened their books, then set them cover-side down on top of their heads. The cover stiffened like any old regular hat brim, while the pages faced upward, before they started to turn on their own.

"I can't believe Aunt Cauldroneyes made hats that are books!" I said, smiling. "No wonder she said she wanted to surprise me. She knew I would love them."

I quickly opened the book and wore it like the older students.

"The spells inside each edition of the book are based on your age," Hartshorn said. "The edition for first wands contains beginner spells. Your aunt also infused the hats with a study potion so that as you wear them, it will help you remember spells and wand movements. I once knew a student who recited a hundred-page enchantment, word for word, when wearing the hat."

The pages on my book started to flip.

"You must be thinking about magic," Hartshorn said. "The pages always turn when you're thinking about cauldrons or conjuring."

Suddenly a long ribbon in the color of my birthstone flopped out of the pages and fell down my forehead, tickling my nose. I thought the ribbon was a bookmark, but when I reached up and tugged on it, it became a solid, sapphire-colored wand in my hand.

I had held plenty of sticks back home in Hungry Snout Forest and whirled them around, pretending they were wands. I'd done the same with Aunt Cauldroneyes' spatula in the kitchen and her old wooden soup spoon, but I'd never held a real wand, until now.

"Okay, that is amazing," Tolden said, before quickly placing his book on his head. A green ribbon fell out of the pages almost immediately. He took hold of the ribbon and it became a wand that matched the color of his cloak.

Hartshorn used his wing to point at our egg shadows behind us. They were rocking back and forth, the tiny bolts of lightning inside them flickering against the shells.

"The shadows always get excited when they know magic is around the corner," he said.

"Wand Keeper Tolden, you're holding it wrong." Rainrattles reached out to push Tolden's hand farther up on the wand. He placed Tolden's thumb on the small bump on the rod.

"That's your wandle wart," Rainrattles said. "That's

how you know how to hold it. Put your thumb on the wart, and the rest of your fingers will naturally follow."

"Did you say 'wandle'?" I asked.

"That's what a beginner wand is," Hartshorn said. "Read the underside."

I turned the wandle over and discovered text that wrote itself as you read it:

> What you hold in your hand is a wandle. It is for the witches and wizards who are just starting their lessons. A wandle cannot conjure anything above fifteen inches. It is primarily used by gnomes to repair tears in their little red hats or by giants to hide their candy.
>
> If you are using this wandle for the first time, remember that you cannot fly with a wandle, you cannot transport, you cannot outrun a unicorn stampede, and you cannot—under any circumstances—stir a boiling potion in a cauldron. But a wandle does work rather well when speaking with snails or slugs, on account of the wandle being slow.
>
> Be mindful that a wandle only has five good spells a day in it. After that it is no better than an old bookmark until the next morning. This will remind you to learn not to be quick to magic, but to be smarter with it. And remember, when in doubt,

bring your wandle out. Give it a spin and find the magic within!

"Five good spells a day?" Tolden groaned.

"Well, I suppose it's five more than we had." I shrugged.

Before we left the Wrinkled Pumpkin, I took the peppermint badge Folklock had given me and handed it over to Ms. Gourd Vines.

She went behind the candy counter to the large glass jar full of peppermint candy shaped as elves. Using a pair of snapping tongs, she filled a paper bag with them.

"They aren't real elves, are they?" I asked.

"Goodness no," she said. "They're only sugar and syrup. They used to be real elves, but thankfully times have changed."

"Some of the stuff in the store, though," I said. "I saw a jar of eyes right over there. And dead men's toes and—"

"Was it really eyes you saw?" she asked, her pumpkin face wrinkling even more with her smile. "Or was it plump mushrooms floating about? And was it really dead men's toes? Or funny-shaped fungus?"

She handed the bag of peppermints over. I shared them with Tolden and our dodos on our way to our first class. Egypt, meanwhile, reached into Tolden's cardigan pocket for another sandwich.

She was already on her second one by the time we got to our classroom.

"Rainrattles and I will meet you after class is over," Hartshorn said. "Oh, and a word of warning to the both of you. The desks at Dragon's Knob are quite old and, therefore, quite grumpy. It's best not to lean on them with your elbows, and it's wise to never leave homework on top of them."

The rest of the students were already inside and at their desks. They each had their spell-book hat on their head, and the room was full of the sound of flipping pages. The whole class was thinking about the magic ahead.

We found a couple of seats by the windows, and though the desks looked as old as Hartshorn said they were, they didn't seem to be anything other than wood with an iron scroll of leaves around the top. As me and Tolden sat down, we couldn't take our eyes off the room. It was delightfully dusty, with cracked clay pots full of desert sand and linen scraps. There were plenty of mummies, from mummified shrew mice to a mummified hand wrapped in blue bandages. Pyramid stones were used as bookends, and sand fell from the crooked corners in the ceiling.

"I think you'll like this class, Egypt," I said as she hopped up on my desk, her cloak hanging off the edge.

As Tolden watched even more sand fall from the cracks in the walls, he rested his elbows upon the desk. Suddenly the lid opened and knocked his elbows off as the desk grumbled.

"One should never put their elbows—" Egypt was cut off mid-sentence when the lid of my desk flapped open and knocked her to the floor.

Grackle and Slithe cackled from their seats, before

their desks started to shake. Soon every student had a desk that was grumbling.

"That's enough!" Wander Mummyheart stepped into the class. "You settle down now."

The desks grumbled one last time before falling quiet. Even though they weren't moving anymore, Egypt decided it was best to sit on my lap.

"I want to welcome you all to my class, the Poetry of the Pyramids." Mummyheart stood in front of us. Her sphinx shadow followed behind her as she tossed up her bright blue cloak. Unlike students, the teachers had cloaks of all colors, fabrics, and patterns. She wore strips of aged linen like bracelets up and down her arms, and her golden rings were sculpted as pyramids rising up from the backs of her fingers. There was a rumor from the older students that Mummyheart was a mummy herself because beneath her shirt collar, you could see more linen sticking out.

She looked rather like her sphinx to me, with light blonde hair that fluffed around her face like a lion's mane, and her teeth were small and sharp like a cat's.

"In my class you will learn about pyramids, mummies, and the magic of sand," she said.

"How can sand have magic?" Slithe asked. "It's like dirt."

"Both dirt and sand are skins of the earth," she said. "And the earth is the most powerful source of magic. The ancients knew that if you put sand into an hourglass, you could travel through time. If you took a hammer and laid it against a single grain of sand, you could build an entire pyramid in the moment it took you to raise the hammer up."

"That's true," Egypt whispered to me.

"As you know, this is the first year at Dragon's Knob that we will teach exclusively about the magic of nature." Mummyheart walked around the room, her cloak sweeping the sand on the floor. "I have taught at Dragon's Knob for many years. I have never used animals in my courses. Instead I have always taught about how the ancients honored animals."

I looked back at Grackle. He was staring down at his dragon-eye ring, which was watching Mummyheart.

"We are lucky to have an example in class today of a mummified cat," Mummyheart said as she came over and lifted Egypt up off my lap. She set her down on the desk and spent the first few minutes of class pointing out the wrappings on Egypt and telling everyone how difficult it was to wrap a cat's whiskers one by one.

"Oh, don't I know it," Egypt said, winking at me.

After the linen lesson, Mummyheart called us up to the front of the class, where a large mummified cauldron sat.

"We will do our magic in the class cauldron," she said. "The linen on the iron infuses it with the power of a mummy. The spell we will be making in it today is not a hot one. However, it does on occasion shoot out fire. So we must flameproof your sleeves. Please remove your vial of dragon spit from your satchels and add two drops to each of your sleeves. For those who are not wearing sleeves today, add the spit directly to your arms. That should do the trick."

She tapped her shoe, waiting impatiently for us to find our vials in our bags. Once we did, she held her nose. We didn't know until we opened the vials that dragon spit smells like dragon breath, which isn't all roses. We quickly added two drops of it to our sleeves. I made sure to add some to Egypt, just to be on the safe side. She frowned as she watched each drop splash against her linen.

"You will notice that there is already a standard potion base in the cauldron," Mummyheart said. She encouraged us all to look into the cauldron. It was half-full of rust-colored sand.

"Now we shall begin." She unrolled a piece of pale green parchment. It was blank, but when she shook some sand out of her sleeve onto it, the sand moved across the parchment and formed words.

"A sand spell," she said. Burrland was standing beside her, so she gave the spell to him to read the ingredients aloud.

"Nineteen practical pig[32*] winks," he said. "Thirty-seven cobra hisses, three desert scorpions, and the song of a scarab beetle."

"Oh, this is going to be a fun one," Mummyheart said as she swept over to a cabinet marked with hieroglyphics.

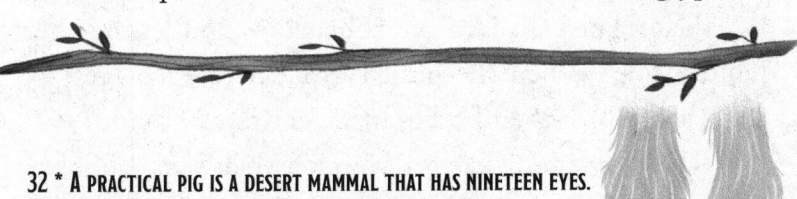

32 * A PRACTICAL PIG IS A DESERT MAMMAL THAT HAS NINETEEN EYES. NOT EVERY EYE IS ON THEIR FACE, WHICH IS VERY PRACTICAL.

She grabbed two glass bottles and one jar, and gave them to her shadow, who carried them back to the cauldron for her.

Mummyheart took the dark green bottle from her shadow. After she pulled out the cork, a loud hissing filled the room.

"This bottle is filled with leaves taken from a plant known as Pyramid Ivy," she said as she turned the bottle over and shook out several leaves into her hand. The leaves unfurled like snake tongues and hissed. She counted the leaves until she got to thirty-seven.

"Pyramid ivy only grows in between the cracks of pyramids," she said. "Because of this, the ivy hisses like an Egyptian cobra and slithers like one, too." She let the leaves slither from her hands and down into the cauldron.

The next bottle she grabbed was labeled as containing winks. "Each time a practical pig winks," she said, "they drop a little stone into the sand." She counted out nineteen of the very tiny black stones, then tossed them into the cauldron, followed by her own spit, which caused the sand to sizzle.

"What's next again?" She asked Burrland to repeat the ingredients. When he came to desert scorpions, she said, "Oh, yes. Those are a delight."

She grabbed the jar from her shadow and reached her hand inside. When she pulled it out, it was covered by three scorpions, their bodies made entirely of sand.

"These may move like real scorpions," she said, "and they may threaten you with their stingers like real scorpions."

Tolden jumped back when one of the scorpions jerked toward him.

"But," Mummyheart said, "they are not real. It is an illusion of the desert." She held her arm over the cauldron, and the scorpions broke apart into nothing but red sand that fell in on top of the other ingredients.

"The last thing it says to add is a scarab beetle song," Burrland said.

"Oh, that I always carry in my pocket." Mummyheart pulled out a small blue vial. When she opened it, a dark violet mist poured into the cauldron.

"The song of a scarab beetle," she said. "Now we shall give it a stir." She handed out large wooden spoons to each of us, their handles covered in gilded centipedes.

As we stirred, the sand moved and behaved like liquid while the golden centipedes on our spoons twinkled brightly. Soon a deep, dark yellow smoke rose and swirled around us as a snorting creature climbed up out of the cauldron and perched his talons on the rim of it.

"A sand dragon!" Tolden shouted while the rest of us gasped, then cheered as we watched the dragon made of sand leap up from the cauldron and fly around the room.

The loose sand fell from his body as Mummyheart laughed and said, "Well done, all of you. A wonderful first day of class."

She called her shadow to her hand. Lightning streaked across the sphinx's face as she turned into a wand. Mummyheart said a spell that gave us each a badge in the shape of the dragon we had just conjured.

CHAPTER 16
Zombie Fingers and Fairy Spit

EGYPT LOVED THE CLASSES. I HAD TO ADMIT, I DID, too. Even though I thought of Aunt Cauldroneyes every day. I wished I could tell her all about the way Wander Babbles Goldswift wore a cloak that was in a pattern like the wings of a red-and-yellow moth and how her classroom fluttered with butterflies of all sizes, some of which were as large as eagles. Goldswift's class was hopping with crickets, and ladybugs were always crawling on our inkwells. Her lessons were all about insects and what she called the discovery of truth. Nearly everyone was trying to discover the truth of what she had in her hair, which was piled up into a messy bun. Every time she put a new pencil into the bun, there would be the noise of something chewing and her pencil would come out sharpened.

"I bet it's some sort of termite," I said to Tolden, who nodded.

But what Goldswift had in her hair was nothing compared to what Wander Ambrosia Wormcake had in hers. She taught the History of the Wand, which also included the most historically accurate wand movements, like the backward flick, the cauldron stir, and what Wormcake called the flying broom arm, which she said was an especially strenuous wand movement. But it felt nice to work up a sweat while waving our wandles because Wormcake tended to keep her classroom quite cold on account of her being a zombie.

"I know you're all dying to know what you will learn in my class," she said with a very dry laugh. When we didn't join in laughing ourselves, she repeated, "I said you're all *dying* to know. Dying, get it? That's an old zombie joke."

She tended to shuffle when she walked, and her voice was very hoarse. Grackle and Slithe would groan every time old, dry skin dropped off her. But she didn't seem to notice most things. She always came to class still wearing her pink hairnet over the curlers in her bright orange hair. The curlers were green zombie fingers, by the way.

"When you're a zombie, someone is always breaking a finger," she said. "I thought I'd put them to good use. A zombie finger curls hair rather nicely."

Sometimes while she was at the blackboard, a finger would fall out of her hair. Like an inchworm, the finger would crawl away, the yellowed fingernail screeching against the floor.

Wormcake's class might have been a bit, well, strange, but at least it was followed by Wander Fairycrumb's. She taught lessons of the smallest wand. She was a fairy herself, with spiderwebs for eyelashes and a wonderful wart on her cheek. Despite Fairycrumb being so small, her wand shadow was a rather large woolly mammoth with giant tusks that became bright white from the lightning. When she called the shadow to her hand, it became a wand that was no larger than a sewing needle.

"It isn't the size of the wand that matters," she said, "but the size of the magic in you." She flew around, waving her tiny wand. "Wands breathe. They have heartbeats. Some smell like chocolate. Others smell like storm clouds. They can unroll like a scroll, predict the future. They can even be mummified." She darted over Egypt, who made a swipe at her in the air. "They can fly and sink. Both float and fall. It's all up to the one who wields the wand. I want you all to make note of this, so bring out your wide-ruled parchment, beige number two, and your fairy quills."

The fairy quill came with a tiny crystal inkwell that exploded with a tinkling of sparkles when opened. Inside the inkwell was pink goo. It was fairy spit, which makes for rather thick ink. It is also very loud ink. When we wrote with it, the class became full of the sound of fairies spitting, which Wander Fairycrumb delighted in.

I was surprised by how quickly I got into the routine of

the classes. And despite the castle having been like a large maze when we first got to it, we were now able to find our way around without our dodos most of the time. I found myself sometimes sitting at an open window on breezy days, talking to the breeze as if it were Aunt Cauldroneyes. I told her all about Tolden, Softfang, and how much Egypt was liking the classes.

"Egypt even likes the homework," I said to the breeze. "I like the homework, too. I'm learning how to use my wandle with all kinds of movements and spells. I'll teach you when you're back, Aunt Cauldroneyes. I'm even learning how to speak unicorn."

We were learning this in Wander Spindle Globemallow's class, which was always after lunch and was the most intensive of lessons, as it involved learning the ancient languages of animals. She started out teaching us how to interpret unicorn neighs. She was excellent at neighing, and her hair was rather long like a mane. Even if Grackle made fun of her bare feet and talons for toes, I liked the hair on them.

"The neighs of unicorns are a very unique language," she told us. "Each group of unicorns has a specific neigh. The frost-horn unicorns sound different from the fire-horn unicorns, and the crystal horns sound different from the wood horns. There are a hundred more unicorn groups, so it takes centuries to master all of their native languages, but you can begin to understand them by starting out with the basic neighs."

Globemallow opened her mouth wide, her teeth

jutting forward like a horse's. She called us all to the front of the class so we could neigh for her. We made the mistake of leaving our parchments of notes on our desks. The lids flopped open and chewed the notes to pieces.

We had to be extra careful of the desks in Wander Noctuary Thunderteeth's class. He had a long gray beard tied with a bright red ribbon that matched the color of his cloak. His shadow was a large bear with nine arms each constantly flashing with lightning.

Thunderteeth taught magical math. The books in his class were so thick, full of endless math equations and formulas, that their pages had to be turned by giant wooden wheels that constantly creaked in the class. His class also had the most note-taking. Bat black was the best ink for note-taking, and the basic quill number 8 was the best to write with, but Tolden made the mistake of using his phoenix feather right when we were in the middle of writing down Thunderteeth's magical multiplications from the chalkboard. Tolden had to wait over two minutes for his feather to rise from the ashes.

"Remind me to trade this quill in at the Wrinkled Pumpkin," he leaned over and whispered to me as I giggled at the growing pile of ashes on his desk.

Candlehour's class was at the end of the day, and it was as she promised. It was about Fuzzlefeatherfoop magic. As she walked around the classroom, she hiccupped out blue frogs.

"I am happy to say that every quill you use at Dragon's Knob," she said, "has been given by the bird freely, or it has been harvested from the forest floor. It's an important change, to protect species. I can't tell you how many birds are hunted each year just for their feathers."

Grackle smiled at his dragon-eye ring as it watched Candlehour very carefully.

"I've already summoned your flying cauldrons," she said, pointing up to the ones floating above our heads. "Feather magic is always best stirred in something that floats."

"Feather magic," Grackle muttered just before his desk lid opened and tried to grab his parchment. "Let go, you stupid desk." He managed to pull the parchment out, but it was shredded.

At the end of class, I pulled Tolden aside and said, "Grackle is up to something with that ring."

"I wouldn't be surprised," Tolden said. "I've heard the eye of a cave dragon will collect secrets for you."

"I told you," Egypt said.

She nudged my leg as Grackle passed us. We watched him turn the corner, then we followed him. He headed outside behind some of the greenhouses. I picked up Egypt, and the three of us peeked out behind a bush as we watched Grackle reach into his pocket and pull out something small. When he tapped it, it expanded into a large notebook.

"A shrinking notebook," Tolden whispered to me. "Grumps uses those all the time to write his poetry in. But once he shrinks them down, he can never remember where he put them."

We watched as Grackle held his dragon-eye ring up to face the notebook. As the dragon eye blinked, words started to write themselves down on the paper.

"The dragon eye is writing the secrets it's collected with each blink," Egypt whispered.

"But what secrets?" I asked.

Grackle tapped the notebook, and it shrank back down small enough to fit into his pocket.

We wondered what secrets Grackle was collecting and who he was collecting them for.

"We should tell Folklock when she's back," Egypt said.

We were already halfway through October, and Folklock had not returned to the school yet after having gone to the house in Hungry Snout Forest to look for clues that might help us find Aunt Cauldroneyes. I would go up to Folklock's office every day, and the chatty clematis would say, "We're sorry, Spella. She's still not here."

I tried to focus on school and the homework assignments, like mastering my unicorn neighs from Wander Globemallow's class. I could hear Tolden practicing his neighs in his room next door. He sounded more like a donkey than a unicorn, but only Egypt had the heart to tell him that to his face.

My growing lack of focus led to a disaster in Wander Wormcake's class. She told us to turn to page 1,095 in the textbook *When Twilight Bubbles* in order to make a potion that we were required to dip our wandles in for a historical wand movement called the potion pucker.

"It's a cold potion," she said, "so you will be using your frost cauldron. It's lined with moonlight and will keep the cauldron cool for the potion. Remember to count your stirs.

An over-stirred potion can have the most *grave* consequences."

But after I put in my ingredients, I was thinking of Aunt Cauldroneyes instead of counting my stirs. Before I knew it, the potion exploded onto Egypt and turned her into an icicle.

"Oh, Egypt, I'm so sorry." I tried to wrap her up in my cloak.

"Not to worry," Wander Wormcake said, "we'll take her to the 99th tower. That's where Wander Hyacinth Buckleberry's office is. She's the school's mender. She'll have to perform an immediate defreeze on Egypt."

I hoped I could cheer up Egypt once she got released from the 99th tower by at least finding out some news about Aunt Cauldroneyes. Later that day, after Candlehour's class ended, I stayed behind to ask her if she'd heard any word from Folklock.

"She's doing everything she can to find your aunt," Candlehour said. "Folklock has found the rarest plants in the world. Plants that people said could never be found, but she did, because she never stops looking. If anyone can find your aunt, she can."

I turned to stare out the window. "I keep hoping I might see Aunt Cauldroneyes flying in on her broom."

Candlehour nodded, then said, "Your aunt made me my hat. Did you know that?" She patted her stovepipe hat. A blue bird had just flown into one of the holes with a beak full of worms for the little chicks I heard chirping inside the hat.

"I knew she had made the hat when I saw it," I said. "I always know her work."

"She makes a hat for everyone, no matter who they are." Candlehour smiled. "No matter if they have hooves or hands, wings or fingers. Whether they are a friend or a stranger. That's what the person who stole your aunt knew, Spella. That if they brought a hat to her, she would try to help them."

She reached down to the little owl in her basket to scratch under his chin.

"I've always loved birds," she said. "It was not a surprise to me that my wand shadow ended up being a griffin. Did you know it was once the law that griffins should be captured to fly chariots across the skies? Griffins are very strong. Stronger than a thousand lions with the wings of an eagle. I've studied all kinds of wings. I want to tell you, Spella, that your aunt has some of the largest wings I've ever known. And I've studied the biggest of hawks, the bravest of dragons. I know you're worried about your aunt, but Mathilda Cauldroneyes will fly free. I know it."

We turned to the sound of a flock of birds passing by the window.

"Oh," Candlehour said. "One should always watch migrating birds. They are powerful sorceresses."

It wasn't until that evening that Egypt was released from the 99th tower and Wander Buckleberry's care. I carried Egypt back to my room. Even though she was no longer covered in ice, she was still shivering.

"I'm so sorry, Egypt," I said, wrapping her in blankets. The hats helped me.

"Oh, I know you didn't mean to, young one," she said. "At least I can say I have built the mighty pyramids and I have now been frozen. And don't worry about the blankets. Wander Buckleberry warmed me up. She said the shivers are just a side effect and they'll go away soon."

I sat down with Egypt in the poufy chair by the fireplace until she stopped shivering. Hartshorn was already asleep and snoring in his floating bed above us, when there came a knock on the door. I opened it, but no one was there and the hall was empty except for my sewing box from home. A small handwritten note lay on top of it.

Dearest Spella,

I spotted this sewing box while I was at your house. I thought you might like to have it. I thought it might remind you of your aunt until we find her. I will tell you more in the morning. For now, sleep well and discover sweet dreams. As the stars come to tell it.

The letter ended with Folklock's signature, which looked more like a vine than a name.

I carried the sewing box into the room, quietly closing the door behind me.

Egypt followed me over to the fireplace, where I sat down. She read Folklock's letter herself, then watched me open the box. I pulled out a drawer, revealing dark wooden spools of thread in every color. There was sleepy thread, angry thread, and happy thread.

"I've always liked to hear the thread giggle," Egypt said as she sat beside me, her head against my arm.

"You'd better go to bed," I told her. "You get real grumpy when you're tired."

"Don't stay up too late yourself," she said. "You have classes in the morning." She made a face. "Oh, bother. I sound more like the old one every day."

She yawned, and popped out of sight. I looked up at the floating bed to see her getting ready to curl up on my pillow.

I turned back to the box and pulled open a drawer that held sewing needles. There were needles carved from wood, shells, and even bones that Aunt Cauldroneyes had found in the forest. I touched a very thin one that was marked with delicate carvings.

"Best for fairy embroidery work," I whispered, remembering Aunt Cauldroneyes' words when she'd first explained the sizes of the needles to me.

In the largest drawer of the box was what looked like a very small roll of fabric. It was printed with flowers like dilly daffys, which reminded me of the wild ones that grew by the porch of our house. When I tugged on the fabric, it kept unrolling. That's when I knew it was a roll of never-ending fabric that also changed colors and patterns with each new pull.

"You think of everything, Aunt Cauldroneyes," I whispered.

"Here you go, Spella." One of the fairy hats flew to my shoulder and held a piece of tulle out toward me.

"Is that from your ribbon?" I asked. "Did it fall off?"

"I took it off," she said. "So you can add it to your hat."

"My hat?"

"The one you're starting to make, Spella."

I looked down at the fabric in my lap.

"That is what you're doing, isn't it?" she asked. "Getting ready to make a new hat?"

I ran my hands over the fabric and smiled.

"Yes, I am going to make a hat." I reached for the spool of shaggy orange thread. It was made from strings that had been shed from Aunt Cauldroneyes' shaggy cloak. I had collected the strands from the attic floor and wrapped them around a spool long ago.

"You can add my tulle to it as one of the bits and baubles," the fairy hat said.

"And this, too." A mouse hat hopped up onto my knee. She was holding a piece of satin from the hem of her skirt.

"Thank you," I said. "Thank you both."

I studied the collection of needles again before choosing the one that was as long as a cat's whisker.[33*] Then I started to measure the fabric, and began.

The fairy hat flew back to her nest of small pillows to

---

33 * A CAT'S WHISKER IS THE PERFECT LENGTH FOR SEWING TOGETHER THINGS YOU REALLY CARE ABOUT.

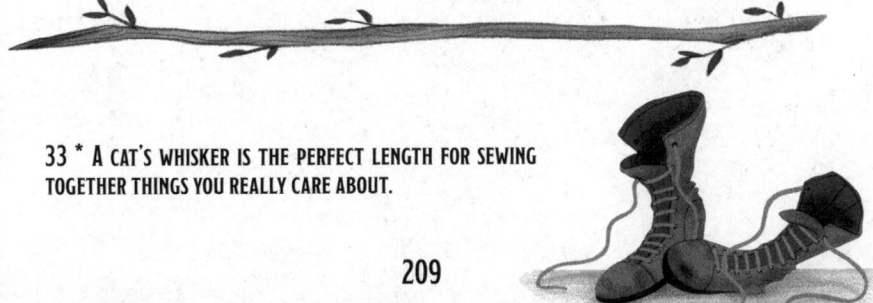

sleep, but the mouse hat stayed and asked, "Who will the new hat be for, Spella?"

"For Aunt Cauldroneyes," I said. "So when she's back, she'll know that we thought of her every day she wasn't here."

The little mouse hat flipped her tail up and stayed on my knee, watching my stitches with a smile.

Spell No. 1,719

Weigh a centaur's heart,
Tell me my path from the start.

Note from the Before Long Witch
Sometimes we want to be a wild dreamer and spend all day sailing the high seas or running with a herd of wild horses. This spell will bring you the comfort of a good cup of tea. When saying this spell, be sure to hold something nice beneath your chin. It could be anything, from two silver bells to a furry wildwisp or even a two-headed sea sponge.

CHAPTER 17
BLUE BUTTONS

I THOUGHT WE WOULD FIND AUNT CAULDRONEYES BY Halloween and she'd be back in time for us to carve jack-o'-lanterns and dress the hats in funny costumes like we did every year. But as the pumpkins growing around the school ripened and the windowpanes in the early morning became spotted with frost, she was still gone.

The morning after Folklock dropped off my sewing box, she came to see me at breakfast just as her note promised she would. She let me skip my first class so I could walk with her through the castle gardens as she told me about her visit to the house in Hungry Snout Forest. She apologized for being gone for the past few weeks, but she said she had stayed longer in order to look for others in Witches' Bells who might have seen or been visited by the mysterious wizard.

"The good news is that I met a couple of witches who had seen one such wizard crossing through town that night," she said. "I was able to get more description of his appearance from them. I have also scratched messages into fern leaves and many elf cups for the Sisterhood of the W.O.L.V.E.S. to inform them that Mathilda has been taken. The Sisters are working hard, too, to find information on where she may be. There's not more I can tell you now, Spella. I hope you understand that some things I must keep to myself for the time being. I also don't want you worrying more than you need to. I want to assure you that even though it will feel like time is passing and nothing is being done, I will be working every moment until we find her."

Folklock stopped walking and turned to me.

"Spella, did your aunt tell you that when we were little witches, we made a promise over a bubbling cauldron that we would always be friends and help one another when needed? I do not intend to break that promise."

While I felt better after speaking with Folklock, I couldn't help but still worry. Aunt Cauldroneyes being gone was all I could think about.

One day in Wander Goldswift's class, I was looking out the window instead of taking notes. By the end of class I had nothing written down for that night's homework, so the girl beside me slid over her parchment and said, "You can copy from mine if you want, Spella." And sometimes at lunch, when Tolden stayed late in art class, I would sit at the dining table by myself. Even though I hardly touched my food, a cookie would drop onto my plate, then another and another as the students passed by. I knew what Aunt Cauldroneyes would have said. "See, little dear. I told you that you would make new friends."

I knew the other students only felt sorry for me, the girl with the blue freckles and the missing aunt.

I tried to take my mind off it by working on the hat every evening. Sewing always made me feel better. I made the stitches Aunt Cauldroneyes had taught me, like the cackling circle and the whirly wise, and used the ancient knots she liked best. The hats brought me pieces of themselves so I could add them to the hat as bits and baubles. The owl hats each gave me a feather. The bat hats gave me parts of their vampire silk and even an extra fang. The spider crawled down from her web and spun lace that she told me would look nice on the brim. The goblin hats brought me little silver bells, and the witch hats gave me their cackles, not to mention one or two of their best warts.

Sometimes I would make a stitch and think it wasn't good enough. I'd pull it out and start over again.

"I think you're afraid to finish the hat," Egypt said, her linen loose around her face and stained with what I knew were the tears of an old cat. "Because if you finish it, and the old one still hasn't appeared, then what will that mean?"

Egypt muttered about pyramids and walked to the

windows. It was where she and the hats spent their time now. They no longer ran around the room, swinging on the curtains or shredding the wallpaper. Maybe they had expected Aunt Cauldroneyes to show up and giggle at their messes the way she always did. But as we got closer to the cold days of winter, they sat at the windows, looking out. The owl hats, however, had decided not to sit at the windows but to fly out them. They would stay out all day and into the night, circling the castle. When they finally came in, they had mist on their feathers and a look in their eyes that said they had not seen her as they had hoped. Mr. Sea Captain would hang outside the windows, each of his tentacles holding a telescope so he could look out across the lands for her.

Egypt would try to take her mind off things by knitting socks for Socky and by mummifying. She had already mummified the dragon's head over the fireplace, books on the shelves, and even the footstools. I was grateful to have schoolwork to distract me, but every time I saw a blue button, I thought of Aunt Cauldroneyes, so I started to collect them. When I saw one on a student's bag or scarf, I would ask, "Can I have your blue button?"

They would look at me, surprised. But then I'd say, "I feed the buttons to my freckles. That's how they stay so blue." That was easier to say than the real reason why I wanted them.

I always offered them a button in return. Being a magical hatmaker, I had pockets full of them. They'd pick out the new button they wanted, and I'd get their blue one.

I didn't tell Tolden I was collecting them. Not even when I asked him for his cardigan. I told him I was going to patch the hole in the sleeve that Slithe had made. I did patch the hole, but I also took the blue button that was on the front. I replaced it with a pink one, the color of Softfang.

Every time I got a new blue button, I would run back to my room and pull the spell book off my head. I studied the spells, hoping to find one that would change the blue buttons into something that didn't make me so sad.

By the time November arrived, I had found no spell and the blue buttons were piling up in my room. I started to hide them under the cushion of the plump chair by the fireplace. At least then I didn't have to see them anymore.

As the autumn continued, me and Tolden started to walk around the school's gardens every day after I told him how much I'd loved walking around Hungry Snout Forest.

"The castle looks great, don't you think, Spella?" he asked one day on our walk. The fabric patches on the brick had darkened to shades of burgundy, purple, and green. Aunt Cauldroneyes had used seasonal fabric that would change with the time of year, while the weather vanes spun up crimson dust.

"Hey, wanna see my new badges?" Tolden asked. I knew he was trying to take my mind off Aunt Cauldroneyes.

"Sure," I said. We sat down by some trees and showed each other our albums and the most recent badges we had earned. I had already sewed other badges to my cloak and Tolden's, like the slug badges we'd received as extra credit for taking care of the plants in the greenhouses. Tolden had also earned extra credit for helping out the giants in the kitchen. His most recent badge from that was a piece of jelly toast.

"Speaking of the kitchen," he said, "wanna go get some pumpkin smash?"[34*]

"We don't have time," I said, looking up at the tower clock. "We have to get to Magical Arts."

The class was called The Painted Cauldron: An Introduction to Magical Arts, and it was taught by Wander Marigold Chimneyelf. She wore potion bottles as earrings, and her long hair flowed down in waves over her cloak, which was vibrant with multicolored triangles and bold black lines that looked like stained glass. Her wand shadow was a fox with a bushy tail. He had a pair of antlers that rose no more than five inches above his head. He always circled her feet as she walked.

Her classroom was in the bottom of a tower that had a brightly painted mural on the walls of abstract unicorns with long square faces and dragons with triangle scales. The tower was full of heavy oak easels and large paintings that floated all the way up to the tower's ceiling.

"Our paintbrushes at the school are made of stiff thistles and soft grasses." Wander Chimneyelf ran her finger

34 * Pumpkin smash is a bubbling juice served in hollowed-out pumpkins.

over the bristles of a brush in her hand. "We have ticklish brushes and stubborn brushes—"

"What's a stubborn brush?" Tolden asked.

"Oh, it's a brush that will paint a tree when you want to paint a flower, or paint a teacup when you want to paint a nose. They are rather tiresome to work with, but not as tiresome as the sleepy brushes. Those I really do not recommend using at all." She pointed to the brushes sleeping on the table.

Tolden loved everything about art class, like how the largest paint drops on the floor would shout out, "Hey, watch where you're going!" whenever someone almost stepped on them. He especially loved drawing and painting. He would stay late after school in the classroom to work. His hands and even Softfang often had paint on them. He also started to carry extra parchment and a graphite quill around with him. The quill was enchanted to stay sharpened.

"I wish I could draw dragons better," he said, sketching the face of Softfang, who posed for him with her head held high.

"I think your dragons look like they can fly off the page," I said.

Tolden had tons of badges from art class. It was his favorite subject, even more than dragon studies. I didn't yet have a favorite subject myself, but I really liked Wander Longfellow Wicklebug's class. He taught what he called Songs of the Stars. It was our astronomy class, and I already had several star-shaped badges from him. His room smelled like the river. Best of all, marsh beetles popped off the desks and into the shallow puddles of water on the floor.

Wicklebug was usually late for class by a couple of minutes. His wand shadow would come into the room first. It was a Ticklish Lizard with stubby hooves and a long tail that was often electrified by bolts of lightning.[35*] He always followed soon after, pausing to pour swamp water out of his oxford shoes.

"Forgive me," he'd say with a *ribbit*.

He wore a hat that was shaped like a large thimble on his head. It had a ball-cap bill and a brown-spotted feather in the top of it. On the thimble itself were rows of mismatched buttons and charms of glass beetles.

"I hope you all noticed the sky last night," he'd say. It was always the first thing he said as he picked up the green chalk and headed to the blackboard while making another *ribbit*.

He had once been turned into a frog. When he was transformed back into a man, the only things that changed were that he became tall again, wore high-waisted pants rolled up to his knees, and had reading glasses on a chain around his neck. His skin had remained as green and slimy as a frog's. And his bulging eyes blinked in shades of brown cattail grass.

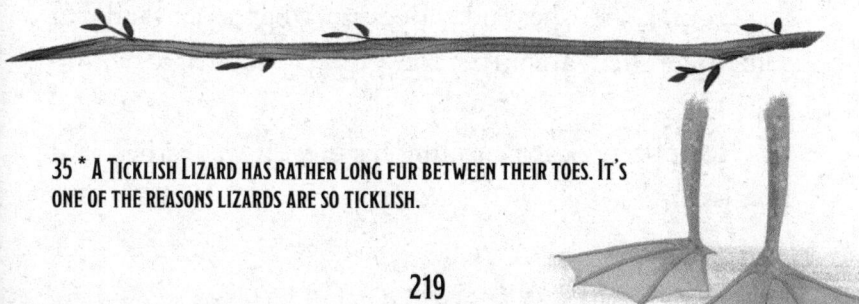

35 * A TICKLISH LIZARD HAS RATHER LONG FUR BETWEEN THEIR TOES. IT'S ONE OF THE REASONS LIZARDS ARE SO TICKLISH.

He spent a good part of his day swimming and often came to class with lily pads stuck to the back of his suspenders. As he spoke of the planets and the orbits of the galaxies, he dripped with water, and ate any fly that came in through the open windows with a flick of his long tongue. I thought he was as fantastic as the frogs back home. Only he spoke about midnight eclipses and writing cauldron prayers on bowls and burying them beneath constellations.

"Because if you're lucky," he said, "you will find your bowl filled with stars."

I thought of Aunt Cauldroneyes and the way she would bury bowls in the fields. She would dig them up and find them bursting with stars that she would then bring inside to sew onto hats.

One day Wicklebug called his lizard shadow to his hand and used his wand to conjure an entire galaxy in front of the chalkboard. He knew more about stars than anyone I'd ever known.

"And why shouldn't I?" he asked. "There is plenty of stargazing from a lily pad, after all. And I'm pleased to teach you everything I know. This is my first year at Dragon's Knob. I wanted to be part of the change. It will take hard work. And we'll be using the oldest wand of all to do it."

"The oldest wand?" I asked. "What's that?"

"Your voice," he said. "Because what is a wand but something that amplifies the power and magic within you?"

He noticed Grackle rolling his eyes. It was rather hard to miss.

"You do not appreciate such changes at this school, do you?" Wicklebug asked him. "Why are you here, then?"

"Generations of Nightcliffs have graduated from Dragon's Knob," Grackle said. "And my family likes to stick to traditions, like using animals in magic. It's not like creatures matter the way we do."

"Why is that, Wand Keeper Grackle?" Wicklebug asked. "Is it because you're bigger than these so-called creatures? And because you're louder than them and you wear clothes and walk on two legs rather than on four or nine or thirteen?"

"Yes, yes, yes." Grackle frowned.

"Well, unicorns might not wear clothes, but they run with herds that will outlive you. You may speak a hundred words a minute, but the whale can silently swim from one end of the ocean to the other with a voice that you will never hear, and yet she is powerful enough to dive on a single breath. Can you do that, Wand Keeper Grackle? Can you run with the herds or swim to the bottom of the sea?"

Wander Wicklebug looked past Grackle's shoulder, at an ant climbing on the window.

"You are bigger than this ant, Wand Keeper Grackle." Wicklebug let the ant crawl onto his fingers. "And yet you will never be able to create a new one. Do you know what creature can create a new ant, Wand Keeper Grackle?"

Grackle was silent.

"Another ant," I said.

"That's right, Wand Keeper Spella." Wicklebug smiled. "Only an ant can ever create another. But how can something so small be more powerful than me? Or you? We who are so big compared to an ant?" He fell quiet before saying, "Because no matter how big we get, we are never more powerful than the smallest creature. And we are no more important."

He returned the ant to the window.

"Now if you will all have a seat and pick up your quills, we are going to take notes about the Anima Mundi trees and how they can make galaxies in the middle of the forest."

Throughout the rest of class, I stared at the one blue button on the back side of Wander Wicklebug's hat. When Tolden noticed, I quickly dropped my eyes to my parchment and copied the notes Wicklebug was writing on the blackboard.

When the bat with the overbite of fangs flew down the hallway, ringing the bell for the end of class, I told Tolden I'd meet him later. Then I stayed behind and went up to Wander Wicklebug's desk.

"Aunt Cauldroneyes made your hat," I said. "I can tell it's her thread and stitches."

"She made me a hat, and I told her about the stars," he said. "We have been dear friends for centuries. That is why I know that wherever she is, she's not giving up. And neither should you."

Later that evening I got all the blue buttons out from under the cushion of the poufy chair. As I collected them into a pile on the floor, someone knocked at my door.

It was Tolden. Softfang was perched on his shoulder with a smile.

"I have something for you, Spella." He opened his hand to reveal the blue button from Wander Wicklebug's hat. "It's okay," he said. "I told Wicklebug I wanted to give the button to you, and he said I could have it. You can add it to your collection."

"How did you know I was collecting them?" I asked.

"I've seen you a few times with blue buttons floating in the air toward you. Then I noticed my blue button had been replaced."

He looked down at the pink one on his red cardigan, and I turned away.

"I'm sorry if I wasn't supposed to know about the buttons," he said.

I didn't say anything, so he laid the blue button down on the floor and turned to leave.

"Wait," I said, picking the button up. "Do you want to see my collection?"

He walked with me to the pile on the floor. I added the new button to it.

"Why do you have all of them?" he asked as Softfang jumped down into the pile. She grabbed a button and hopped back up to Tolden's shoulder with it.

"When Aunt Cauldroneyes cried, blue buttons were her tears," I said. "She was that type of witch." I sat down beside the pile. "I've been trying to find a spell to change the buttons to any other color but blue. They make me think of her tears."

I knocked the pile over, sending the buttons scattering. I wiped my eyes as Tolden left.

He came back a couple of minutes later and said, "I had to go to my room to get some paint and brushes."

He sat down in front of the buttons and opened the small jar of yellow paint he had brought with him. He dipped his brush in, and the bristles started to squeal happily.

"I brought ticklish brushes," he said. "They always make me smile."

He began to paint the buttons.

"I think yellow will be nice," he said as Softfang nodded. "You said your aunt grows sunflowers in her garden back home. I thought we could make the buttons look like them."

He gave me the extra brush. I dipped it into the paint until it squealed with delight.

"They really are ticklish," I said, starting to smile. Egypt came over and laid her paw on my leg as we painted the buttons until we had a garden of sunflowers in front of us.

CHAPTER 18
A Waterfall of Books

THE WHOLE CASTLE SMELLED OF PEPPERMINT. SILVER fairy bells, no larger than thimbles, were hung on the staircases. Flurries fell from the thick cathedral beams in the ceiling, causing drifts of snow at the edges of the hallways, which Egypt liked to leave her footprints in.

I helped hang the popcorn strings in the hallways, along with bright red cranberry wreathes, as treats for the critters who lived there. The castle's baker had made a gigantic flock of gingerbread geese and set them on the longest of the dining tables. There were rumors the geese would lift up the table at night and fly it outside the castle, filling the December air with the smell of gingerbread.

All the students had headed home for Christmas break, including Tolden. He returned to the sea to be with his grams and grumps. He offered to stay at the castle with me, but I knew he would be missed by his grandparents. I also knew that he and Softfang were missing them.

"It's the longest I've been away," he said, reaching for a sandwich from his pocket. He held it to his nose, breathing in his grams' perfume. "Why don't you come with me and Softfang, Spella? You'd love the sea in the winter. Sometimes the waves get so cold, they freeze and break against the shore like glass. You ever held a frozen wave in your hand? When you hold them too long, they thaw. They smell salty and nice, like the skin of a whale. Grumps loves to eat the ice. He has no teeth, so it melts in his mouth. He always smiles, and it dribbles down his chin."

Tolden and Softfang grinned at the thought.

"I can't leave the school," I said. "I'd like to be here close in case there's any word about Aunt Cauldroneyes."

He nodded and said quietly, "I know, Spella. I just thought I'd ask."

I was going to be the only student who didn't go home for Christmas break that year. A few of the wanders stayed behind, like Wicklebug, who swam in the river.

Headwander Folklock stayed, too, while Candlehour went with Burrland to their family cottage.

"With her hiccupping all the time," Burrland said to me before he left, "Aunt Rose Harriet is gonna leave blue frogs everywhere in the house. Mom will be so upset.

Last Christmas, Aunty had a terrible case of autumn cough. You know what autumn cough is, don't you? It's when you cough out leaves and acorns. It took Mom three months to get rid of the acorns. They were everywhere, even under the rugs."

As I thought of Burrland and Tolden enjoying their Christmases at home, I couldn't help but think of how me and Aunt Cauldroneyes had decorated our tree in the attic with tiny hat ornaments. Grandma's Boot would put the star on top, while the bats and owls would hang the wreath outside. As the snow fell, we would go out into the fields with old incantation bowls and turn them upside down, over bits of straw so the bowls could make warm homes for hice.[36*]

We would take gifts of seed into the forest for birds, and fresh greens for the wild onedeer. Like their unicorn cousins, the onedeer had a single antler that twisted like an old branch. As we fed them, snow would fall onto our faces and Aunt Cauldroneyes would wrap her long braids around my shoulders like scarves.

"I wonder if the old one is warm where she is," Egypt said one day.

"I know she is," I said. "She has her long braids. She'll wrap them around her neck like scarves."

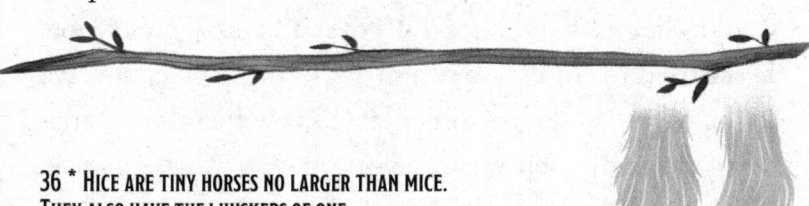

36 * Hice are tiny horses no larger than mice. They also have the whiskers of one.

Egypt nodded, but I knew she still worried. I did, too.

I kept working on Aunt Cauldroneyes' hat. I added all the bits and baubles, like the jigsaw piece Grandma's Boot gave, and the scrap of salty felt from Mr. Sea Captain's pirate hat. There were leaves from Green Toes and a jeweled beetle from Wormella. I'd even sewn on some linen from Egypt. Because of this, the hat had the most charms of any I'd ever made. But it still felt undone. Or maybe it was because I was afraid to finish the hat, like Egypt had said.

"Looks like you're getting close." Egypt meowed as she sat down beside me on the poufy chair. She stared at the hat. "You could finish it tonight, young one."

I laid the hat down and stood up.

"I can't," I said quickly. "I have to go to the library to study."

"Study?" she said. "There are no classes. There is no homework. It's Christmas Eve."

"I'll see you and the hats later." I kissed her on the head. "There's a lamp over there that I don't think you've mummified yet." I pointed to the lamp, but Egypt only watched me leave.

I thought about her and the hats on my walk to the library. I knew they couldn't wait until I found Aunt Cauldroneyes. Ever since I'd arrived at Dragon's Knob, I had tried to think about how it all might be connected to the wizard and Growling Hat. I knew there was something that Folklock wasn't telling me about the man in the dragon's-wing cloak. But what was it?

Secretly I hoped the answer might be as easy as finding a book in the library. I loved the library. There I could find the atlases of the gods. The myths of the monsters. The poetry of the heroes. It was the largest room in the castle. It was also the most recently built because of the fire over the summer. It had started in the stacks of books.

Aunt Cauldroneyes told me about the fire when she'd heard about it. She'd said that Folklock was the one who saw the flames. The headwander had been moving plants into her office when the chatty clematis told her they smelled smoke. The fire raged long enough to burn many books. When they rebuilt the library, they made it look like it always had.

There was a large, glass dome that was a window to the sky, and on top of the highest bookshelves were plants that were said to grow only amongst books, making the vines seem as rare as manuscripts written in languages no longer known.

One of the most famous parts of the library was the waterfall of books. It flowed from the tallest shelf, and came pouring into a river of even more books that circled the entire library. At any time someone could reach into the river or fish a book out with one of the fishing poles that were collected in an umbrella stand by the river. Each pole had a ribbon bookmark for a lure. The ribbons squirmed like worms.

But the waterfall and river weren't the most amazing things about the library. The shadows were. There were shadows that looked like three-headed crocodiles and winged camels. There was a long-necked dinosaur that towered above, and whales that went swimming by. Whenever Egypt visited the library, she especially loved the shadows of the fish and their scales that pulsed with lightning.

"Hello, child." An aged whisper came from behind me.

It was Wander Tansy Velvetfoot. Grackle and Slithe made fun of her. She was part 'possum and had a pink, knobby nose. Her cheeks were covered in pale gray fur that darkened out to her ears, which were rounded and high on her head.

"Hello, Wander Velvetfoot," I said in the same whisper she had used.

I could tell she was very old. She had gray whiskers, and pearly eyes behind eyeglasses whose lenses were filled with sloshing water. The water magnified her eyes, which otherwise would have been quite small. She walked with a little hunch and a limp. I knew she must have kept a chill in the large, drafty library because she always wore at least three cardigans.

"Oh, here they come." She chuckled at the herd of dust bunnies hopping by our feet and racing around the corner of a shelf. "I don't think any library should be free from dust," she said. "It makes such wonderful bunnies." She smiled at me, her small ears twitching. "May I help you find a book, Spella?"

I was surprised she knew my name. All the times I'd been in the library, I hadn't ever spoken to her. She'd always been over at her large desk, reading in such deep thought, I had never wanted to disturb her.

"I was just going to study some," I said. "If that's okay?"

"Certainly," she said. "You know, usually it's just me and the books on Christmas Eve."

A large bird shadow flew overhead and crossed our faces.

"Well," she said, "me and the books and all our shadow friends, of course."

"Who are the shadows?" I asked.

"Sometimes a witch or wizard loses their wand and the shadows become lost," she said. "But wand shadows have to go somewhere. They tend to like libraries. I suppose because books make you feel magical. That's why some people are frightened of books. That's why some people even try to ban them. Or worse, burn them."

The shadow of a horse galloped by. Wander Velvetfoot giggled, and it sounded like the tinkling of small bells.

"Why don't you have a shadow?" I asked her.

"My magic isn't a wand," she said. "My magic is the books. I have always loved the library." She started to walk ahead, waving her little hand for me to follow. I could feel cold air coming off some of the books as we passed by. And hot air coming off others. Spilling out from pages were things like pebbles, leaves, and even roots.

"Sometimes books are so full," she said, "they can't help but spill out a little." She held her hand beneath the sand pouring out from a corner of a large book. The sand fell between her fingers as if from an hourglass.

She pulled out a book that had a cover made entirely

of oak leaves. Above it were several books trembling on a shelf.

"Are they scared of something?" I asked.

"Yes." She sighed. "They hide amongst the shelves."

We watched the books slide themselves back into the shadows.

"They've been that way ever since the fire," she said.

Something started to tug on the back of her long skirt. It was a small book.

"He's a little attached," she said, scooping the book up in her arms. "I saved him from the fire." She wiped a tear that had started to fall down the cover of the small book. "So many books were burned. I tried to save all I could."

She pushed up the sleeves of her cardigans. The gray fur had been burned off her thin arms, and there were now scars that rippled like crumpled paper.

"Aunt Cauldroneyes told me about the fire," I said. "But not about how it started."

Wander Velvetfoot looked down at the small book, cradling it like a baby in her arms as she said, "That would be the work of the former headwander. He was not a gentle wizard. When it was announced that Dragon's Knob would be the first school to do away with using creatures in spells, the headwander was told he would be dismissed unless he agreed to the new rules. He refused, so he was removed as headwander. He did not take it well. He believed he was king of the castle. I wasn't surprised that he started a fire in the library. Books are often the first to be attacked."

The little book cooed in her arms.

"When monsters are out," Velvetfoot said, "they tend to destroy the things with wings. Books have some of the biggest wings of all. Big enough to fly the world to the stars and back. So he tried to burn them. But books are phoenixes. Their stories rise from the ashes."

She continued to cradle the small book, who nuzzled against her arms.

"I best leave you to your studying, Spella," she said, before pointing toward a rounded doorway that had a stained glass window above it. The window had a faint glow, as if a single candle was behind it, lighting up the dragons in the glass and the words ANCIENT ARCHIVES.

"If you'd like to learn more about the castle, the library, and even the Dragon King," she said, "those are our oldest books."

As she walked away, the little book crawled out of her arms and back down to her pale blue skirt, where it clutched the swishing fabric, waving to me with its pages until she disappeared around the corner.

I quickly headed into the archives. The room was even more unswept than the rest of the library. I saw a much larger herd of at least fifty dust bunnies hopping off with an even dustier carrot. The dark wooden shelves were close together, making for narrow passages between. When I heard a scratching sound, I peeked though the shelves, but saw only the hairy, black legs of a tarantula passing by on the other side.

The books in the room were old enough to actually have wrinkles, like ancient faces. The deep wrinkles bunched and pinched the tattered covers until they looked as though they had deep-set eyes that watched me walk along the shelves. There was one book that had bright orange smoke swirling from its spine. I reached up and grabbed it. It was warm in my hands as I carried it over to one of the desks. Inside, the words were revealed to be written in fire ink, which flickered like flames.

"Every dragon has a fire bone in their throat," I read aloud. "It is the source of their fiery breath. But in the hands of a Wand Keeper, the bone becomes a fire wand. And unless great care is taken by those who wield it, the world may burn in its power. The Dragon King rarely breathed fire, which means that all his power was stored up inside the fire bone."

In the margin of the page someone had written, *Fire stored in bone. Must find it. Must find the tomb of the Dragon King. Must wield the fire wand.*

I continued to read the book long into the evening. I flipped through page after page. Whoever had written the notes in the margins had done so throughout the chapters. They seemed to be obsessed with finding the tomb. Just as I stopped at a page with an illustration of the Dragon King, a flash of something blue jumped onto the book.

"Fleabag!"

He licked me on the cheek. His bifocals were steamed up from his heavy breathing.

"What are you doing here?" I asked. "Did Egypt send you to get me?"

He nodded, and a string of drool dropped from his mouth onto the table.

I looked over at the grandfather clock. I had been reading for hours.

"It's after midnight!" I closed the book. "C'mon, Fleabag."

Wander Velvetfoot was behind her desk, dusting off the cover of a book that was tall enough to dwarf most giants. I stared at the book's title.

Into the Fire by **Nogard Bmot**.

"Nogard Bmot." I said the author's name aloud, and Wander Velvetfoot nearly dropped her dust rag.

"Oh, Spella! You're still here?" She started to gently push the book. "You get on," she told it. "Get to your shelf now. It's time for bed."

The book slowly walked, bopping from one bottom corner of its cover to the other, over to a shelf, where it tucked itself in between the tall books already there. Fleabag trotted over to sniff them as Wander Velvetfoot giggled.

"The biggest part of a librarian's work is making sure every book gets to bed." She laid the dusting rag on her desk and stared at the book in my arms. "Like to check that one out?"

"Yes, please." I handed it to her. She opened it to the paper pocket on the back flap. Inside it was a checkout card. It had the names of everyone who had previously checked the book out. She handed me the card with a quill that had a big fluffy feather as long as my arm.

"If you'll just sign the card," she said.

I read the last two names before mine. Folklock and

someone named Stonescare. The signature looked familiar. It was the same handwriting I'd seen in the margins of the book.

"Who is Stonescare, Wander Velvetfoot?" I asked as I signed the card.

"Oh, he's a bad cackle, that one."

I waited for her to say something more about Stonescare, but instead she asked for my card back. She slipped it into the pocket before punching it with a stamp that read PLEASE RETURN THIS BOOK ON TIME, OR ELSE YOU'LL OWE A DRAGON'S DIME.

"Happy reading," she said, handing the book back to me.

"I wanted to ask you something else, Wander Velvetfoot. Do you know where the tomb of the Dragon King is?"

The water in her eyeglass lenses started to quickly slosh before her eyes.

"The tomb of the Dragon King?" she said. "Well, some say he is buried beneath the longest fingernail of Headwander Folklock herself. And others say he is laid so deep in the earth, he is only a foot away from running out of ground. I've also heard tell that he is hidden inside a book that has never been read. But then again, how would one know, if the book has never been read?"

"So the Dragon King was buried in secret?" I asked.

"Oh yes. Now, when he died is not secret. It was in March of his most ancient year. They called the day he died the hour of the candle. People used to believe that a dragon was born every time a candle was lit. That's how mysterious dragons were to even the most magical of folks. They are of course not born by wick and wax, but the fable stuck. And because it was said they were born by lighting a candle, it was said they died when one was blown out. When the Dragon King passed, it was called the hour of the candle because he was such a great leader. They said it took an hour for a breath to extinguish his flame."

She bent down to pick up Fleabag and hold him.

"But even if you found the tomb of the Dragon King," she said, "you wouldn't be able to enter it. The tomb is enchanted. You might have read in the book about the fire bone. The Dragon King knew there could be grave robbers, so he enchanted his tomb to prevent the bone from being stolen."

She gave Fleabag a few more head scratches before letting him out of her arms.

"Best get to your room now, Spella," she said. "It's quite late for a student to be up past their bedtime."

She started to hum as she walked more books over to their shelves, to tuck them in.

I thought about the Dragon King's tomb on the walk back. When Fleabag whimpered, I looked up and realized we were in a hallway I wasn't familiar with.

"We must have taken a wrong turn," I said. "I've never been this far on the north side of the castle. It's colder here."

Unlike the rest of the castle, which was bright, this hall was dimly lit. At the end of it, there appeared to be a staircase going down.

"I bet those go to the dungeons," I whispered as Fleabag stayed closed. "Let's go back the other way."

We turned quickly, but heard a loud creak.

"Something is coming up from the dungeons." I grabbed Fleabag and hid beside a cabinet up against the wall, just as a large creature appeared. He stood at least fifteen feet tall and was covered in shaggy fur, as green as the swamp.

He had a pointed snout and floppy ears that hung nearly to his feet, and he slobbered yellow slime that fizzed wherever it landed. His claws were so long, they clacked against the floor, no matter how quietly he tried to step.

"A g-g-g-goblin dog,"[37*] I finally managed to whisper as Fleabag pushed his bifocals against his eyes. I knew he couldn't believe what he was seeing.

The goblin dog held his snout up, sniffing the air. He could smell us.

I quietly pulled my wandle out of my vest. I would be conjuring a spell for the swamp, so I thought back to what I had studied about wet spells. I knew I had to hold my wandle pointing down. Then I had to flick it like I was flicking water off.

"Make us smell like the swamp," I whispered, *"so the goblin will not chomp."*

[37 *] MOST WILL MEET A GOBLIN DOG NOT IN THE SWAMP BUT IN A STRAWBERRY PATCH. THEY CANNOT RESIST STRAWBERRIES.

Mud started to drip off the wandle before it turned limp. I had used my last spell for the day, just as I felt my clothes getting heavier. When I reached my hand into my pocket, I found clumps of mud. I looked at Fleabag. He was dripping with swamp water, too, but at least we no longer smelled like a girl and a hat.

The goblin dog wheezed and turned away from us. His nose was leading him farther down the hall.

"He's looking for something," I said to Fleabag, who nodded.

Goblin dogs were not known to stray from their swamplands. They were generally avoided because of their size. And their smell. There was also a persistent rumor that a goblin dog devoured anyone who couldn't solve riddles, but Aunt Cauldroneyes said that was only gossip started by the dogs themselves so that others would leave them alone.

They were known as excellent trackers. It was said they could catch a scent from miles away. But what could be in a castle that a goblin dog would want?

"We have to make him leave the castle," I said to Fleabag very quietly. "I used the last spell in my wandle, so I need you to give the goblin dog some of your fleas."

Fleabag made a face and shook his head. He loved his fleas, and not even Aunt Cauldroneyes could convince him to give them up at bath time.

"Please, Fleabag," I said. "The goblin dog is not supposed to be in the castle. He could harm the others if we don't get him to leave."

That was enough for Fleabag to agree. He checked to make sure his bifocals were steady. Then he took off running down the hall toward the goblin dog. He jumped high in the air and landed on top of the dog's head.

"Who are you?" the dog asked, his voice softer than I'd expected.

Fleabag started to scratch, knocking a great cloud of fleas onto the dog.

"Why are you making me all itchy?" The dog shook.

He sat down and started to use his hind legs to scratch at his ears, his eyes bulging until they looked ready to pop out of his head.

"Please stop," he said. "You're making me dizzy and itchy."

As he scratched, I heard a tinkling sound. It was coming from the chains and shackles around his ankles. When he pawed at his neck, I saw he also wore a tight collar.

"Why are you doing this to me?" The dog started to whimper. "What did I ever do to you?"

"Fleabag," I said, running to stand in front of the dog, "call your fleas back."

Happily the old hat whistled, and the fleas hopped off the dog.

"I thank you very much," the goblin dog said as Fleabag jumped down to the floor. "I'm not supposed to be seen in the castle. Are you the type of Wand Keeper to tell secrets?"

"What are you doing here?" I asked.

"I don't want to be here, I assure you," he said. "If it

was up to me, I'd be back at the swamp tucking in with a nice bowl of strawberry ice cream right about now. It was at the swamp that I was caught by a spell while I was sleeping. Then I was forced to come here."

"You're a prisoner?" I asked.

"Yes." He wiped his cheek on his shoulder. "My captor has enchanted these chains and shackles that I wear to keep me from running away."

"Let me help you," I said.

I tried to pull off the shackles, but he said, "I can't let you remove them. He will hurt my students back at the swamp. I'm a teacher, you know. I run the school for swamp pups."

"I'll go get the headwander of this school," I said. "She'll be able to help you."

"I don't think so." The goblin dog whimpered some more. "The one who took me is a night sorcerer."

"A night sorcerer?"

"That's what I call him," the goblin dog said. "His teeth are broken from eating wands. That's how you become a night sorcerer. That's how I know he'll eat me, and eat my students back at the swamp. That's what he says will happen if I don't find what he's looking for."

"What is he looking for?" I asked.

"I can't tell you," the goblin dog said. "I shouldn't even be speaking to you. If the night sorcerer found out, you would be in danger, too."

"Maybe I can help you," I said.

"You're kind." The dog smiled. "I can tell. A goblin

dog knows these things. Please don't tell anyone I was here. I didn't mess up any of the paintings or even the rug."

He looked down at the rug beneath his feet.

"I slobber a bit," he said, "but a goblin dog's slime dries in a few seconds. I haven't been a bother. If you really want to help me, you'll not tell anyone I was here."

The chains and shackles clinked as he stepped backward. Even though I wanted to run and tell Folklock, I didn't, because the goblin dog had so much fear in his face. I knew it was for the pups back at his school. I didn't want to do something that put them in any danger. I had to trust him.

"All right," I said. "I won't tell anyone."

He thanked me before quickly leaving and disappearing into the darkness at the end of the hallway.

I looked down at Fleabag. He was still dripping with swamp water. "We have to find a bathroom and clean up," I said. "We look like we both came out of the swamp, and that's the first thing Egypt will say. We can't tell her about the goblin dog. Agreed, Fleabag?"

He blinked his eyes behind his bifocals and nodded.

Spell No. 4,003

**If a witch is late, find a broom. Do not wait.
Count her whiskers, six to eight,
And disappear down the straight.**

Note from the Before Long Witch

You must spin a pendant while reciting this spell and point your wandle directly at the top of your head. You will disappear quickly and be invisible. Please note that after being invisible, you might find that you are abnormally thirsty. You should have a gallon of loopy woopy berry juice prepared. But be warned, loopy woopy berry juice is the favorite drink of lawn gnomes, so you'll likely hear several small knocks at your door. It is always best not to ignore thirsty lawn gnomes. If you do, you might discover that you haven't any daisies in your yard come morning.

CHAPTER 19
As the Stars Come to Tell It

ON CHRISTMAS MORNING HEADWANDER FOLKLOCK knocked on my door. The hats were sleeping in a pile with Socky in front of the fireplace. Egypt was on top, lying flat on her back, her feet up in the air. They were snoring at different times, the deep bellows of the large hats followed by the high wheezing of the small ones. On occasion Socky would bark in a dream, which would then cause Egypt to hiss in hers.

"There's something delightful about seeing a pile of creatures snoring on Christmas morning," Folklock said with a smile. "I came by to ask you if you'd like to join me for a cup of tea in my office, Spella?"

She looked as though she had just come in from the

fields. Her muddy pants were tucked into even muddier books. Strands of her hair were sticking out the way mine did when it got caught on a stick in the forest.

"Would you like to come, too?" Folklock asked Hartshorn. "I know how much you love a good tea."

He was wrapped in a blanket with his wings over his ears, trying to escape the snores.

"Thank you," he said, "but I should be here when they wake up. Those little bat hats have started to eat my blanket." He pulled the blanket tighter around him, his feathers poking through new fang holes. "No matter how many times I tell them it's not made of chocolate."

Me and Folklock held our laughter until we were out in the hall. I put on my cloak to keep out the flurries falling from the ceiling. Folklock looked at my brooch and said, "September's sapphire. We were born in the same month. We shall be September sisters. We are already sisters of the W.O.L.V.E.S."

She showed me the tiny lightning bolts tattooed around her left wrist like a charm bracelet. The same bracelet that all the elders in the Sisterhood had. I watched the lightning flicker ever so slightly in its hidden message as we walked to her office.

It was my first time inside it. It was a large rectangular room, with an entire wall devoted to windows that overlooked the grounds. I knew she had traveled far and wide. Hanging on the wall were framed photographs of her in jungles and on mountaintops, in wetlands and meadows. Always she was with plants, looking at the tiniest of them through her microscope or standing beneath giant leaves that made her look small.

She had brought many of the plants into her office. They hung from the ceiling and grew from every available space, while thick research books on ancient botany were littered about.

"It's more like a greenhouse than an office," I said as she slipped out of her rubber boots. She knocked the mud off against her desk before dropping them to the floor.

"I went out early this morning," she said, "to gather Terrific Toadstones."[38*]

She picked up a copper kettle from the small woodburning stove in the corner. The kettle was shaped like a woodland cottage, the copper hammered into little windows and even a chimney, out of which the steam of the water boiling inside rose. Folklock plucked two leaves off the plant by the stove. Instantly the leaves curled into cups that she poured the hot water into. She reached into her pocket and took a pinch of Terrific Toadstones to drop into the water.

"Wait for the tea to bloom," she said. The water rippled before spotted petals pushed up to form a flower.

"Toadfire!" I said as she handed me my cup. We blew on the flowers, causing the petals to fly out around the room.

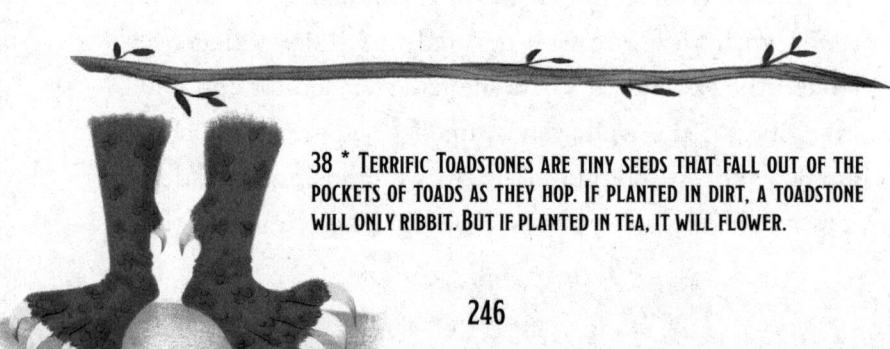

38 * Terrific Toadstones are tiny seeds that fall out of the pockets of toads as they hop. If planted in dirt, a toadstone will only ribbit. But if planted in tea, it will flower.

As I sipped the tea, I looked at her desk. It was cluttered with parchment.

"Everything is a little messy," she said, "because I'm currently researching my next book. I'm detailing the life of aquatic plants, like ones found here by the river."

She pointed to it out the window. Her office was situated high enough that you could see well into the distance, causing the river to look like a winding snake. You could also see some of the protestors on the bridge. There were still a few, even on Christmas Day.

Instead of looking at the protestors, I looked at the drops of water on the glass left from that morning's rain.

"Raindrops on window glass are telescopes to the stars, no matter how far," I said, leaning in to stare through the raindrops until I saw billions of twinkling lights.

"Who told you something that beautiful?" Folklock asked.

"Aunt Cauldroneyes." I went to the sofa to drink my tea. On the coffee table were several thick books. I pulled one to my lap. It was full of photographs.

"Do you recognize the witch in this photograph?" Folklock came over and laid her finger on a young woman with black braids down to her wide bare feet.

"That's Aunt Cauldroneyes," I said. "She's so young there."

She was standing in front of a brick factory with the name Nightcliff Manufacturing on the side of it. Puffs of black smoke rose out of the chimneys. I read what was written beneath the photo.

Activists gathered to protect trees as more old-growth forests were cut down to break ground for a new one-thousand-acre unicorn ranch owned by Nightcliff Manufacturing. The activists were also protesting the capture of wild unicorns to be raised at the ranch.

"Your aunt has worked for a long time to make things better in the world," Folklock said. "As the stars come to tell it."

"What does 'as the stars come to tell it' mean?" I asked. "I've heard you say it before. I think it's wonderful."

"My mother would say that stars are storytellers of time that live up in the sky, and the shining that we see is the ends of their quills, writing the myths of the world. So she would say, 'Herbalia, do good things in the world. Do kind things. Do things that will keep the lights shining as the stars come to tell it.' So I say those words to remind myself to be kind. To be decent. So that at the end of my story, the stars will be able to continue to shine."

She drank the last of her tea. As soon as she sat the cup down, the leaf unfurled and floated back into the air, returning to the plant as a leaf once more as she headed to her desk.

"I've gotten you a little Christmas present," she said. "Now, where did I put it?"

As she searched the many drawers of her desk, I saw they were full of roots, leaves, and several caps off Burps-Forever cola bottles. There was one drawer that was nothing but seeds, and another that had a very bushy fern growing in it. I went over to pet the leaves.

"That's a drawer fern," she said. "They only grow in dark, tight spaces."

She pulled out the drawer above it, and suddenly white blobs of marshmallow floated up into our faces.

"Oh, my marshmallow ghosts,"[39*] she said. She shooed them out of the way, then lifted out the box beneath.

"Merry Christmas, Spella."

I hoped the gift might have something to do with Aunt Cauldroneyes, but then I saw it was a board game.

"It's called Cauldron Hop," Folklock said. "It's the oldest known board game, developed in the first century of the world. Why don't we play a round?" She smiled. "You can practice with me and get good at it for when your friends return from Christmas break."

"I really only have Tolden for a friend," I said.

"You have more than you think." She winked, opening the box. She carried it over to the window seat, where she pulled out the little wand-shaped game pieces and handed one to me. It didn't seem to do any real magic, except move my token across the board and flip the dice.

"This is a game of strategy and spell memory," she said. "You get a wart on your face for each round you're ahead. The one with the most warts wins, and the loser gets their

39 * Marshmallow ghosts are the ghosts of sugar and flour that have been spilled on the floor. They are very common sightings in kitchens that have not been swept for some time.

nose pinched." She chuckled. "Some say my nose has been pinched quite a few times." She held the furry orange dice out to me. "You roll first, Spella."

I wasn't sure if I would be very good at the game. It was my first time playing it. But by the end, I had enough warts on my face to be a toad.

"I've never been very good at Cauldron Hop." Folklock laughed as I reached over and pinched her nose.

"What happens to my warts?" I asked.

"Oh, they go away."

I crossed my eyes to watch them disappear from my nose.

Folklock asked if I wanted to play another round, but I said I had to get back to the hats.

"It'll be their first Christmas without Aunt Cauldron-eyes. I don't want them to be alone."

She gave me a box of marshmallow ghosts to take with me. I had to keep the lid on tight the whole walk back. The ghosts kept bumping up against it. When I got to my room, Hartshorn was doing his best to stop the mice hats from taking off with the fruitcake he'd brought up from the kitchen, while Socky was collecting all the socks Grandma's Boot had knitted for gifts.

"I see everyone is having a nice Christmas." I laughed.

When they saw me, all the hats came running and knocked the box out of my hands, sending the marshmallow ghosts floating up to the ceiling.

"I'm happy to see all of you, too." I hugged them back as we settled in on the rug in front of the fireplace. Hartshorn fought off the bat hats as he carried a flat package toward me. I knew Egypt had wrapped it. It was covered in mummy linen. When I opened it, I saw it was a Venom Spitters record.

"Tolden left that for you," Hartshorn said. "I told him I'd make sure you got it on Christmas. He used some of his badges at the Wrinkled Pumpkin to get it."

"And here is a gift from all of us, young one." Egypt handed me a soft package wrapped in more linen. I opened it, revealing a pair of knitted socks that Socky hadn't stolen just yet.

"Thanks, Egypt." I hugged her. "I love them."

"Check what's inside the right sock," Hartshorn said.

I reached in and pulled out a piece of wood that was only a couple of inches long.

"It's a wood worm," Hartshorn said. "That's from me."

"I've never heard of a wood worm," I said, turning it over in my hands.

"They're born from a tree's spit,"[40*] he said. "Best of all is that you get to make a wish on a wood worm."

"A wish?" I sat up taller. "I can wish for Aunt Cauldroneyes to come back home!"

Hartshorn fell quiet as he looked down at the piece of wood.

40 * Trees spit for a variety of reasons. Sometimes it's because they've entered the annual forest-spitting contest. Other times it's because they've simply swallowed a bug.

"I'm sorry," he said. "That's not a wood worm at all. It's a piece of broken firewood. I've had it ever since I was in the dungeons. That piece of broken firewood was the only thing I had to wish on, so I believed it was a wood worm. And when I held it, I made the wish that me and the other dodos would be free from the dungeons. And look at us now. My wish did come true. So if you make a wish on that piece of firewood about your aunt, maybe your wish will come true, too. I know it will."

I looked down at the piece of wood and smiled as I said, "Thank you, Hartshorn."

He nodded, his cheeks growing red. "You're welcome, Wand Keeper Spella."

He started to run after the mice hats to try to get the fruitcake back from them one last time so he could cut everyone a slice. Egypt watched him before leaning in and whispering, "Fleabag told me about the goblin dog."

I looked over at Fleabag, who blinked behind his bifocals.

"I told him not to say anything." I groaned.

"There are three things I know about goblin dogs, young one." Egypt held up her paw and started to count. "First, they look like the swamp. Second, they love homemade strawberry ice cream. And third, they have an excellent sense of smell. But their sense of smell is not for finding chocolates or lost keys or their way through a garden. They can smell bones."

"Bones?" I turned to look into her glowing yellow eyes.

"Yes." She nodded. "The kind that have been buried."

CHAPTER 20
Brooms with Cackling Engines

I FINISHED THE LINING OF THE HAT I WAS MAKING for Aunt Cauldroneyes in January. I decided to use silk the color of the bright orange pumpkins that grew beneath her bedroom windows back home. All over the hat I embroidered my memories, like the time we found the feather of the River Eagle. I embroidered Aunt Cauldroneyes holding it toward the sky.

I sewed on scenes like us drinking chocolate curl by the fire. I even embroidered us together at the sewing table in the attic. I used thread called snake silk for all the embroidery.

"Any stitch you make with snake silk," Aunt

Cauldroneyes had told me, "will move. If you embroider a river, you will see the water ripple. If you stitch a leaf onto a branch, you will see the leaf wiggle and waggle as if caught in a breeze."

When the embroidered images moved, they made me believe, if only for a moment, that Aunt Cauldroneyes was there with me.

"There I am." Egypt pointed her paw toward the thread image of herself. I had even embroidered her linen wrappings.

I also sewed scenes of all the hats, like Mr. Sea Captain hanging out the window with his tentacles, and the fairy hats flying with their little wings.

"I do believe this is the most beautiful hat you have ever made," Egypt said. "When the old one is back, she will be most pleased with it."

"When she's back." I repeated those words as I pulled the thread into a very tiny knot on the hat. The knot was called "the blue freckle". Aunt Cauldroneyes had named it after me.

During this time, I thought often about the goblin dog. If he was in the castle to pick up the scent of bones, like Egypt said a goblin dog could, then I knew it had something to do with the tomb of the Dragon King, but I didn't know how Aunt Cauldroneyes fit into everything. When Tolden returned from Christmas break, I told him all about it.

"A goblin dog?" He sighed as Softfang did the same. "All I did over Christmas break was help Grumps find his wooden teeth and help Grams wrap my Christmas presents, then pretend to be surprised when I opened them an hour later."

Me and Tolden, along with Egypt, started to walk the halls late at night in search of the goblin dog. We always had to wait until our dodos fell asleep. But as the weeks passed, there were no more sightings.

Winter ended, Tolden finally mastered sounding less like a screaming donkey and more like a neighing unicorn for Globemallow's class, and Egypt managed to potty train the bat hats. I was still trying to fit together the pieces of the fire wand, the goblin dog, and the tomb of the Dragon King. I knew the goblin dog had to have been looking for the tomb. I could only hope that he didn't find it before we found him.

But by spring, the only thing all the other first wands could talk about was flying brooms. I found myself thinking less of the goblin dog and more about the brooms, too.

"I can't wait to fly one!" Tolden said.

Wander Willa Wuthering Winds was finally going to let us on a broom, after months of studying them in the classroom, where the closest we got to flying brooms was staring at the ones hanging on the wall like art. The desks in her class seemed to be especially grumpy. It was as though even they wanted us to fly on brooms.

Wuthering Winds had the most tongue-twisting name to say out of all the wanders. There was a rumor that she had been born on a mountain peak, thereby honored by the winds. It was why her wand shadow was a round bird with four wings and taller than she was. And she was pretty tall. She wore her hair in low ponytails that lay over her shoulders like broom bristles. She was usually dressed in thick tweed shorts, no matter the season, that fell in wide cuffs to her knees, her socks stretched on her strong calves. On the tool belt cinched around her waist, she had every tool you would ever need, should a broom break down. She had twig tweezers, lantern clamps, and extra-strength wood jelly for any handle that might snap.

Our first flying lesson was in the flattest meadow that surrounded the school. Wander Wuthering Winds lined us up and handed out our skeleton keys, which we would use to start our brooms with. Because they were school brooms, the part of the key that went into the keyhole had the silhouette of the castle on it. The shaft of the key was engraved to resemble dragon scales.

The brooms were already laid out in the meadow. The end of each handle was curved and curled into a hook that held a lantern.

"Very useful come nightfall," Wander Wuthering Winds said. On the back of the broom, just behind the padded seat, was a shallow indentation and a belt with a buckle.

"To hold a traveling cauldron," she said.

Each broom also had a horn called a goose beak, because it made a sound just like an angry goose. Wuthering Winds honked Burrland's horn as she passed his broom.

"The goose beaks are especially good at night, to warn any birds flying in your path so you can avoid colliding with them," she said. "As broom riders it's important to be respectful of those we share the sky with."

I could tell the brooms had been used for centuries at the school. Past students had stuck gum under the seats, and mine even had names carved into the handle, which had been whittled down by students' grips over the years.

"All right, you goblins and ghouls, start your broom's engine," Wuthering Winds said. She loved calling everyone goblins and ghouls.

We put our keys into the castle-shaped holes. With a turn of the key, the brooms started to cackle as they hovered up by our sides. Tolden's seemed to cackle quite a bit.

"All great broom engines run on cackling gas,"[41*] Wuthering Winds said. "Now, without further delay, put on your broom-riding gloves."

We reached into our satchels and pulled out the large, bulky gloves. They had wide sleeves embroidered with broom mythology, and on the fingers were tiny stiff hairs, like the stiff hairs on a tarantula's legs.

"The very best to grip on to broom handles with," Wuthering Winds said.

I had two pairs of the gloves in my bag. One pair for me and one for Egypt. She tossed her cloak back and waited patiently for me to put the gloves on over her linen

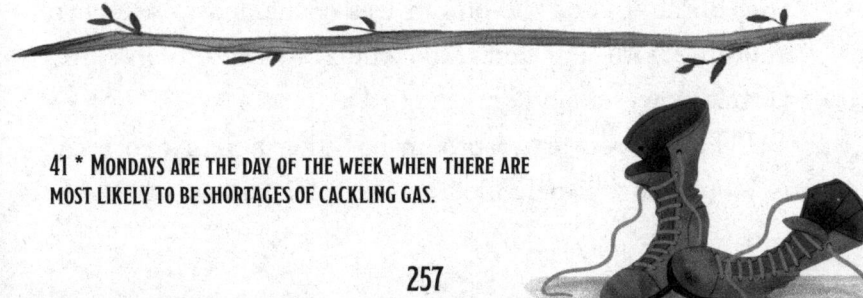

41 * Mondays are the day of the week when there are most likely to be shortages of cackling gas.

wrappings. Her pair was identical to all of ours, though made much smaller and in a special shape to fit her paws.

After I put them on her, she sat straight and tall with her paws close together, the wide sleeves of the gloves fanning out from her thin arms.

As I put my gloves on, Wuthering Winds walked around the group of us and said, "These are training brooms, so they will only fly you two feet off the ground for safety. To keep the brooms from going as fast as they can, each has a stone bat tied to it."

The stone bats fell out from the bristles to the ground at our feet.

"We can't have you flying off into the upper regions of space, now, can we?" she said.

"These brooms are the shabbiest I've ever seen," Grackle said.

"They're nothing like the Dragon Chaser." Slithe pulled a small yellow feather from his pocket.

A few of the others cackled when they saw the feather.

"That's the Dragon Chaser?" Tolden himself laughed.

Slithe only held the feather high with a smile, then let it go. We watched as the feather floated down through the air before instantly turning into a flying broom covered in shiny warts. And instead of bristles, the broom had fire. Slithe told us the broom was enchanted to not burn anything with its flames, like the grass the broom softly floated down to land on.

"The more warts a broom has, the more expensive it is," someone whispered loud enough for Slithe to hear. He smiled wider as some stepped closer to the broom to marvel at its red velvet seat trimmed with little golden dragons that roared whenever you touched their bellies.

"All right, Slithe," Wuthering Winds said. "Put your fancy broom away. I'll have you know that no matter how many warts they put on brooms in the store, no broom is safer than a good old-fashioned one. I've heard those Dragon Chasers don't chase down anything but very small dragonflies and that they're prone to crashing into water at the most important moments."

"That's hog rubbish," Slithe said. He picked up his broom and shook it in his hand until it became a small yellow feather once more. He put the feather into his pocket and groaned at the school broom in front of him.

Wuthering Winds turned with a smile to face us all. "Go ahead and mount your brooms. Be sure to grip your handles tightly with both hands," she instructed.

Egypt jumped up onto the front of my broom. Once I mounted, we rose only a couple of feet in the air.

"Now practice turning your handle to go forward," Wuthering Winds said.

I turned the end of the handle slightly up, the stone bat dragging on the ground and anchoring us. I looked over at Tolden. He was having a blast, but Softfang was gripping his collar tight, her eyes wide.

"Now the stone bats will lighten just a little," Wander Wuthering Winds said, "to let you pick up some speed."

Though we got no higher, my broom started to go fast enough that Egypt's linen blew back on either side of her face. She laughed, and honked the goose beak as Tolden flew past, nearly startling him off his broom.

Wuthering Winds called her bird shadow, who flew into her hand and turned into a wand with four tiny wings along its sides. She dipped it into the bucket of storm water she had brought with her. Then she cast a spell, bringing rain and wind to the meadow, so that we could practice flying in stormy weather.

"Notice how when the rain falls onto your broom, it immediately dries," she said. "That's because the handles have a rain-repellent potion. However, that potion can be easily removed."

She dipped her wand into the bucket again, and at once our brooms became wet and slippery.

"Hold on tight!" She conjured more rain by spitting onto the end of her wand. "You must learn how to keep steady in a storm."

While the day remained sunny and bright, lightning flashed in the meadow and thunder roared as Wuthering Winds conjured storm clouds above our heads. If not for my broom-riding gloves, my hands would have slipped off. Egypt was holding tight to the handle, too. A couple of her claws had broken through the gloves, and she dug them into the wood.

"All right. Now let's learn to fly in some wind!" Wander Wuthering Winds stood with her feet very wide and kicked her legs, which cast a spell that blew away the storm clouds and stirred up a mighty wind.

It blew so strong, it spun us in circles around the stone bats.

"You must learn how to steer your broom in a hurricane," Wuthering Winds said loudly over the whoosh. "You never know when one will come when you're flying high."

Egypt was hugging the broom handle tightly, her face pressed against it, as we spun around the stone bat.

"*MEEOOOOOOOOOOOOOWWWWWWW!*"

"Hold on, Egypt!" I held firm to the handle and turned my bootheels down just as Wuthering Winds instructed. Instead of working against the wind, I worked with it and started to straighten my broom until Egypt was finally able to sit up, though she continued to grip the handle tightly and her yellow eyes were still spinning in her head.

"Sorry, Egypt," I said with a chuckle.

"You did very well, Spella," Wuthering Winds said. She held up her wand and created a badge. It looked like a flying broom with wings. The badge flew over to me and sewed itself onto my cloak. "You earned that, Spella."

I couldn't wait to show the badge to Tolden. I looked over at him. He was spinning so fast, he was a blur. I especially delighted in seeing Grackle spinning. Slithe was already on the ground, having been thrown off his broom. He quickly tried to get back on before anyone else noticed.

The one who was spinning the most was Burrland. His broom was turning so fast, he was thrown off into a nearby tree. Then he slid down its trunk to the ground.

Wander Wuthering Winds immediately ceased the wind, and all the brooms slowly stopped spinning.

"Are you all right?" I asked Burrland as I was the first to fly over to him.

"I think so," he said, standing up just as a small twig popped out of his forehead.

"Hey, you got a . . ." I motioned toward his head.

He reached up and felt the leaves at the end of the twig.

"Oh no," Wuthering Winds cried out as she came running up.

Tolden and the others were flying on their brooms behind her, though many were still flying dizzily.

"You've got branch pox," Wuthering Winds said to Burrland. "Very contagious. Everyone, fly back!"

Another small twig shot out from Burrland's chin. Even more twigs popped out from his shoulder, his kneecap, and both ears. Twigs even pushed up through his shoes, having grown out of his toes.

"I'll have to take you to the 99th tower at once," Wuthering Winds said. "The rest of you, continue to practice. And stay away from that tree." She pointed to the tree, who seemed to lower its branches in embarrassment. "It will have to be disinfected immediately, or the whole school will come down with branch pox. We can't have another outbreak like we had in 1567."

As she walked Burrland back toward the school, Grackle said, "Burrland is a fool just like his aunt Candlehour."

"Wander Candlehour isn't a fool," I said. "And neither is Burrland."

Grackle rolled his eyes at me, then looked at the new dragon badge on Tolden's cloak. He had gotten it in Candlehour's class for his report on dragon wings. Grackle quickly flew over and ripped the badge off Tolden's cloak.

"Give that back," Tolden said.

Grackle looked at the mist behind us.

"Let's race through the Misty Mile," he said. "If you win, you'll get the badge back."

We'd all heard the rumors about the Misty Mile. It had once been the location of the annual broom race, but that had been canceled a century ago. First, a wizard had disappeared while competing in the race, never to be heard from again. Then a witch had come flying out, backward, and had never gotten turned right. But what really did the race in was when a witch came out with broomsticks for fingers.

It was decided that the trail had been cursed by the sweat and hopelessness of the witches and wizards who had come in last place during all the races that came before. From that day forward the whole trail had been covered in a mist.

"If I race you," Tolden said, "you'll give my badge back?"

"Of course." Grackle smiled at Slithe.

"He's lying," I said. "He's not going to give it back, even if you win."

"I'll tell you what, cauldron baby." Grackle turned his broom around to face me. "You can race, too. And if either of you win, then I'll give the badge back. But we won't get far with these stupid stone bats."

Remembering the lessons from our classes, Grackle held up his wandle and started to fly it like a flapping bat, then cast, *"Say goodbye to rocks and stones. Give me a broom that's all my own!"*

He pointed his wandle at each of our stone bats. They started to flap before breaking away from the brooms and flying off above our heads.

"Never seen bats made out of stone fly before," Egypt said, watching them as if she expected they would drop out of the sky at any moment.

She then turned her eyes to me. "I don't think it's a good idea for you all to do this race, young one," she said. "Monsters tend to hide in the mist."

"It'll be fine," I told her. "It's no scarier than the mist of the swamp back home."

I lined up with Tolden at the starting line determined by the handful of bristles Grackle yanked out of his broom and threw down onto the ground. Then Slithe flew to hover in front of us. He flipped back his school cloak to the tiger cloak he always wore beneath it.

"On your brooms," he said. "Get ready. Fly!"

Slithe threw up his tiger cape until it roared, starting the race.

The three of us turned the handles of our brooms up and headed into the mist. Without the stone bats we could go as high as we wanted, but the mist was so thick, I had to keep close to the ground.

When I nearly flew into a tree branch I said, "I'm going to land, Egypt. I can't see anything."

Egypt started to honk the goose beak. "Just in case there's anything in our way," she said.

I turned the broom handle down to land, and the engine started to cackle louder. That was the warning we were getting close to the ground. I kept my feet down until my boots touched the grass.

Egypt hopped off the broom first. Then I took the key out. The engine made one last cackle before turning off. I started to use the broom to sweep away the mist, the way Aunt Cauldroneyes would when she'd sweep fog off the front porch in the early mornings.

But no matter how much I swept, the mist quickly returned. It was so thick, I got turned around. I didn't realize Egypt wasn't by my side until several minutes later.

"Egypt? Egypt! You walked too far ahead. I can't see you anymore!"

I swept even harder, the mist swirling like dust on the ground. No matter how much I swept, I couldn't find Egypt. Then I heard something. A cracking and crunching sound. I noticed the mist was thinning up ahead. I continued to sweep, getting closer and closer to the sound.

Crack, crack, crunch.

The sounds led me to a clearing in the mist where a wizard was hunched over a pile of wands, eating them. I could hear his teeth breaking against each wand every time he took a bite.

Crack, crack, crunch.

The wizard wasn't alone. He had a creature by his side. "*Grrrr.*"

It was Growling Hat and he was staring right at me.

"*Grrrrrrr.*" The hat growled louder until the wizard stopped eating the wands and slowly stood up to face me. His cloak was a dragon's wing, and as his hood fell back off his head, I saw his bushy red sideburns and wrinkled nose. His hair was even wilder than before. In the daylight, I got a good look at him. He was dressed like the pirates who came in to get hats from Aunt Cauldroneyes. He wore a coat that had an assortment of buttons made out of bone and horn. The coat had wide cuffs covered in feathers, and around his waist, over his vest, was a sash made of night cloth. The stars on it twinkled brightly.

"Ah, the blue-freckled girl." He smiled, showing his broken teeth, before eating the last bite of the wand in his hand.

"You took Aunt Cauldroneyes!" I said as I held the broom like a sword. "What have you done with her?"

He laughed and removed his cloak. It fluttered before falling still on the ground behind him. Without his cloak, I saw his wand shadow draped across his back. The creature was a tangle of tusks, claws, and fangs lit up by strikes of lightning. The shadow had also been ripped in half, and bled faint black smoke that rolled down to the wizard's feet. The smoke disappeared before it touched the ground.

"Tell me where Aunt Cauldroneyes is!" I screamed at him.

"She's busy," he said before flicking a piece of wand from a tooth. "Maybe she is tossing thimbles or somewhere stirring buttons in a cauldron." He grinned. "Isn't that what magical hatmakers do?"

I could tell that the silver talons on the toes of his boots had recently been polished because of how they gleamed.

"Tell me where she is!" I shouted again.

"*Grrrrrr!*" Growling Hat bared his teeth.

The wizard turned to the hat and shouted, "Get her!"

The hat leapt toward me. I quickly held the broom up, catching his mouth on the handle. He bit down so hard, he snapped it, and I fell back onto the ground. As I struggled to get to my feet, the hat grabbed hold of my ankle.

"No!" I screamed. "Let me go!"

The wizard laughed, and I saw he had a wand, broken in half, pushed through the center of his right hand. The wand looked like the creature that had made it. There were patches of reptilian skin, tangles of fur, and gnarled fangs of all sizes. I knew it had been stabbed through his hand long ago. There was already a scar formed around it. A shiny black scar like dried ink.

I could only imagine what horrid spells he would cast, and I tried even harder to get away from Growling Hat. His teeth were clamped down on my pant leg and tearing into the fabric.

I could hear a goose beak honking in the distance.

"Tolden!" I screamed as loud as I could. "I'm over here! Help me!"

Growling Hat started to drag me by the pant leg across the ground toward the wizard, who had a wicked smile across his face.

"Bring her to me!" the wizard ordered.

I tried to grab hold of what I could on the ground. Anything from a tree root to a heavy rock, but Growling Hat only pulled me harder and caused my hands to slip off.

"No!" I cried out just as a creature flew out of the mist.

I didn't realize it was Egypt at first. She had come in so fast, like a streak of lightning.

"Meeeeeooooowwwww!" She dug her claws into the hat. Together they fought, rolling across the ground in a ball of linen and gray fur.

"Foul beast!" The wizard reached into the fight and grabbed Egypt by the linen on the back of her neck. He threw her against a tree. She fell to the ground and didn't move.

"Egypt!" I got up quickly and ran to her.

"I'm okay, Spella." She tried to stand, but couldn't. "It's just my arm," she said. "I'm okay. You must go back to the castle, where you will be safe. I will fight them off. I have built the pyramids. I have—"

The wizard only laughed.

"I'd never leave you," I said to Egypt as I grabbed her up with one hand and laid my other against the tree.

Help us, I wrote on the tree with my fingers in the ancient Elflock language. *Please help us. We need you.*

My freckles started to glow as the tree bark swirled. The woodland unicorn had heard my pleas. I stood back, cradling Egypt, as the ground shifted beneath our feet.

"You can speak to the tees?" the wizard shouted. "That is not possible!"

All around us, trees started to uproot themselves until they became horns on the heads of woodland unicorns rising up from the ground. They snorted and flared their nostrils as they walked toward the wizard. The boulders that made their hooves shook the earth with each step.

"How did you call the herd of the woodland unicorns?" the wizard shouted at me. "No one can do that anymore. I ate the wand of the last tree speaker!"

The unicorns neighed loudly and stomped their hooves. The wizard quickly grabbed his dragon's-wing cloak and Growling Hat.

"Hear my words well, blue-freckled witch," he said with a snarl. "I will one day devour your wand, too."

The mighty unicorns reared up with their own fierce cries before galloping after him until he disappeared into the mist.

Spell No. 1,011

**The witch's cat has a name,
Orange and hot like a flame.
Meow, meow, a whisker's game.
I will take a mad lion's fame.**

Note from the Before Long Witch

If you've ever been bitten by a troll, you'll know it makes for a very bad day. The bite itches like dragon pox, it burns like goblin boils, and it stinks like horseradish. To remedy the bite of a troll, say this spell, because trolls are frightened of cats, and just hearing the word "meow" will be enough to heal any wound from them. This one is best said in the presence of a cat who has just recently purred.

CHAPTER 21
THE WIZARD'S NAME

ONCE THE WIZARD WAS GONE, THE UNICORNS CAME galloping back, churning up green dust with their heels.

"Will one of you please help my cat?" I asked, not bothering to wipe the tears out of my eyes. "Quickly, please. She's hurt."

The largest of the unicorns stepped forward. Her horn was a tall, twisting willow tree. "My name is Earthula," she said. "I will help you."

She came close enough to Egypt to sniff her. Earthula's nostrils flared until I saw moss growing inside them.

"She has a broken arm," Earthula said as I continued

to softly cry. "Not to worry, tree speaker. A broken bone is like a broken branch, and we woodland unicorns know how to mend that."

Earthula dropped her head low enough to point her horn at Egypt's arm. Its willow branches creaked as they swung back and forth. The leaves shook and started to glow.

The unicorns around us pawed at the ground with their boulder hooves, then started to drum them as their neighs turned into chants that I knew were in the ancient Elflock language. They were calling forth the old spirits. They shook their horns, shaking out ghostly strands of pale blue. These phantoms galloped toward Egypt, where they grew smaller and smaller until they disappeared into her broken arm like they were entering a doorway.

"The cat's bone is now mended," Earthula said. "It has been healed by the ghosts of our ancestors."

Egypt held up her arm and moved it as she asked, "You mean I have the ghosts of woodland unicorns in my arm now?"

"That's right," Earthula said.

"I suppose that will mean I will have to gallop every so often to keep them happy." Egypt smiled at her own joke, then said to the unicorn, "Thank you for helping me."

The herd neighed and Egypt meowed with them.

"Oh, Egypt!" I couldn't help but shout out as I grabbed her in a tight hug. "I thought I'd lose you." I buried my face in her linen, which was starting to soak up my tears.

"Lose me?" She purred up against my cheek. "An old, mummied cat like me? You're not going to get rid of me that easy. Besides, I have more chocolate mice left to eat."

She held a piece of her linen up and waited for me to blow my nose on it. Then she wiped the rest of my tears, just as Aunt Cauldroneyes would have.

"We best get out of this forest now," she said. "And back to the school where you're safer, Spella."

"Me and my herd will take you both back to the school, tree speaker," Earthula said. She lowered her head so we could reach the willow's branches and climb up.

The branches wrapped themselves around us as we held tight to the tree's trunk and Earthula galloped through the mist. Egypt quickly learned it's not a good idea to smile with your mouth open when riding a woodland unicorn. She got a mouthful of leaves that she spent the rest of the way spitting out.

The herd came with us. Their hooves pounded the ground while their breath blew out and cleared the mist in front of us until the castle started to come into view.

Waiting at the edge of the Misty Mile were Grackle and Tolden. They were standing with the rest of the students. Wander Wuthering Winds had returned from taking Burrland to Wander Buckleberry in the 99th tower. Folklock stood beside her.

"Wow! Those unicorns are gigantic!" I heard a student say.

"They have trees for horns!" another added.

"I've never seen any like them before!"

They watched as Earthula lowered her head and her branches gently carried me and Egypt back down to the ground.

"Never hesitate to call on us again should you ever need our help, tree speaker," Earthula said with a smile. Then she and the others galloped around us. Their heavy hooves left indentations in the ground that I knew would make rather wonderful ponds for the meadow after the next rain.

They gave one last neigh before returning back into the forest.

"I couldn't find you in the mist, Spella," Tolden said, running up to me. "I tried honking my goose beak, hoping you'd hear it. I didn't get very far and ended up crashing brooms with Grackle." Tolden leaned in closer to whisper, "He used his dragon eye ring to see our way out of the mist. The eye seemed to know the secret of how to get out."

"I have something to tell you that's going to top that," I said. "The wizard who took Aunt Cauldroneyes was in the mist! He was eating wands."

The other students gasped while Wuthering Winds and Folklock looked at each other.

"That means he's back, Herbalia," Wuthering Winds said.

"Take your students inside, Wander Wuthering Winds," Folklock said. "I have to see Spella in my office, immediately."

Egypt stayed with Tolden as I followed Folklock. Her Pegasus shadow flew above our heads as we walked quickly back to the castle.

Once we were in her office, she grabbed a book off the shelf.

"I want to show you a photograph of someone, Spella."

She flipped through the pages. "Tell me if the wizard you saw looked like this."

She pointed to a wizard with red sideburns and eyes that glowed like fire.

"That's him, Headwander!" I slammed my finger down on the photo and pointed it at his face. "That's who has Aunt Cauldroneyes."

His wand shadow was in the photo with him. It was a creature that had horns and tusks, a long fanged snout, and several legs that were crooked and sharp. They were all around the creature's body as if on a wheel.

"I've never seen a wand shadow like that," I said.

"It's a wonderbeast," Folklock said. "When a Wand Keeper corrupts their magic, they corrupt their shadow."

"But who is the wizard?"

"His name is Stonescare," she said.

"Stonescare!" I nearly fell off my feet. "That name was in the library book about the Dragon King. I saw it!"

Folklock nodded. "I saw that book, too. I checked it out myself to try to learn what Stonescare may be up to." She looked down at the photograph. "Your aunt and I have crossed paths with him many times over the centuries, and it has never been pleasant. This photograph of him was taken at a rally *against* plant magic."

"Against it?" I said. "That must be why he hunted down the tree speakers."

"How do you know about that?" she asked.

"He told me in the Misty Mile."

She closed the book. "Did you know that a tree stump

was the first cauldron ever stirred, Spella? That's how close to nature we once were. The first witches spoke the language of the trees and aligned themselves with the great thunderbird. The thunderbird is said to be the oldest magic of all. She is the one who gave the eggs to the first Wand Keepers. As part of his war against plants, Stonescare started to hunt thunderbirds and tree speakers because they represented everything he hated. It was said that he hunted down the last tree speaker eight years ago."

"He hunted them down and ate their wand," I said.

I cringed and thought back to the *crunch* and *crack* sound of him eating the wands in the Misty Mile. Then I remembered his writing in the book at the library and how he had written, *Must find the fire bone. Must wield the fire wand.*

"Headwander Folklock, what would happen if Stonescare were to get one of the most powerful wands of all?" I asked. "What if he were to use the fire wand?"

"He would bring about the volcano world," she said. "Lava would flow across the land. Everything would be on fire. Forests and fields would burn. Rivers and lakes would dry up. We would lose untold species. Our planet would become so hot, no magic would be able to fix it. If Stonescare were to find the fire wand, he would destroy the world."

I looked down at my hand, imagining what it would be like to have a wand pushed through the center of it like Stonescare had.

"His wand was broken in half," I said. "It was through his hand. Why?"

"Do you know why a wand has a shadow, Spella? Because you have to have light to make a shadow. But sometimes a witch or a wizard can be so overcome by darkness that there is not enough light for a shadow, and their wand will force itself through their hand, forever cursing them. Stonescare was doubly cursed, because his shadow ripped in half. One half lives as the lifeless creature on his back, to be carried for the rest of time. The other became the wand, half-formed in his hand."

She stepped over to the window and looked out. From her office you could see the library and the sunlight reflecting in the windows like fire.

"His wand pushed through his hand the night he started the fire in the library," she said.

"But I thought the fire was started by the former headwander?" I asked.

"Stonescare *is* the former headwander of Dragon's Knob, Spella."

CHAPTER 22
A CASE OF GIRAFFE NECK

"THE FORMER HEADWANDER IS THE WIZARD WHO took your aunt?" Tolden asked.

I had run to find both him and Egypt as soon as I left Folklock's office. I didn't have to look far for them. They were in my room, waiting with the hats for me. Egypt was halfway into Tolden's pocket, pulling out sandwich after sandwich until she got a peanut butter and jelly. She was tossing the rest into the tentacles of Mr. Sea Captain, who was handing them out to the hats.

They all listened, holding their breath, as I told them what Folklock had shared.

"Stonescare was the one who had the book in the

library," I said. "He was trying to find out where the Dragon King's tomb is. That's why he sent the goblin dog into the castle."

"To sniff out the Dragon King's bones!" Egypt said. She was growling, and her linen was popping out of its knots. It always did when she got upset.

"If Stonescare can use the goblin dog to track down the bones of the Dragon King," I said, "then Stonescare will find the tomb. He'll be able to wield the fire wand. And that's also why he was reading the book in the library. He was learning about the fire bone and trying to find a hint about where the tomb may be."

"We have to find Stonescare," Egypt said. She was tying her linen back up in knots. I knew she was getting ready to practice the pyramid pinch for the next time she saw him.

"That's the problem," I said. "Folklock doesn't know where he is. She told me in her office that the reason she was gone so long when she returned to the house and Hungry Snout Forest is that she was trying to find out where Stonescare was. She had a feeling he was the one who had taken Aunt Cauldroneyes because of how I had described him with the dragon's-wing cloak and the fiery eyes, but she told me that she didn't want to tell me it might be him in the beginning. She said she knew I would only worry even more if I found out how horrible he was. She went to all the places he usually hung out at to find any information, but he had seemingly disappeared the same night the hat took Aunt Cauldroneyes. No one had seen him since, until I saw him in the Misty Mile."

"But why has he taken the old one?" Egypt asked.

"What reason could he have to kidnap a magical hatmaker?" Tolden asked. He was rubbing his chin in deep thought, while Softfang did the same to hers.

"That I still don't know," I said. "All I do know is we have to find him before he finds the tomb."

"And when we do," Egypt said, "I'll be ready." Her yellow eyes flickered.

The mice hats, overwhelmed by the news, started to whimper. Tolden patted them on their heads, then said, "The good thing is, at least we now know who has Aunt Cauldroneyes. And we know what Stonescare is after. The fire wand. So don't worry," he told the hats. "We've learned a lot. And I guess we have Grackle to thank."

"Grackle?" I said. "Why Grackle?"

"If he hadn't taken my badge, we wouldn't have gone into the Misty Mile, and you wouldn't have seen Stonescare and known he was the same person who took your aunt."

"Don't expect me to thank Grackle Nightcliff for anything." Egypt crossed her arms.

Even by the end of March, the whole school was still talking about the Misty Mile and Stonescare. It was a wonder anyone got through classes without whispering about the former headwander. Added to that, everyone was growing distracted by the warm spring weather, even if it was still frigid in Wander Wormcake's classroom. She had started fresh lessons on wand movements that she said had historically been very popular in the springtime.

"Like the fluttering flap," she said, whipping her wand in front of the blackboard. "There's also the kettle arm. To make this movement, your wand should swoop up, then pour. Everyone, please follow with your wandles. Swoop up and pour."

"Swoop up and pour," we repeated as we swooped our wandles through the air.

"No, no, Burrland." Wormcake shuffled over to his desk. "You're doing far too much swoop and not a long enough pour. It's called the kettle arm, not the swooping arm. Watch how I do it one more time. Swoop—" She started her wand low and raised it up into the air with such a jerk, a piece of zombie skin flicked off her wrist and landed with a splat in front of Egypt. As usual Wander Wormcake didn't notice, and continued from the swoop to the pour.

"Look how long I hold the pour," she said to Burrland, "as if I am filling a large cup with plenty of tea. That is the swoop and pour, and it is a movement you will do well to master because many of the basic spells utilize either a swoop or a pour."

She watched Burrland do the movement again before telling him he would get better if he practiced holding a teakettle for his homework.

Burrland continued to work on the movement as Wander Wormcake shuffled back to the front of the class.

Egypt shook her head at Burrland, who only seemed to get worse with the pouring motion. I think he was just happy to return to classes after his branch pox was healed up by Wander Buckleberry.

When Burrland first came back, he'd told us all about it. He said she'd had to rub a horrible-smelling pink ointment on the branches and leaves coming out of his skin until they dried up and fell off. He said nighttime had been the worst because at any time, a new branch would pop out from his ear and shoot his head off the pillow. He swore to everyone he wasn't still contagious, though we all held our breath each time a small leaf shook out of his hair and fell to the floor.

"Wander Buckleberry said that will happen from time to time." He had sighed when telling it to us. "For the rest of my life, apparently."

Seeing leaves fall out of his hair always made Egypt particularly cautious. As Burrland continued to practice his kettle arm movement, another leaf popped out of his hair there in the classroom. As it floated over the desks, Egypt shouted out, "Nobody touch it!" She ran over and used deep breaths to blow the leaf out one of the open windows.

Wander Wormcake waited for Egypt to hop back up on my desk before she began to teach us about another wand movement.

"It's called the jam jumber," she said. "Hold your wandle out like you're spreading jam on toast, and just keep spreading that jam." She waved her wand back and forth, as a zombie finger rolled out of one of her curls. It dropped to the floor, and I watched it crawl away as Wormcake stepped over to Tolden.

"You are very familiar with sandwiches," she told him. "I can tell. You have an excellent jam-spreading technique. I bet the jam jumber will become one of your signature moves."

She laid a toadstool badge down on his desk. He groaned as she shuffled back up to her desk. He knew toadstool badges tended to give spots to those who touched them, like Softfang, who jumped down onto the desk to grab it. She instantly became covered in purple spots.

"Don't worry," Tolden told her. "The spots only last a few seconds."

We were happy to get out of the chill of Wormcake's classroom and into the warm gardens for Wander Sorcery Fieldfeather's class. He taught agrostology.[42*] We didn't have his class the whole year. It had just started that spring.

"I will teach you the magic of mosses, the language of liverworts," he said, his long beard hanging to his waist. "You will come to learn of the power in a single blade of grass."

He had the type of voice that was great for the theater stage. It was why he was also the drama teacher for third-year students and up. He was currently writing his own one-wizard play. There was a rumor it was going to be all

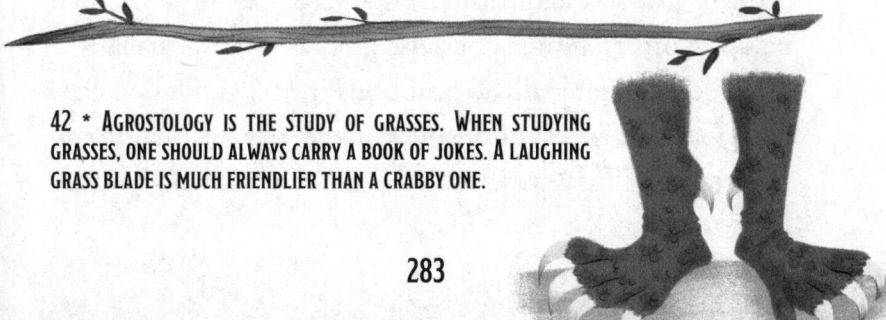

42 * AGROSTOLOGY IS THE STUDY OF GRASSES. WHEN STUDYING GRASSES, ONE SHOULD ALWAYS CARRY A BOOK OF JOKES. A LAUGHING GRASS BLADE IS MUCH FRIENDLIER THAN A CRABBY ONE.

about his wand shadow, which was a grass-backed tortoise nearly as tall as Fieldfeather himself.

It was not unusual to see wheat growing out of Fieldfeather's pockets quite suddenly in the middle of class. And though his lessons were all about fields and meadows, they were also about our cloaks. He was rather obsessed with making sure we swished them just right.

"Like grass in the wind," he said as he asked us to stand up and swing our cloaks from side to side. *"No, no, no."* He ran over to Grackle. "You are swinging too hard, Mr. Nightcliff. *Gently*, like grass in the wind. *Whoosh, whoosh, whoosh.*"

Our quills in Fieldfeather's class were long blades of grass, and the ink, which he said he had made himself, was crushed flower petals.

"I'm a hobby ink maker," he said. No one but Grackle had the heart to tell him the ink was lumpy with petals.

We started out using our pocket-sized cauldrons in his class. The built-in timers came in handy, especially because we used a lot of seeds in his potions. The seeds were always hopping and popping about. By the time we chased them down, we might have overboiled our cauldrons if not for the timers.

"We cannot, however, use a pocket-sized cauldron for growing grass," Fieldfeather announced. "For that, we shall be using dirt cauldrons, because grass is ever so special."

He had arranged the cauldrons in the garden's courtyard for us. The cauldrons were large and sat directly on the ground. They were sculpted entirely of dirt. Because of this, you'd sometimes have an earthworm pop out the side of it or a funny sort of moss suddenly spring to life on the rim.

"That's smoke moss," Fieldfeather told us. "It grows from any condensation that collects on the rim of a cauldron from potion smoke and such. Now, when you're working with dirt cauldrons, you're bound to have a plant grow here and there."

"I got weeds growing inside mine," Grackle said, peering over the rim of his cauldron at the dandelions inside.

"There is no such thing as a weed," Fieldfeather told him. "All plants matter—remember this now, class. And all you have to do when you find some dandelions in your dirt cauldrons is plan to have an especially yellow potion."

I loved having classes outside in the courtyard. The gardens were one of my favorites places. They were full of walking sticks as tall as me, slithering ivy, and roses that changed color to reflect the mood of whoever smelled them. With it being spring, everything was blooming.

"I adore this season," Fieldfeather said in his deep, drawn-out voice. "It is such a wonderful time to grow some grass."

Grackle rolled his eyes and kicked his cauldron, causing a large chunk of dirt to drop off. He quickly knocked it under the cauldron before Fieldfeather saw. I noticed Grackle's dragon-eye ring, which had begun to glow as it watched Fieldfeather's shadow walk around and deliver us each a piece of parchment with the spell written on it.

We all started to arrange our ingredients for the potion

on the wooden tables set up by each of our cauldrons. The ingredients looked more like a compost pile than anything else. There were purple apple peelings coiled around chunks of cabbage noses and rinds of old, mushy pumpkins. Then we had our seeds. There were thistle trick seeds and some flat ones that were called dragon buttons. Egypt helped me count the seeds and troll beans.

"Grass magic is very temperamental," Fieldfeather reminded us as we began to add the ingredients to the cauldron. "If you are one seed off, you risk an explosion."

Right when he said it, a loud explosion popped off in the back of the courtyard. All of us quickly turned around to see Grackle. His entire face was covered in green grass growing out of his skin. The only thing that was longer than the grass was the very end of his nose.

"I told you." Fieldfeather tsk-tsked. "Didn't I tell you? One seed off. That's all it takes. Mr. Nightcliff, you'll have to go see Wander Buckleberry now. She'll need to mow your face."

Fieldfeather reached into a pocket of his long robes and pulled out a very small push lawnmower that fit in the palm of his hand.

"I've kept one of these with me to have handy ever since the same thing happened to me once in my youth," he said. "Only it wasn't grass growing on my face. It was growing on the bottoms of my feet. And I'll have you know, Mr. Nightcliff, feet are even more ticklish when they're being mowed."

He gave the lawnmower to Grackle, who could barely see out of the grass. He took a wobbly step forward, but the grass was growing too fast and was now farther than his nose.

"I can't see anything!" He groaned. "I hate this school! And all these dumb plant spells!"

Egypt whispered to me that she was disappointed grass hadn't grown over his mouth.

"Mr. Wolfice." Fieldfeather sighed. "Take Mr. Nightcliff to the 99th tower."

Slithe led Grackle by the arm back to the castle while the rest of us looked down into our cauldrons, trying to remember how many seeds we'd already put in so the same thing wouldn't happen to us.

"Be very careful, young one," Egypt said as she perched on the rim of my cauldron. "I have already been frozen this year and gone to see Wander Buckleberry. I do not wish see her again in order to be mowed."

"You and me both, Egypt," Tolden said. He was re-counting the seeds on his table to see how many he'd already used.

Meanwhile, Wander Fieldfeather was walking around each student, looking into their cauldrons. When he came to mine, he said, "Very good start, but your potion is too thin."

"So, if I use some more troll beans," I said, "I can thicken it?"

"That's right."

I grabbed some and plunked a couple in. I gave the potion another stir before adding more, just to make sure I didn't add too many.

"I need some more, too," Tolden said, reaching for his sack of troll beans. He dumped the entire lot in, and by the time he stirred his potion, it was as thick as porridge.

"Oh." Fieldfeather made a face. "Mr. Tutters. You'll never grow any grass with a potion that thick."

I chuckled and kept stirring mine until tall blades of fuchsia grass started to grow. They rose up high above the rim of the cauldron and became feathered on top with pale yellow cattails. I could smell the sweet scent coming off the grass.

"It smells and tastes like raspberries," Wander Fieldfeather said, "but one should never eat the purple parts of the grass."

It was too late. Egypt, still sitting on the rim of my cauldron, took a big lick of the grass as soon as Fieldfeather said it tasted like raspberries.

"What will happen?" Egypt asked as grass grew from her nostrils like fuchsia nose hair.

"Oh, nothing that you won't be able to trim," Fieldfeather said, smothering a laugh. "Now, if you had eaten the grass instead of licking it, that would be a different story."

"What magic does the grass do?" Burrland asked.

"Wait for it," Fieldfeather said.

As the cattails blew, their pollen shook off into the wind. Not long after, small winged creatures came flying toward the grass. They were no larger than bees.

"Giraffe flies,"[43*] Fieldfeather said. "Notice how long their necks are."

Whenever one of the giraffe flies landed on a blade of grass, the giraffe would gallop, rather than fly, to the top of the pale yellow cattails.

"Fuchsia grass is becoming quite rare as more of our forests are cut down," Fieldfeather said. "And without fuchsia grass in the world, we will lose the giraffe flies because they only eat this one particular strain of grass. You'll notice they're not eating the purple part, but rather the pale yellow cattails. So to answer your question, Mr. Candlehour, the magic of this grass is the creatures it feeds."

I watched as a bee went buzzing toward the grass and took a bite out of it. Instantly the bee's neck grew until it was like a giraffe's, only striped black and yellow.

"Oh, that happens from time to time," Fieldfeather said. "The grass is full of all the vitamins and minerals that a neck needs to grow long. Don't worry about the bee. Hives have the magic to take care of their own."

Fieldfeather called his shadow to his hand, where it turned into a tortoiseshell-covered wand. With it, he conjured a badge that was shaped like a giraffe fly and handed it to me.

43 * Giraffe flies look identical to land giraffes, only they're much smaller and have the wings of a dragonfly.

"Well done, Spella," he said.

As he continued to walk around and look over the shoulders of the other students, I watched the bee with the long neck buzz away. Then I picked off a grass blade and put it in my pocket just as rain started to fall.

"Oh no." Fieldfeather held his arms up. "Rain is never good for dirt cauldrons."

The fat drops of water landed on the cauldrons and started to turn the dirt into mud.

"Everyone, back inside!" Fieldfeather led the way, his cloak swishing behind him.

His classoom was next to the courtyard. Once we were back inside it, we stared out the windows at the cauldrons melting down into mud puddles.

While the others watched out the windows, I reached into my pocket and pulled out the blade of grass.

"What are you doing with that?" Tolden asked me.

"I'll show you after class."

As soon as Wander Fieldfeather ended the lesson for the day, I ran with Tolden and Egypt up to Hisses and Hoots Hall.

"There's something up there," I said, pointing to the ceiling at the end of the hallway.

It was lined with exposed trusses that were covered in spiderwebs spun over the centuries. There were even a few bats swinging from their feet. And in the highest parts of the ceiling, where it was dark, you saw only pairs of eyes.

"What are we searching for, exactly?" Tolden asked. He and Softfang were looking together.

"The web," I said.

"Which one?" Egypt shrugged. "There's thousands of them."

"I know," I said. "That's why I have to get closer, so I can be sure it is what I think it is. I saw it this morning and I thought about asking Mr. Sea Captain to use one of his tentacles to hold me up there, but I didn't want to get his or the other hats' hopes up just yet."

"What do you mean, young one?" Egypt asked.

"I mean that one of those webs up there isn't from a spider," I said. "At least, I don't think it is. That's why I got this, so I can be sure." I pulled the grass out of my pocket. "You saw what it did to the bee that ate it. Well, I'm in need a rather long neck at the moment."

"Don't you dare eat that grass," Egypt said, but I quickly took a bite before she could stop me.

Almost immediately my collar started to stretch. The buttons popped off my shirt, and my neck started to grow so long, I was looking down on Tolden and Egypt, who were looking up at me.

"You've got spots on your neck just like a giraffe," Tolden said as he watched my long neck sway under the weight of my head. "You'll have to go see Wander Buckleberry for that."

But I wasn't thinking about being a girl with a giraffe neck or having to go see Wander Buckleberry. I was only thinking about seeing the web in the corner up close. My long neck kept making my head wobble, but finally I was able to control it enough to lean toward the web.

"I didn't notice that one until now," Egypt said, her eyes starting to shine.

"Isn't it an ordinary spiderweb?" Tolden asked with a shrug.

"It's not like the other ones," I said, my head swaying on my neck. "It's not made out of spider silk. It's made out of thread. Aunt Cauldroneyes' thread!"

Spell No. 801

Shake, shake, shiver.
Like a snake, you will slither.
Shake, shake, shiver.
Bring forth the river.

Note from the Before Long Witch

Tie a blue ribbon around the end of your wandle while you speak these words, and you will summon enough water to fill a glass. Not useful for extreme thirst, but this spell is particularly handy if you find yourself in the desert with a sphinx. And on a unicorn's birthday you can use this spell to wash away the white frosted cake crumbs that you'll be sure to have around your mouth.

CHAPTER 23
INTO THE DUNGEONS

AUNT CAULDRONEYES USED TO TELL ME A STORY OF Grandmother Spider. She said that in the beginning of the world, only part of it was in the light. Seeking to be free of the darkness, the animals banded together. They decided to go to the part of the world that had the sun, and take some of it for themselves. The 'possum offered to go first, and hid the light in his furry tail. But the sun was too bright and burned his fur away.

"It's why the 'possum has a bald tail to this day," Aunt Cauldroneyes told me.

The buzzard tried next. He flew to the sun, taking some to carry upon his head. But the light scorched his feathers.

"To this day," Aunt Cauldroneyes said, "he is bald-headed."

Then Grandmother Spider, the woman with webs between her hands, made herself tiny and took a lump of clay that she formed into a bowl. She spun her web and strung it across the world until she reached the sun. She was so very small that no one saw her scoop pieces of the light and drop them into her bowl. She followed her web back home, carrying the sun in her bowl and bringing light to the world.

"She is the mother of witches," Aunt Cauldroneyes said. "Because we are all spiders at heart."

I was reminded of the story of Grandmother Spider when I spotted the web in the corner and I knew immediately that it had to do with Aunt Cauldroneyes.

After all, I had learned all about thread from the best hatmaker in the world. I knew how some could be thin enough to hold the tiny seeds of toadstools, and how others were so heavy that it could only be found with the rocks.

"Keep your eyes open to the world, Spella," Aunt Cauldroneyes had told me. "There are many spools of thread. An owl's talon, a fire's whorl, a telescope that has seen the farthest stars. If you pull at things in life, you will find that thread unravels from them. Make from it what you will, but try to make something wonderful and wise."

She had taught me how to reach into the darkness of a keyhole and pull black thread out, and how to lift the leaves of an ivy just right to find the coil of something green and earthy to sew with. Spools of thread for me were things in the world, but to her, the spools were her hands. Over the years, I had studied her thread. The thickness. The shine. The tension. Out of a thousand strands collected together, I would be able to recognize Aunt Cauldroneyes' thread anywhere.

After I found the web in the corner of the hallway, I wanted to immediately find more. But Egypt said I had to go see Wander Buckleberry first to get rid of my giraffe neck. I spent the rest of that afternoon in the 99th tower drinking a bitter potion to de-stretch my neck. I still had a few giraffe spots on my skin, but Buckleberry said those would go away in a few days.

Egypt had stayed with me while I drank the potion, and watched my neck get shorter and shorter. Egpyt had to drink her own potion to get the grass out of her nose. Once we were finally away from the tower, I grabbed her up into a hug and spun her around until we were both dizzy.

"Aunt Cauldroneyes has to be leaving us messages in the thread!" I said. "I don't know how she's doing it yet. But she's making the webs appear somehow, from wherever she is trapped. I just know it, Egypt! You remember the story she would tell us of Grandmother Spider? Once the world was dark, but Grandmother Spider found the light and took it back home by following her web. That's what we'll do. We'll follow Aunt Cauldroneyes' webs."

That night, I snuck out of my room with Egypt while

Hartshorn snored from his bed. We tiptoed down the hall and met Tolden, who waited for us.

"Good thing my dodo is a heavy sleeper, too," he said. Softfang was yawning by his ear, but Tolden was wide awake. "Ready to find some webs?" he asked.

We followed the first one from the corner in Hisses and Hoots Hallway. It wasn't long before we spotted another between the arms of a chandelier, then one wrapped around the corks of potion bottles on a shelf. The webs were leading us through the castle like breadcrumbs.

Egypt was especially excited, running up ahead, her eyes darting to find the next. Softfang was no longer yawning. She was skipping across Tolden's head, her little hand over her eyes and on the lookout.

We found webs lying like lacy handkerchiefs on the rugs and in the corners of the windows. Even between the hands of the largest of the grandfather clocks. Each web we found made us so excited, we would shout out in whispers so as not to wake anyone else, "There's another one and another one!"

Before we knew it, we had followed the webs all the way to a darkened hallway that ended at a staircase going down.

"I've never been on this side of the castle before," Tolden said in a whisper.

But I had. It was the hallway where I'd seen the goblin dog.

As Egypt held her nose in the air and sniffed as if doing so would help her find the next web, I walked over to the staircase. I could feel cold air coming up the steps.

"Hey, there's the spider," Tolden said, pointing above my head.

I looked up to see a silver spider working quickly to spin the thread that was wrapped around her body, as if she were a spool.

"Never seen a spider like that," Tolden said. "She's shiny, like she's covered in diamonds."

"She's the last of her kind," I said. "She's a Star Spider. She lives in Aunt Cauldroneyes' hair."

"The old one gave some of her thread to the spider," Egypt said, "to weave it into webs. In an old castle, one spiderweb could be lost among others like it. But a web made out of thread would catch the eye of a fellow hatmaker. You, Spella." Egypt winked at me.

"The spider crawled to the other side of the world," I said, remembering the words from the story of Grandmother Spider, "and she was so very small that no one noticed her."

"Hey, don't you guys think that the web is shaped like an arrow?" Tolden asked. "An arrow pointing down." He looked toward the staircase. More cold air was coming up the steps. "Where do you think they go?"

"To the dungeons."

We turned around to see Hartshorn.

"What are you doing on this side of the castle, Wand Keepers?" he asked.

"Aunt Cauldroneyes is here, Hartshorn!" I said. I spoke as fast as my heart was racing. "I know she's left these webs for us to find. We have to go down there!"

He stepped over to stand at the top of the staircase. "I should have known Stonescare might keep her in the dungeons," he said. "It's where he likes to keep everything he traps. We can't go down there. He's far too dangerous."

"If Aunt Cauldroneyes is in the dungeons, I'm going." I started to walk past him, but he held his wing out. The one like a ship's sail.

"Do you want to know what happened to my wing?" he asked. "And why we dodos have silver scars on our ankles? When Stonescare was the headwander, he would chain us in the dungeons. There was no warmth except from our hot breath, until he stole our fire."

Hartshorn raised his eyes to mine.

"Once upon a time I was a fire-breather," he said. "But a dodo dragon doesn't have a fire bone. We are birds half the time, and we have only a gift from our mother that is as fragile as a single flame. A wizard can extinguish that easily. After Stonescare stole our fire I tried to fly away, so he took my wing to punish me." He looked down at the artificial wing. "I can't go down to the dungeons again. I'm sorry, Wand Keeper Spella. I'm just not that brave."

He ran back down the hall.

"He's going to get Folklock," Egypt said.

"I'm not waiting," I said, turning to the staircase. "None of you have to go with me, but I need to see if Aunt Cauldroneyes is in the dungeons."

"I go where you go, young one," Egypt said.

"Me too, Spella." Tolden didn't hesitate. Softfang had wrapped her tail around his ear and was nodding. She held a piece of Tolden's floppy hair like a sword pointed forward.

"Be very quiet," Egypt told us as we walked down the staircase. "We don't want anyone to know we're coming."

Two-headed lizards quickly scurried up the stone walls and across our fingers as we felt our way down the stairs. It was darker at first, but as we went deeper into the dungeons, we saw the lower portions were lit by torches on the walls.

"Look there." Egypt pointed at the faint glow casting out from under a closed door. We could hear voices from inside the room.

"I want that hat finished tonight!" A man shouted. I had heard that voice before. It belonged to Stonescare.

"I'm trying," a woman said, her voice like the warmth of soup, even in a dungeon. "Hat-making takes time."

"Aunt Cauldroneyes!" I whispered. We ran to the closed door. There were old claw marks that had left gaps wide enough in the wood to see into the room.

"It's her, young one." Egypt kept her voice low as she laid her paw on my arm.

"You found her, Spella." Tolden grabbed my other hand, and we shared a gap to look at Aunt Cauldroneyes. She was sitting at a sewing table. Her back was to us, so I couldn't tell what type of hat she was working on. I could only see her shadow cast on the dungeon's wall, showing the thread spinning from her hands. I knew she wasn't sewing quickly. Her braids hung down to her bare feet, which were dirty with the dust of the dungeon.

She looked thinner. I could only imagine what Stonescare had fed her. Certainly no cinnamon buttons or chocolate curl or caramel thread, all the things a magical hatmaker likes most.

Worst of all, I saw a shackle around each of Aunt Cauldroneyes' ankles, chaining her to the leg of the sewing table.

"Aren't you the best magical hatmaker in the world?" Stonescare shouted, his shaggy red sideburns framing the fire in his eyes.

He was pacing in front of the table. The silver talons on his black boots clacked against the stone floor. He had Growling Hat on top of his head and was wearing robes made of night cloth. The fabric glowed in a full moon, while clouds swirled on his long sleeves. The stars shining from his collar lit up the dragon's wing of his cloak, speckling it with billions of tiny lights.

"I have the best magical hatmaker right in front of me," he said. "And yet it takes you months to make a single hat!"

"This is no ordinary hat," Aunt Cauldroneyes said. She kept her stitches steady despite his rage.

"I know what you've been doing all this time." He slammed his fists onto the sewing table and leaned in toward her. "Do you think me stupid? I am fast as lightning, quick as sand. I am the wand in the hand. I know *everything*."

He smiled, showing her his broken teeth. There were pieces of wand stuck to them like crumbs.

"You've been sewing slowly on purpose," he said, stepping away from the table. "I know that. But I also know we had a deal. You were to make my hat or I would have another magical hatmaker make it for me. A blue-freckled hatmaker. Know of anyone by that description, Cauldroneyes?"

He took Growling Hat off his head.

"Grrrrr." The hat snarled as Stonescare turned him upside down and held him against Aunt Cauldroneyes' ear.

"This hat is full of many frightful caves," Stonescare said. "You know that, hatmaker. Luckily for you, I let you out of the hat. But if I were to capture the blue-freckled girl, I would not be so kind. And there are many monsters in those caves who eat nothing but blue freckles."

"No, you will leave her alone!" Aunt Cauldroneyes shouted. "I'm nearly finished."

"Ha! You've been saying that every single night." Stonescare let Growling Hat down to scurry across the dungeon floor and chew on an old bone in the corner.

"Tell me that hat will be finished now!" Stonescare threw his arms up into the air. I stared at the wand stabbed through his right hand.

"Yes, yes," Aunt Cauldroneyes said, sewing fast enough for her braids to start to rise.

"Grrrrrrrrr." The hat was growling at something in the corner of the dungeon.

It was the goblin dog. He whimpered while the hat snapped at his legs.

"How many times do I have to tell you to stop bothering that beast!" Stonescare used his boot to knock Growling Hat back. "He hasn't fulfilled his purpose yet."

Stonescare turned his flaming eyes upon the dog.

"Leave him alone." Aunt Cauldroneyes stood from the sewing table.

"I can't," Stonescare said, stepping closer to the dog, who backed up against the wall, his chains and shackles shaking with him. "He still hasn't found me the bones of the Dragon King."

"I've tried," the dog said. "I haven't smelled dragon bones anywhere in the castle, and I've looked as best as I can. 'Course, I never have had such good a nose after my own brother shoved swamp mud up it one time."

"You fool!" Stonescare raised his hand to slap the dog, but Aunt Cauldroneyes spun threads across the dungeon and wrapped them around his wrist before he could.

"I told you to leave him alone," she said.

The fire in Stonescare's eyes burned so fiercely, smoke rose to his bushy eyebrows.

"Ah," he said, his voice eerily calm, "the threads of a spider witch. But the thing about spiders is that their webs are so easily broken."

He used his teeth to snap the threads, then moved toward Aunt Cauldroneyes.

"Speaking of spiders, let's see how yours is doing," he said.

He reached into the pocket of his shirt and pulled out a small glass bottle. He held it up in front of Aunt Cauldroneyes' face, before realizing the bottle was empty. He bared his teeth and snarled.

"One should never keep a Star Spider in a glass bottle," Aunt Cauldroneyes said. "If you had cared to know more about them, you would have known that a Star Spider can weave a sword. It takes many months, of course, to weave one that is strong enough to break through glass."

Stonescare's face twisted in fury as he turned the bottle over and saw that the glass had been broken. The hole was just large enough for a Star Spider to escape.

Stonescare roared and threw the bottle, shattering it against the wall.

"This means we have even less time," he said. "I'm sure you've sent your spider on an errand, clever hatmaker."

He flung up his cloak and faced the wall, his breath racing with his thoughts.

"You've left me no choice," he said, jerking around to Aunt Cauldroneyes. "I'm going to get the blue-freckled girl."

"No!" Aunt Cauldroneyes cried out. "You promised you wouldn't hurt her, Stonescare."

"I only promised that as long as you kept your promise to make me my hat!" he shouted back. "You have not kept your end of the bargain, so I will not keep mine."

"He's coming." Tolden's whisper was full of fear as the three of us fell back from the door.

Just before it opened, Aunt Cauldroneyes shouted, "Wait! I have finished your hat, Stonescare."

We slowly crawled back to the cracks in the door to see Stonescare turn on his heel to face Aunt Cauldroneyes as she made the last stitch and cut the thread. She stood away from the table, her chains only allowing her to take a single step, but enough to reveal what she had made. It was not a hat at all but a crown.

"The crown of the Dragon King," Tolden whispered.

You might think a king's crown would be made of gold and jewels. But the Dragon King was beloved by all, because it wasn't riches that he valued, but rather the kingdom he had served. Instead of gold, the crown was woven with the ancient wood of Warps, which I knew took months to become soft enough to braid. The jewels were not emeralds and diamonds, but rather knotted twigs and leaves, and there was a garland of moss with charms of starlight crystals. Arches carved from tree rings encircled the crown, and patches of fabric filled the center.

Unlike the hats I had made with Aunt Cauldroneyes, I knew the crown would have taken the longest. Tree rings can only be carved on nights the wind blows in from the west. Starlight crystals will only be found in the foam of raging seas and the type of fabric she had used was woven from the layers of the earth.

"It's incredible," Tolden whispered.

"I thought it would have been bigger," Egypt said in a hushed voice.

"She had to make it in a size to fit a wizard," I said quietly as Stonescare took the crown in his hands.

"Grrrrrr."

Growling Hat was close to the door. We could hear his claws dragging across the stone on the other side. He was sniffing like a dog tracking a scent. Then I smelled it, too. Tolden's grams' perfume wafting up from his pocket.

"Grrrrrrrrrrrr."

"Oh, shut up, you!" Stonescare shouted at the hat.

"Grrrrrrrrrrrrrrrrrr." The hat scratched harder at the door.

"C'mon." Egypt grabbed me by the arm. "We have to get out of here. We have to get Folklock."

"I can't leave Aunt Cauldroneyes," I said.

Growling Hat was clawing so hard, we could hear the wood splintering just before the door was thrown open. Stonescare stood there, looking down at us.

"Ah, welcome to my dungeons!" He grinned, then held up his right hand. He pointed the broken end of his wand at the stone walls and waved it like a fast-moving snake as he cast a spell. *"Make them stay as if caught in a cage. Make them stay until old age."*

"Run!" Egypt shouted. But it was too late. Chains and shackles flew out from the walls and wrapped around our ankles, pulling us back. Egypt tried to dig her claws into the stone floor, but she only left scratch marks.

"Spella!" Aunt Cauldroneyes cried out. She tried to run to me, but her chains were too short and she was yanked backward toward the table.

I tried to run to her, but my chains weren't long enough, either.

"Oh, Spella, what are you doing here?" she asked as blue buttons fell down her cheeks.

"I followed the thread webs to find you," I said.

"Oh, little dear." Aunt Cauldroneyes sighed. "Those were for Folklock to see. I never meant to put you in any danger."

"What a lovely little reunion of the hatmakers," Stonescare said as Growling Hat rumbled at his side. "Now I have everything I want. My new crown, and all of you left to rot in these dungeons."

"Let us go!" Tolden tried to twist out of his shackles. Softfang was doing her best to help him by trying to chew the iron, but her fangs were too soft.

"You don't need them, Stonescare," Aunt Cauldroneyes pleaded. "I made your hat. Now let them go."

Egypt hissed and bared her teeth at Stonescare.

"I never let anything go," he said. "You should know that, hatmaker."

Egypt clawed the air toward him. He raised his wand and pointed it at her.

"Wait!" I shouted. "I'll tell you where the tomb of the Dragon King is, if you let everyone go."

"Spella, no!" Aunt Cauldroneyes cried out.

"How could someone like you possibly know where the tomb is, when I don't?" Stonescare stepped closer to me. "I am curious about you, I will admit. Curious about how you spoke to the trees, you little blue-freckled witch. Maybe you are only a trickster. Maybe you are trying to trick me now."

He held his up wand again, this time pointing it at Aunt Cauldroneyes.

"The library!" I shouted. "The tomb is in the library. I'll take you to where it is. If you agree to let them go."

"Don't show him where it is, Spella!" Tolden said.

"I have to! He'll hurt all of you."

Stonescare knelt down to stare into my eyes, the fires in his flickering out toward me.

"Chains be gone, you are now free." He circled his wand like he was stirring a cauldron over my chains and shackles. *"But do not think you can ever flee."*

The iron broke away, releasing me. He quickly grabbed my hand and yanked me by it.

"You will show me where the tomb is," he said, picking up the crown off the sewing table as we passed it.

"I said let them go first!" I tried to pull away. "Let them go!"

He lost his grip on my hand, pulling off my spider glove instead and sending me barreling to the floor. Before he could grab my hand again, a shadow fell over his face.

We looked up to see a dragon stepping in through the door, his irises split with bolts of lightning.

CHAPTER 24

A Battle between Dragons

"HARTSHORN!" I SMILED.

"You came back!" Tolden's eyes lit up, as did Softfang's.

"Let them go, Stonescare," Hartshorn boomed.

"Dodo, nice to see you again," Stonescare said, laughing. "Ah, you've gotten your wing replaced, I see. I rather like wearing your old one as my cloak."

Stonescare threw the winged cloak up behind him. It flapped in the air as I got to my feet and ran into Aunt Cauldroneyes' open arms. As soon as I did, shackles came back out of the dungeon's walls and chained me. But at least I was with Aunt Cauldroneyes this time.

"Oh, how I've missed you, little dear." She started to

check me all over like how she would check the hats after they'd played in the forest. "Are you hurt anywhere?"

"I'm fine now that I've found you." I hugged her tighter. I only wished Egypt and Tolden were closer. Their chains were on the other dungeon wall, too far away.

"I want you to leave Dragon's Knob," Hartshorn said as he started to circle Stonescare. "And never return."

"Does a dodo dare tell me what to do?" Stonescare raised the crown in his hands.

"Don't let him put it on!" Aunt Cauldroneyes shouted.

Hartshorn quickly used his tail to knock Stonescare's feet out from under him. He fell against the stone floor, striking his head and knocking himself out. The crown rolled across the floor, close to Tolden. He tried to grab it, but his chains were too short.

"I can't reach it!" He gritted his teeth and stretched his fingers as far as he could.

Hartshorn headed toward the crown himself, but Growling Hat ran over and bit him on the foot, drawing blood. The hat then jumped high up in the air and landed on Hartshorn's head.

"Be careful!" Aunt Cauldroneyes shouted. "The hat will pull you in."

Growling Hat quickly started to yank Hartshorn up in a swirling wind, just like what had happened back home in the attic when the hat stole Aunt Cauldroneyes. Hartshorn roared as his large body twisted through the air and he began to disappear into the hat, until the last we saw of him was the talon on his smallest toe.

"Hartshorn—" I buried my face into Aunt Cauldroneyes' side.

She patted my back and said, "I don't think we've seen the last of your Hartshorn."

Growling Hat burped. I looked up and saw he was absolutely stuffed. His gray fabric was stretched so tight, clumps of fur were popping off and his thread had started to spread at the seams.

"He looks about ready to burst," I said.

His tail whipped from side to side, shedding more gray fur as he burped again. One of the knots of fur popped right off and struck Stonescare in the nose. He was still lying on the floor. He blinked his fiery eyes and sat up.

Shaking his head, Stonescare turned to see the crown and quickly rose to his feet. As he ran toward it, I shouted to Tolden, "Your sandwiches!"

Tolden looked confused.

"Your sandwiches!" I shouted again, and made a throwing motion with my arm.

Tolden nodded with a grin, then reached into the pocket of his cardigan and pulled out one of his grams' peanut butter and jelly sandwiches. He threw it at Stonescare. It smacked him in the forehead and left a trail of jelly down his nose as the bread slid down.

"I knew I liked that boy and his sandwiches!" Egypt meowed.

Tolden reached into his pocket for another and threw. This time it was egg salad, which left bits of mayonnaise in Stonescare's sideburns.

"Aaaagh!" Stonescare's rage echoed off the dungeon walls as he tried to wipe egg out of his eyes.

Tolden quickly threw another.

"Grilled cheese," he said, smiling. "My favorite!"

The gooey cheese covered Stonescare's face, and he started to sneeze.

"That'll be Grams' perfume!" Tolden shouted. He kept reaching into his pocket, pulling out sandwich after sandwich. They hurled through the air and hit Stonescare in the face, until he held up his right hand.

"At three and four the centaurs snore," Stonescare cast. *"Knock on the door, a noise no more."*

Stonescare's wand howled and shot forth a flaming sword that struck Tolden down. He landed on the floor with a thud, his eyes closed.

"Tolden!" I shouted, but Aunt Cauldroneyes held me tight.

"He'll be okay," she said. "It's only a sleeping spell."

Tolden wasn't the only one enchanted. Softfang lay asleep on his shoulder.

"How dare anyone throw sandwiches at me!" Stonescare wiped the bits of food off his face and shook his head, causing tomato and lettuce to fly from his bushy hair.

Knocking a bread slice off his shoulder, he noticed the crown.

"Finally it's mine!" He showed his broken teeth in a smile as he picked the crown up, just as Growling Hat burped again. This time it was so loud, it rumbled the stone walls.

Even Stonescare stopped to stare at the hat and the thread snapping along the fabric's seams.

"How many times have I told you not to eat so fast?" Stonescare said just as a button popped off the hat and smacked him in the nose.

"Thank goodness for big dragons," Aunt Cauldroneyes whispered to me as the fabric on Growling Hat ripped down the middle and Hartshorn's tail pushed through.

"*Grrrrrrrrr.*" The hat growled one final time before he was torn apart in a cloud of smoke and puffs of gray fur that, when cleared, revealed Hartshorn the dragon.

Stonescare quickly put the crown on.

"No!" Aunt Cauldroneyes yelled.

A tail shout out from Stonescare, while scales ripped apart his clothing and horns rose from his wild hair as the crown grew with him. His shaggy red sideburns thickened as his face twisted into a long snout. He had become a dragon that dwarfed Hartshorn.

"I'm not afraid of you anymore, Stonescare," Hartshorn said, standing taller.

"Then I will make you afraid." Stonescare lunged at Hartshorn and bit the side of his face.

"Leave him alone!" I picked up stones from the dungeon floor and hurled them at Stonescare, but they only bounced off his hard scales as if they were nothing more than pebbles.

Stonescare laughed and grabbed Hartshorn by the back of the neck. The two dragons rolled in a twisted tangle of arms and legs, until they slammed into the wall. Stonescare opened his mouth wide, but no fire came out.

"No matter what you think," Hartshorn told him, "you're not a real dragon. You can't breathe fire."

"Neither can you!" Stonescare grabbed Hartshorn and started to spin him around by the tail.

Hartshorn's claws dragged across the dungeon walls, creating sparks, as he tried to catch hold of something to stop the spinning.

"You have always been nothing but a weak dodo," Stonescare yelled.

When he let Hartshorn's tail go, the dodo dragon flew through the air. Though he tried to flap his wings to steady himself, he was going too fast. He hit the wall with a hard smack and slid down, his heavy head landing on the floor. His body fell still.

"Hartshorn! Oh no, Hartshorn!" I called his name over and over again.

"What have you done, Stonescare?" Aunt Cauldroneyes cried out.

He wiped the sweat off his brow, then stomped toward us.

"No." Aunt Cauldroneyes threw herself in front of me. "You're not hurting her!"

"Don't worry," he told her. "You're coming, too. I want to make sure the girl knows that if she doesn't show me exactly where the tomb is, she will see just how angry a dragon wizard can be toward an old magical hatmaker."

Spell No. 420

Funny apples and gray owls,
I'll stop you with a goblin's growl.

Note from the Before Long Witch
Be sure to howl and growl when speaking this combat spell. You must be convincing, or the spell will sense your hesitation and not cast. This spell is especially helpful when exploring ancient ruins, because you're likely to cross paths with the rock warts, a fearsome group of predators who like to steal shoes and make you walk home on rocks barefoot.

CHAPTER 25
The Tomb of the Dragon King

EGYPT WAS STILL CHAINED TO THE DUNGEON'S WALL and could only growl and hiss at Stonescare as he grabbed me and Aunt Cauldroneyes with his talons. He held us tightly as he carried us past Hartshorn, who was lying on the floor, his eyes closed.

"Hartshorn!" I called his name as I wiped the tears from my cheeks. "Please be okay, Hartshorn."

"He never did have the heart of a dragon," Stonescare said.

"You will not get away with this!" Aunt Cauldroneyes shouted as Stonescare flew us back up the staircase.

Like the dungeons, the castle had been built for a

Dragon King, with hallways wide enough for wings. As Stonescare flew, there were no staircases too narrow for him, no doorways too small. I hoped there might be someone up, wandering the halls. But everyone was in bed, unaware that Stonescare was about to take the fire wand for his own.

Having once been the headwander, he knew the fastest way to the library. He dived into its doors and threw them open, startling Wander Velvetfoot, who was sitting at her desk, reading.

"What is going on here?" she shouted, rising to her feet. Stonescare ignored her and instead held me close to his face.

"Where is the tomb, blue-freckled girl?" he roared.

"Let them go!" Wander Velvetfoot said as the little book whimpered and ran up her skirt. "Let them go, then get out of my library."

"You know where it is, don't you, old 'possum?" He turned his eyes to hers. She recognized them at once.

"Stonescare?" Velvetfoot's voice trembled. "But how are you a dragon?"

He tilted his head at her and she gasped when she saw the crown.

"I am the king now," he said, to which the candles in the library blew out, leaving only the moonlight cast through the dome in the ceiling and the lamp burning from Velvetfoot's desk.

"What do you want?" she asked.

"You know what I want." He ran his long dragon tongue

over his teeth. "I want to know where the tomb is. Tell me, old librarian, or this hatmaker and her blue-freckled girl will be nothing but a dragon's dessert."

He gripped me and Aunt Cauldroneyes more tightly in his claws.

"Don't hurt them," Velvetfoot said, before stepping over to the tall books on the shelf behind her desk. She tenderly pulled one out and helped it stand in front of us. It was the book *Into the Fire* by Nogard Bmot.

"I don't want a stupid book!" Stonescare bellowed and stomped his feet. "I want the tomb."

"It is the tomb," I said. "'Nogard Bmot' is 'Dragon Tomb' written backward."

Wander Velvetfoot looked at me. "You are a smart girl, Spella."

"It's probably just another trick from a blue-freckled witch," Stonescare snarled.

"Isn't it funny?" Velvetfoot said to Stonescare. "Had you succeeded in burning down the library, you would have destroyed the very thing you sought."

He gnashed his teeth at her before saying, "Out of the way, old 'possum." He shoved her back, then threw me and Aunt Cauldroneyes to the floor. He stomped toward the book.

"Are you okay, little dear?" Aunt Cauldroneyes quickly grabbed me up. Velvetfoot huddled with us.

"You made him the crown of the king, Mathilda?" Velvetfoot asked.

"I had to," Aunt Cauldroneyes said. "He was going to

harm Spella. I tried to sew as slow as I could, hoping to escape or be found before I finished the crown."

"He'll be able to get into the tomb now." Velvetfoot's voice was soft but frightened.

"I thought the tomb was enchanted," I said.

"Oh, it is," she said. "No one but the Dragon King can enter it. And since the Dragon King is already buried inside the tomb, well, Stonescare had to come up with a different way to get in. By wearing the king's crown, he becomes the king. The tomb will be tricked into unlocking itself."

As soon as Stonescare stood in front of the book, the cover flew open and the pages started to flip themselves until a large doorway was revealed, leading into what appeared to be a very long hallway.

A draft of cold air blew through, rustling Velvetfoot's skirt and Aunt Cauldroneyes' braids as we started to back away.

"We have to get help," Velvetfoot whispered, but Stonescare used his long tail to stop us.

"You're not going anywhere," he said.

His tail pushed us into the book, and he followed behind us, his large body blocking any chance of escape.

The hallway opened into a huge oval chamber. It was lined with windows that looked out upon the kingdom. It was another room of the castle. An invisible one that could only be entered through the doorway of the book. In the center were five statues carved from old gray trees, some of the smaller branches left in place to shed bright crimson leaves to the floor. Each statue was carved into a creature from the kingdom. There was a unicorn, a troll, a goblin, a centaur, and a griffin. They were dressed in soldier armor. They stood around the sarcophagus of the Dragon King as the last of his army.

"Open the tomb of the creaking bones." Stonescare read the words engraved on the outside of the coffin. *"Tell me the secrets of the throne."*

The lid of the coffin slid off, and a heavy mist escaped. Once it cleared, the Dragon King's skeleton was revealed.

"The fire wand," Stonescare said, his eyes widening as he reached toward the long bone that lay where the dragon's throat had once been.

"Stonescare, don't!" Aunt Cauldroneyes pleaded. "If you wield that wand, the world will be nothing but a volcano. You will destroy everything and everyone."

"It will only be the end for your precious plants," he snarled. "Then you will see they have no power at all. The trees will melt. Your herbs will burn. Your green vines will wither away. And in that world of fire, I will show you true magic." He smiled. "I will be the new Dragon King!"

Once he wrapped his fingers around the fire bone, it ignited. He pointed the burning wand at one of the windows. A bolt burst out and broke through the glass to set fire to the trees and fields around the castle. Smoke rose into the sky as birds flew to escape and herds of animals fled the forest.

"We have to do something," Wander Velvetfoot said, tears falling down her cheeks. "He's going to burn it all to ash."

Stonescare pointed the fiery wand at every window until they were all broken by the flames that flew out into the world.

"Do you still have the feather from the River Eagle?" I asked Aunt Cauldroneyes.

She looked at me, her eyes starting to twinkle. "Yes, of course I still have that feather." She reached into her pocket and pulled it out. "A forager is a woman of many pockets, after all."

She handed the feather to me, and I held it up toward Stonescare as if it were a better wand than his.

He laughed and said, "You think a feather will stop me?"

I whirled the feather through the air.

"Thank you, kind eagle, for your magic," I chanted. *"From one, I make you many. Bring a rain of plenty."*

"From one, I make you many," Aunt Cauldroneyes and Velvetfoot chanted with me. *"Bring a rain of plenty. From one, I make you many. Bring a rain of plenty!"*

The feather flew out of my hand and up above our heads. It divided and grew, becoming a flock of hundreds of River Eagles.

Stonescare turned the wand upon them, but the water of their bodies only extinguished each bolt of fire he sent their way. Sweat poured down Stonescare's face as the birds dove through the air and circled him. They wrapped him in a swirl of water that flowed from their bodies like the mighty rivers they had been born from.

"No!" he shouted as the water overtook the fire burning

up and down the wand, extinguishing it until all he held was a bone.

"My wand," he cried out. "My fire wand!"

He cast the bone aside and dropped to his knees, his dragon wings fallen down by his sides.

The eagles screeched to one another, before flying out the broken windows. As they soared above the fiery fields and forests, the mighty flock dropped their feathers of water, putting the flames out.

Stonescare raised his head to watch the fire become nothing more than a cloud of smoke, drifting away into the distance. While the feathers fell like rain outside the windows, he turned to look at me, his face twisted in anger.

"You!" he shouted. "You think you've won? I am the Dragon King!"

"No, you're not!" Tolden yelled as he came running in.

Folklock was behind him, along with Hartshorn, Egypt, and even the goblin dog, who growled at Stonescare.

"Graveyard dirt and cemetery stones," Folklock said, holding her Pegasus wand high. *"I raise your ghost from dragon bones."*

She pointed her wand at the skeleton in the coffin, and as her wand neighed, a bright light beamed out, causing the bones to rattle and shift.

"Don't you dare, Folklock!" Stonescare screamed.

The bones creaked and groaned as they sat up in the coffin. The skull of the Dragon King turned to look at us with deep, dark hollows.

"Who calls me from the land of forever back to this

mortal world?" the king asked. When he saw Stonescare, he asked, "Why do you wear my crown?"

"I am the Dragon King!" Stonescare shouted, though his voice was shaking.

"You cannot be." The bones stood up and walked out of the coffin toward Stonescare. "For I am!"

The king's roar was so loud that the five statues surrounding the coffin began to move, their armor shining before our eyes. The unicorn neighed, the troll grunted, the goblin stomped, the centaur circled, and the griffin waited for the king's order.

"Take back my crown," the king said.

In response, the griffin quickly launched into the air and stole the crown from Stonescare's head.

"No!" Stonescare cried out as he began to transform back into a wizard, not even tall enough to reach the knee of the true king. Left in the shreds of his robes and the fluttering of his dragon's-wing cape, Stonescare started to step back from the approaching soldiers. He pointed his wand at them, but his hand shook too much to cast a spell.

"This is not over," he said just before running to jump out of one of the broken windows. The statues followed him.

The Dragon King walked over to pick the crown up off the floor.

"Who has made this for a fake king?" he asked.

Aunt Cauldroneyes stepped forward. "It was me," she said. "I was forced to make it in order to keep a loved one safe."

"Then you had good reason," the king said. "Just as I have good reason to get rid of it."

He broke the crown with his hands until it fell away into dust.

"I've never seen a Dragon King before." Tolden looked up at him in awe.

"And you won't for long, young man." The Dragon King smiled down at him, the bones in his skull creaking. "I've got to get back to the forever lands. I was having a rather good time in the forest there with old friends until I was called back here to my coffin."

He saw the fire bone lying on the floor. Once he picked it up, it ignited once more.

"It still holds my fire. I must destroy it now that I'm a skeleton and able to hold it for the first time. I had hoped that by enchanting my tomb, it would prevent anyone from entering it. But I have been outsmarted by a wizard."

He held the bone up between his hands, about to snap it.

"Wait!" I yelled.

"Spella." Aunt Cauldroneyes turned to me. "It must be destroyed."

I looked up at Hartshorn. "I want to give it to you," I told him. "And the rest of the dodos."

"It's too powerful," Wander Velvetfoot said. "It holds all the fire of the Dragon King himself."

"Well." Folklock stepped forward. "As a single wand, yes. But if the bone were to be broken up and given to each dodo, its power would be shared. Am I right, Dragon King?"

He laughed, and it was hearty and warm. "That you are. And I can think of no better use of this fire than to share it among friends."

He broke the bone into enough pieces for every dodo and handed the first to me. It was cool to the touch as I carried it to Hartshorn. He carefully used his dragon's talon to pick it up from my hand. He held the bone for a moment before placing it in his mouth. We watched it light in a flame down to his throat, where it blazed like an orange jewel.

"Why don't you try it out?" the Dragon King asked him.

Hartshorn opened his mouth and blew out a stream of fire that made the king clap and say, "Well done, dragon. Well done."

Before the king returned to the sunny skies and the forests of the forever lands, he gave us the remaining pieces of the bone. Me and Aunt Cauldroneyes put them into our pockets. Then we all waved goodbye to the king as his skeleton lay back down in the tomb.

As the coffin's lid slid itself back over him, lava started to flow from the walls and down to the floor.

"We better leave now," the goblin dog said.

We ran quickly down the hallway as it started to grow smaller behind us, closing up.

Even though Egypt was running as fast as we were, Aunt Cauldroneyes still picked her up and held her tight as we jumped out from the book and to the library. The book slammed itself shut, and a last drop of lava fell to the floor and solidified into a smooth rock.

The other students and their dodos were already gathered in the library, having heard the commotion.

"Mr. Hartshorn, is everything okay?" several of the dodos asked as they all came running up.

Hartshorn roared, blowing a small flame toward the ceiling.

"Not around my books!" Velvetfoot said, but she still smiled at him.

"You have your fire back, Hartshorn?" Magis asked, his old eyes growing wide. "But how?"

"From my Wand Keeper," Hartshorn said, smiling at me as he changed back into a dodo. "And she has fire for the rest of you, too."

Me and Aunt Cauldroneyes pulled the pieces of fire bone from our pockets, and Hartshorn handed them to his fellow dodos.

"I best get this book back to its shelf," Wander Velvetfoot said as she walked the book away, the lava having hardened and sealed the pages. "The tomb is now closed," she said, helping the book up onto the shelf.

"Thank you for coming back to the dungeons to help us," I said to Hartshorn as I grabbed him into a hug.

"I was on my way to Folklock's office," he said, "when I knew I had to go back to face the dungeons. I couldn't leave you all to fight Stonescare alone."

As Hartshorn and the goblin dog began to tell the other students and dodos about everything that happened, Tolden stepped over to me.

"Softfang is glad this night is going to be over soon." He was petting the little dragon on the head. She still looked rather startled and jumped at any sudden movements, like when Egypt came over and reached her paw into Tolden's cardigan pocket.

"And I'm glad to see these," Egypt said before taking a big bite of the sandwich she'd pulled out.

"Where do you think Stonescare went?" Tolden asked.

"Wherever he is, he's not finished," Folklock answered. She was staring out the windows at the River Eagles flying by.

"Who called forth the ancient birds?" Folklock asked.

"Oh, that was Spella," Aunt Cauldroneyes answered with a smile. "She's the one who saved us all."

"It was wise of you to conjure the River Eagles, Spella." Folklock turned to me, before catching sight of the smooth rock of lava left on the floor where the book had been. She picked the stone up.

"Have you ever heard the magic word '*Caie-a-rolda*'?" She spoke it in an ancient accent that made the word slow and dreamy.

"I've never heard of it," I said. "What does it mean?"

"It's old plant language. It means, 'The world takes care of us. We must take care of it in return.' *Caie-a-rolda*."

The lava rock transformed into a badge in her hand. It had the image of a flock of eagles.

"You'll need to turn that into more than one badge," I said. "I didn't do any of this on my own. We all did it together."

"Oh, I've missed you for centuries, Spella." Aunt Cauldroneyes grabbed me into a hug just as the Star Spider returned, crawling up her braid and to her ear.

"What is she saying?" I asked Aunt Cauldroneyes.

"She's apologizing," Aunt Cauldroneyes said as she

listened to the little spider speak in her ear, "for not going to Folklock's office and weaving the webs for her as I told her to. She said she's sorry that she put you in danger by leading you into the dungeons, but she knew she had to show you the webs because you are the only one who would be able to recognize my thread."

"That's not fair," Egypt meowed. "I would have saved the day sooner or later." She smiled, showing all her teeth.

Aunt Cauldroneyes laughed, then asked, "How are the hats, little dear?"

"They're here at the school," I said. "They are gonna be so excited to see you! They're going to pop all their buttons."

"As the stars come to tell it," Folklock said, to applause.

CHAPTER 26
Going Home

IT WAS THE END OF APRIL, AND IN A FEW HOURS THE students would all be flying on the dodo dragons to go back to the valleys and the villages, the mountains and the cliffs of the seaside. And though I had come to love Dragon's Knob, I couldn't wait to see Hungry Snout Forest again and that narrow lane leading to the old stone house with the crooked attic tower and its puffs of violet-colored smoke.

After our reunion, Aunt Cauldroneyes stayed at the castle. She shared my room with me and the hats. They enjoyed chomping on the curtains in the evenings as I told Aunt Cauldroneyes all about the spells I'd learned, and we drank chocolate curl in front of the fire. Sometimes Folklock and Candlehour would join us, and sometimes Wander Wicklebug would come in from the river. He would pour water out from his shoes and talk with Aunt Cauldroneyes about the stars he had seen from the lily pads. She would smile and close her eyes at the thought.

During the last month, everyone had been talking about the tomb of the Dragon King and how I had extinguished the fire wand. Other kids would call my name and cheer. And though some had started to exaggerate the battle between me and Stonescare, for the first time in my life, I thought I might be more than just the blue-freckled girl who'd been left in the purple cauldron. I thought I might be free to be myself, even if I wasn't sure who that was yet. I knew I'd have a great adventure finding it out.

"Will you miss the castle, little dear?" Aunt Cauldroneyes asked as she looked around the room, making sure all my clothes had been packed into Moonsplash.

"I'll miss the stars that float in at night," I said. "And watching the hats eat the chocolate curtains. And I'll miss Socky." I patted him on the head just before he ran back into his corner to chew on a fresh sock.

"What about me?" Tolden asked from the doorway. "Will you miss me, Spella?"

Softfang was hanging upside down from his ear, her tail wrapped around it.

"Maybe not as much as Egypt will miss your perfumed sandwiches," I said with a laugh.

He laughed, too, as he reached into his pocket and pulled out a sandwich, which he handed to Egypt.

"All right, everyone." Aunt Cauldroneyes turned to face the hats. "It's time for you all to get packed for our journey home."

She held up Moonsplash and waited for the hats to fly, hop, or crawl in. She counted each one, and when the last bat hat had flown in, she said, "There's one missing."

She turned to the sound of a tiny yawn coming from one of the chocolate curl mugs on the table.

"Ah, there you are." She reached into the mug and lifted out the sleepy fairy hat. "You'd best finish your nap in there." Aunt Cauldroneyes dropped the fairy hat down into her pocket. "A forager is a woman of many pockets, after all. And some of the pockets make the most wonderful little beds for the littlest of souls."

She then turned Moonsplash over and cradled him in the crook of her arm.

"Now, I know I'm forgetting someone." She smiled, then whistled. Answering was Socky, who flew across the room to her so fast, he nearly lost a sock. "Come on, you old dog, you," she said as she fed him a sock from her pocket. "You're coming home with us for the summer. I'll meet you in front of the castle, Spella," she said to me, and smiled at Tolden on her way out.

"I'll tell you what I'm gonna miss," Tolden said as Moonsplash waved to him with his ribbon. "All those hats."

I noticed that Tolden was holding a rolled-up piece of parchment.

"What's that?" I asked.

"Oh, it's what I wanted to show you."

He unrolled the paper. Drawn in illuminated ink was a sketch of me holding the fire wand. Behind me was the Dragon King, roaring out a great breath of fire. Tolden had used ember ink, so the fire smoldered and smoked.

"I wish I could draw dragons better," he muttered.

"I think it's toadfire," I said.

"Let me see, young artist." Egypt reached out and grabbed the parchment. She was chewing on the last bite of sandwich, and dropped crumbs down onto her linen. "Why am I not in the drawing?" She looked up at him, a serious look in her yellow eyes, before she smiled, showing all her teeth. "I think you may become well known in your time for your paintings, young artist." She rolled the parchment up and handed it to him, but he gave it to me.

"So you don't forget me over the summer," he said.

"Aren't you going to come visit me, Egypt, and the hats over break?" I asked "You'll love the tower where Aunt Cauldroneyes and me make the hats. The octopus hat, Mr. Sea Captain, will fly us outside the windows, and then we can go chasing after barkchewers and stumpthumpers in the forest."

Tolden smiled wide. "And you'll come visit me, Grams, and Grumps by the sea? You can have some of Grams' sandwiches fresh so they won't taste like her perfume. Say you'll come!"

"I promise on a pinkie," I said. "If I break it, I'll lose a spell, and be forever stinky."

We shook hands above our heads like we had when we'd first told each other our names.

"Well." Egypt tilted her cheek to the side in thought. "What if I still want a sandwich that tastes like perfume?"

"You can have those anytime." Tolden reached into his pocket and pulled out another for her.

We laughed as the three of us headed out of the room and down the hall.

The rest of the students and the wanders were outside in the tall grass, where the dodos waited for their Wand Keepers.

"Hey, watch where you're going, cauldron baby," Grackle said, elbowing my arm as he passed. Slithe was by his side.

"You ran into her," Tolden said.

"You both think you're so special because of that dumb Dragon King." Grackle crossed his arms. "I would have found the tomb if I'd been looking for it. I had better things to do."

Both boys turned, throwing their cloaks up in our faces as they walked away. The dragon-eye ring stared back at me. I knew it was full of secrets from the school year. I would have to wait to find out why.

"They need some peanut butter," Egypt said, staring with a frown at Grackle and Slithe walking away.

"Why do they need some peanut butter?" Tolden asked.

"For their jelly." Egypt laughed into her paw. When we didn't laugh, she said, "Because they're jealous."

"I do believe that is your best joke of the school year,"

I told her. "And, of course, it has to do with a sandwich."

"It seems as though I've learned something this year, too." She flicked her tail and walked to Aunt Cauldron-eyes, who was standing by Hartshorn, while Socky ran around them.

"I'd better get to my dodo," Tolden said. "See you soon, Spella."

"Yeah, see you soon."

We waved to each other one last time. Then he made his way through the crowd, Softfang swinging from his ear. I watched the students around me, many with cloaks sewn with badges from the year. I looked down at the badges I'd earned, from a lightning bolt to a stack of books to even a telescope from Wander Wicklebug's class.

"I just hate the end of the school year."

I turned around to see Wander Candlehour standing there. Her hair blew in front of her eyes, but I could still see they were teary. Headwander Folklock was beside her.

"You shouldn't think of the end of the school year as something that's over," Folklock told her, "but rather as a new summer adventure about to begin."

"I can't." Candlehour sniffed. "It's just so sad to see everyone flying off." She hiccupped out a bubble. It floated before suddenly popping and releasing the blue frog inside.

Headwander Folklock watched the frog hop away before saying, "That reminds me." She looked up into the branches above us. "Candlehour, what's up in that tree?"

"Where?" Candlehour turned to look up.

At that moment a tree wart toad[44*] dropped down through the branches and landed right on her face. A very easy feat for a tree wart troll, seeing how they're no bigger than the average foot. He wrapped all four of his thin green arms around her face as Candlehour screamed and hiccupped at the same time. Bubbles of blue frogs came out in a great rush. Then she stopped hiccupping.

The tree wart toad laughed as he climbed down Candlehour's cloak and hopped to the ground.

"Thank you." Folklock bowed to him.

"Hot cauldrons!" Candlehour held her hand to her chest. "That about scared me nearly to death!"

"And your hiccups are now gone." Folklock smiled at her.

"They are." Candlehour's eyes grew wide. "They are diddly-gone! How wonderful."

She suddenly sneezed, and out came nearly every creeping, crawling bug imaginable.

"Oh no," she groaned. "I've got the bug snots now. Only way to get rid of them is to be frightened, nearly to death, by a grumpy hog." Her voice shook.

"We'll take care of you." Folklock wrapped her arm around Candlehour's heaving shoulders as they walked back toward the castle.

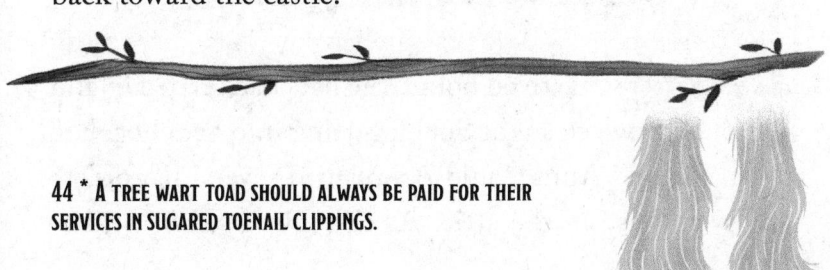

44 * A TREE WART TOAD SHOULD ALWAYS BE PAID FOR THEIR SERVICES IN SUGARED TOENAIL CLIPPINGS.

A shadow crossed over, and I looked up to see Hartshorn the dragon staring down at me.

"Ready to go home, Wand Keeper Spella?"

I nodded and ran over to Aunt Cauldroneyes, who was climbing up his back.

"Just let me know if I'm stepping too hard," she told him.

I picked up Egypt and carried her with me to sit down beside Socky and Aunt Cauldroneyes, who wrapped her arms around us. Hartshorn's wings started to flap faster and faster, raising us up into the air. As Egypt's linen blew back on either side of her face, I looked down at Dragon's Knob. Folklock and all the other wanders were out, waving goodbye to a sky full of dragons.

I waved back, surprised by how excited I already was for the next school year.

As Hartshorn flew us higher, Aunt Cauldroneyes started to sing.

"Cauldron fires and magic swirls, find me a star with a wandy twirl. Blue freckles on a magic girl, no one braver in this world."

I laid my head against her, my freckles sparkling.

A week after we arrived home, the hats had settled in and Egypt had twice caught Socky getting into her chocolate mice. Me and Aunt Cauldroneyes had several hat orders and were busy in the attic. As she sewed superfast, her braids stuck up in the air, until she saw a hat peeking out from behind the poufy chair in the corner.

"Who is that hat, little dear?" Aunt Cauldroneyes asked, standing up from the sewing table. "I don't recognize that one."

"Oh." I ran over and picked the hat up. "I made this one at Dragon's Knob. I forgot to tell you about her. She has bits and baubles from all the other hats."

I pointed out all the buttons, patches, and feathers that the other hats had given me. But even with everything the hat had, I couldn't help but feel something was missing.

"Here you go, little dear." Aunt Cauldroneyes removed her mauve shawl.

I took it and wrapped it around the hat like a ribbon, the long ends trailing in the back.

"She's finished now," I said, holding the hat out toward Aunt Cauldroneyes, but my old aunt only shook her head.

"Little dear, that's not my hat," she said.

"But I made her when I was trying to find you."

"I think that's all the more reason why the hat belongs to you, Spella." She smiled.

"To me?" I looked down at the hat.

"Why don't you try her on?" Aunt Cauldroneyes gently nudged me toward the mirror in the corner of the attic. "See if she fits?"

I turned to face the mirror as Socky ran up and leaned against my leg. Aunt Cauldroneyes and the hats came to stand behind me, to see for themselves.

"*Meooooooow.*" Egypt climbed up Aunt Cauldroneyes' skirt and into her arms.

"You silly old cat." Aunt Cauldroneyes hugged her close, and Egypt purred.

I stared into the mirror and put the hat on. So many times before, I had tried on hat after hat, thinking I would feel something that would tell me who I was. Where I had come from. But as I stood there now, it wasn't the hat I stared at in the mirror. It was the reflection of Aunt Cauldroneyes, Egypt, and all our hats. Not to mention Socky, who was nuzzling his sock nose into my leg.

For so long, I had been looking for my family. I realized then that they had been there all along.

"How about a walk in Hungry Snout Forest?" I asked, turning to them with a smile.

"I quite like that idea." Aunt Cauldroneyes smiled back.

The bat hats led the way, and we didn't even have to push Grandma's Boot out the door this time.

As the others followed the bat hats, Aunt Cauldroneyes stopped by the sewing table and reached back for my hand.

Spell No. 107

A dragonfly's wing and a goblin's book.
Open the pages, have a look.

Note from the Before Long Witch

A sock. Keys. Homework. What do these things have in common? They are objects that are easily lost. If you need to find something hidden, then whip out your wandle and, in the presence of a phoenix, repeat these words. You must say them in the presence of a phoenix because no one can tell a lie if the bird is there. Have you ever heard the phrase "Liar, liar, pants on fire"? It started because someone told a lie in front of a phoenix, and the phoenix set that person's pants on fire. I always say it's best not to ruin a good pair of pants, or a good story.

Acknowledgments

From the time I was a kid, I have loved fantasy and magic. I want to thank my parents, Betty and Glen, for raising me in gardens with trolls and fairies. Thank you to my sisters, Jennifer and Dina, for stirring cauldrons with me.

Thank you to the team at Simon & Schuster Books for Young Readers, including my editor Nicole Ellul, managing editors Amanda Brenner and Morgan York, production manager Chava Wolin, copyeditor Bara MacNeill, proofreader Valerie Shea, designer Sarah Creech, interior designer Tom Daly, rights manager Deane Norton, marketing manager Amaris Mang, publicist Mitch Thorpe, editorial director Kendra Levin, and publisher Justin Chanda.

Many thanks to the artist, Ayesha Rubio, for the beautiful cover and interior illustrations.

I want to thank my longtime Italian publisher, Simone Caltabellota, and the team at Atlantide Edizioni, including Francesco Pedicini, Matteo Trevisani, Beatrice La Tella, Erika Repetto, Francesco Sanesi, and translators

Luca Fusari and Sara Prencipe. And my French publishing house, Gallmeister Editions, including Oliver Gallmeister and translator François Happe.

Lastly, thank you, readers, for making the journey into this magical world. I hope this book gives you joy, adventure, and plenty of spells to cast.